The Rise of the Saxons
and the Legend of Hengest and Horsa

Ryan West

authorHOUSE®

AuthorHouse™ UK Ltd.
500 Avebury Boulevard
Central Milton Keynes, MK9 2BE
www.authorhouse.co.uk
Phone: 08001974150

© 2008 Ryan West. All rights reserved.

No part of this book may be reproduced, stored in a retrieval system, or transmitted by any means without the written permission of the author.

First published by AuthorHouse 10/28/2008

ISBN: 978-1-4389-2400-7 (sc)

Printed in the United States of America
Bloomington, Indiana

This book is printed on acid-free paper.

Index

Prologue ix
Chapter One: The Wicca Prophecy 1
Chapter Two: The Wolf Tamer 7
Chapter Three: The Darkness Consumes 17
Chapter Four: Wyrd! 31
Chapter Five: Return of the White Horse 45
Chapter Six: The Children of Woden 55
Chapter Seven: Under the Boar-Crest 65
Chapter Eight: The Whale Road 81
Chapter Nine: The Saxon Shore 93
Chapter Ten: Touched by the hand of Hel 105
Chapter Eleven: The Battle of Finnesburh-Part One 121
Chapter Twelve: The Battle of Finnesburh-Part Two ...137
Chapter Thirteen: Tides of Destiny 151
Chapter Fourteen: Puddles of Crimson 163
Chapter Fifteen: A New Dawn 171
Chapter Sixteen: The Great Lake of Fire 185
Chapter Seventeen: The War of the Dragons 195
Chapter Eighteen: Night of the Long Knives 203
Chapter Nineteen: England Rising! 211
Epilogue 225
Historical Note: Fact or Fiction? 227

'Gaeth a wyrd swa hio scel!'

'Fate goes ever as fate must!'

Prologue

I'm an old king now as I sit peacefully on my throne in my timbered mead-hall that is beautifully decorated in gold and silver, the spoils of war. My son Aesc is away in battle fighting against the waelisc vermin that inhabits this island. We came to Britain many summers ago and we have rarely known peace in these strange and ancient lands. The kingdom of Cent that lies on the south eastern coast of Britain is still a young nation that some of us are still calling 'England', named after our homelands from across the sea.

I've heard the tale a thousand times before, of how me and my brother Horsa came to these lands and destroyed an ancient race of *Frost- Giants* and how the two of us slain the red fire-breathing dragon that wished to incinerate us all. The poets sing tales of it in my mead-hall and they will continue to do so whilst ever I'm a generous giver of rings and treasures. But one day I will take leave of this life and enter the realm of *Asgard* and dine with the Gods in *Valhalla*, the hall of the slain.

I know that once I'm gone and no longer giving out treasures that my stories will blow into the winds along with my earthly ashes. And the story of Hengest and Horsa will be replaced with new sagas from young champions that are making their names known to the Gods. I hear of them now, the poets in my own hall sing of them. I hear about some Scylding arsehole from Geatland named Beowulf and how he slain the demon *Grendel* that once haunted the Black Forest near my childhood home across the northern seas.

Many of my thanes that are away in battle fighting against the waelisc are too young to remember where they came from and many of them have already forgotten the wars that have been fought for them. I believe that it's important to know the line in which you came, even if that line is riddled with corpses. My brother and I have since been ascended to the status of gods. But we were born as ordinary men that have simply trodden the path that were given to us by the *Norn* sisters, the three witches that decide our *wyrd*, our fate.

They say that I'm a hero, an honest and kind man, a great king and a powerful god, but I'm old now and not long of this world and I'm bored with the same old tales. And so it is my wish to tell you the truth about how my people came to this enchanted little blood isle from across the northern seas. It is my wish to tell you the truth about our origins before it's too late and everyone that was there is turned to ashes and blown to the winds. I no longer care for gimmicks and children's stories as the truth is far more violent and far more glorious than anything else that the poets can come up with to entertain the crowds.

My thrall Derfel is the one writing my sagas and telling you my story, he will tell you how things really happened. Derfel is an old man now; he has been crippled since the day he tried to run away to the northern moors and back to his own kind. Once I had caught him I hit him in the face with the hilt of my sword, smashing his eye socket and permanently blinding him in one eye. My brother Horsa and I then snapped his ankles like twigs and smashed his knees with rocks. We then tied him to my horse, *Chestnut*, and dragged him all the back to Cent and then beat him unconscious, Derfel was always a good for a laugh.

He was once a pious Christian like all of the British, but he has since witnessed the weakness of his god and felt the might of Woden. He had abandoned his god many years ago, just as his god had abandoned him.

Derfel once told me that he curses the day that he first met me, when we were both just children, and he wishes that he had died that day by my blade just like all the others. He now spends his time dragging his worthless corpse around my hall floor with his lifeless, quivering legs dragging behind. His tasks are to clean up the puke from my mead-hall and clean the shit off the floor from the dogs. He now has the status of a worm and often stinks of piss and shit and I've even seen the dogs cock their legs up and spray him in the face as they relieve themselves upon him.

Derfel now hates the Gods and all the races that they have created on this earth; he is now full of hatred for all living things. He is a passionate man and he is angry and bitter in his old age. And so he is perfect to be the one that shall write the sagas of Hengest and Horsa and tell the story of how our people came to these fertile lands.

I know Derfel will take great pleasure in telling the truth of the misery and suffering of my kind that he simply calls 'Saxons'. And he will take great delight in telling of the pain and starvation that we have endured over the years, the screams of my people will bring a smile to his toothless face. And I know he'll be happy to tell of the horrors that we have brought to his homeland in Britain and the holocausts that we brought with us.

Derfel will tell the truth of how we came to this land and butchered his people like vermin and held down the holy women face first in the flames. And tell of how we drowned and burned the worthless children of the Celts as we made way for our own people to settle. You are about to read the beginnings
of a proud nation that
I like to call
England.

*"There is a forgotten,
nay almost forbidden word,
which means more to me
than any other.
That word is England"*

Sir Winston Churchill 1874-1965

Chapter One:
The Wicca Prophecy

Jutland 412 AD
(Northern Denmark)

Many winters ago, Woden the story teller, God of war and ruler of the great warrior-hall in the sky *Valhalla* were born in these lands. He and His wife Frigg had a son Wecta, he too had a son Witta and Witta fathered Whitgils and it was Whitgils who fathered Hengest. I am Hengest son of Whitgils. My parents had named me Aesc, but for my own safety I later became known as Hengest, meaning stallion.

The three hags that sit at the bottom of the world had planned for a spectacular and violent life for me before I was even born. The *Fates* that weave their tangled webs had given me a *wyrd*, almost a burden, a crushing weight on my shoulders. It began the moment Freyja, the Goddess of peace and fertility, the Goddess of childbirth, delivered me into the arms of my overjoyed mother. They tell me that it was a hot night and half the village had been flooded only days earlier, surely a bad omen for the unborn child.

Priestesses were a common feature in our village, protecting the divine springs and hollowed groves from the bad spirits and the elves. They were loved by the people, often casting healing spells and delivering the newborns. At births the wise women would cast their magic rune sticks predicting the future. They were a gift from the divine, coded with the language of the Gods. After examining the rune sticks, the priestess would tell the future of the newborn, predicting health, sickness, marriage, births and deaths.

I had heard the story many times, how on that night, as I lay cradled in my mother's arms, we had a visit from the most feared of priestesses, the Wicca named Modthryth. She came during the hot sticky night as bats swept above the village, screeching as they searched for juicy insects that roamed the forest floor and often shared our beds. She appeared out of the shadows of the woods with only the sound of an owl and the distant cry of the wolves that roamed freely through our sacred lands, singing to the moon, waiting for their chance to swallow it whole. Modthryth and her companions only ever appeared from the depths of the forest to deliver terrible predictions of death, disease and chaos concerning the new one amongst the tribe.

Some say she was a messenger from *Hel* herself, daughter of *Loki*, and guardian of *Niflheim*, the frozen underworld. They say Woden sent *Hel* to the land of cold, mist and darkness to guard those who die as weaklings, disease or old age. And now Modthryth had come to our home on the night of my birth with a message from the Gods.

They tell me that Modthryth removed the bear skin that covered the entrance to the queen's dwellings and stepped over the mistletoe that marked the sacred threshold. And as she entered, the female thralls attending my mother nodded their heads in great respect and great fear. My father, the king, was sat by her side as I lay sleeping still in the arms of my mother.

Modthryth was a short woman with long uncut white hair that fell loosely below her waist like the tail of a horse. She was an old woman with a weather beaten face, maybe sixty summers old. My mother wasn't happy to see her and didn't wish to listen to Modthryth, but not even my father would dare disrespect the Gods wishes and refuse the company of the Wicca.

Speaking in a high clear voice so the villagers outside could hear her clearly, Modthryth spoke: 'I come with a message from Woden. He will grow big and strong like a war stallion. He will be a leader amongst men and a king with the strength of Thor.' Modthryth talked of cursed lands, war and death. She predicted more floods, famines and disease, bringing terror to the villagers as they listened outside. She read the rune sticks as her eyes began to flicker and roll into the back of her head. Modthryth continued: 'He will dance with the *Valkyries*; he will know pain and suffering, he will befriend death and death will know him well. The ground will shake beneath him and the seas will disappear at his command. Dragons will come and fire will reign over all that oppose him. I see bones and ashes consumed by the creatures of the sea. I see the eyes of the primeval wolf guiding him. I smell rivers of blood and fields of corpses. Your child, descendant of Woden, will be the bringer of death and pain.'

They tell me that Modthryth walked over to me placing an herb mixture across my forehead as she continued speaking to my parents: 'Death and chaos will be his ruler and ambition will be his master, but he need not fear death, only love will cause him suffering.' It's strange to hear such words about my *wyrd*, both frightening and wonderful at the same time. I had doubted her words many times, but the *Fates* do not lie and our destinies are not ours to decide. We are simply the tools of which the Gods like to play.

The following night my parents had ordered a celebration to mark the birth of their healthy baby boy and had invited all the tribes from Jutland, England and as far away as Saxony. They tell me of a blood-soaked sacrifice of a hundred sheep, a hundred cows and a hundred boars in Woden's name and in my honour. The fresh blood was dripped onto the floor and walls of my dwellings. And I was blessed dearly as I was bathed in the blood whilst it was still warm.

I was just a baby and I could not have known
that I had just been born
into a blood-feud.

*"The words and promises you bring are fair enough,
but because they are new to us and doubtful,
I cannot consent to accept them and forsake those beliefs
which I and the whole English race
have held so long"*

*King Athelbert of Kent
writing a letter to St Augustine,
AD 597
(Hengest's great grand son)*

Chapter Two:
The Wolf Tamer

Jutland 419 AD
(Northern Denmark)

It was now my seventh summer and I had grown into a healthy and adventurous child. I had big brown eyes and fair shaggy brown hair that my father said reminded him of the wrong end of a mule. My father was away viking in Britain and I had still not heard of his *wyrd*. He should have been back many weeks ago with silver and gold as a gift for my new baby brother or sister, but still no word. It was a hot day making my throat dry and my eyes water from the bright sky. I was bare chested, wearing nothing but brown linen leggings that were beautifully decorated with birds and animals. And around my neck I wore a wooden emblem in the shape of Thor's hammer; it was a precious emblem of the God of thunder bringing luck and protection to the bearer.

All I had with me that hot afternoon was a basket and my long knife called a sax that I used for chopping wood, gutting fish and for eating with. My sax was two feet long and sharp and was made of steel and bone; it was a gift from my father. It was decorated with strange markings that were called death runes.

The sax was an honoured weapon amongst my people and even the mightiest warrior would keep one at the front of his belt in a leather sheath or scabbard. My father had encouraged me to name it, but I told him that I would only name it when I knew of a special word.

I was alone in the Black Forest, enjoying the calming sounds of the birds and the splashing of ocean waves beating against the rocks in the distance. I could smell the trees and the salt in the air, the sweet smell of Jutland. I had surprised several rabbits in a forest opening as I walked past the white pebbles from the beach marking the southern borders of Jutland with the tribes of England, the home of the Angles. I was a Jute and I was not to cross the border without permission from Hoc, the king of all the tribes in England.

I was collecting the finest apples from the sacred tree of Freyja, as her apples bring immortality, and the Gods themselves feast upon them to keep their youthful looks. I was taking great care to choose the biggest and the juiciest, making sure they weren't homes to worms or rotten inside. As I picked the apples I noticed a falcon sitting proudly high above a tree. It was a beautiful bird with dark black flexes across its golden-brown chest. It looked at me with its predatory eyes, spreading its long black wings. Was this Freyja guarding her apples? I wondered.

I then picked out the biggest of the apples, it was green with a reddish tint on one side, and I gently placed it on the floor next to the tree as a gesture to the Goddess of nature. Then the falcon flew away high in the blue sky under the snow-white clouds and I knew I had made her happy.

The apples were a gift to my mother, the queen. Apples represent health and prosperity, an appropriate gift for a woman with child. I prayed to the spirits in the forest and the lakes and to the mighty Gods themselves, that my sibling would be born healthy, as the Wicca Modthryth had predicted death and sorrow.

At my mother's birth she was told that on the day of her third child she and the baby would be cruelly torn away from *Midgard* and taken into the next world over *Bifrost*, the rainbow bridge of fire.

My sister Helgi was fifteen and was ready for marriage and it was she that ordered me to go to Freyja's tree to fetch the sacred apples that bring life whilst she stayed and looked after the queen.

Whilst I began my long journey back home, I suddenly became aware of something behind me. I could hear it scuffling in the bushes. It was watching me with its huge brown eyes. And as I turned around, the evil spirits from the woods that were trying to posses me jumped out of my body with fright, causing me to drop the basket of apples. And there stood a wolf.

My instinct was to run, but I simply froze unable to move. It was the most beautiful thing I had ever laid eyes on. Its fur was as white as the waves crashing against the rocks in the evening tide. Was it an ancient spirit that roamed the forest? I wondered.

The wolf watched me with curiosity, sniffing at the air, desperately trying to catch my scent in the warm breeze. I knew it must have crawled from its den as it was clearly an infant. I then made a bold attempt to walk towards it and pick up the tiny creature. I picked up the magnificent beast with childhood innocence and youthful enthusiasm. The cub struggled to break free from my grip as it furiously kicked its back legs and its claws scratched at my bare chest and thighs. But I didn't mind. I was in awe.

Whilst admiring the softness of its untamed fur, I remembered the stories I had heard of the beasts we Jutes called the 'teachers'. I had been taught that the wolves fight in packs for the survival of the group and never leave one of their own behind, always fighting to the death for their honour. Even with limbs torn off, they never surrender. My father once told me: 'It's not the wolf that fights with the courage of warriors; it's the warriors that fight with the courage of the wolf.'

With the sun on the back of my neck, I was running my fingers through its soft white fur as I thought of the leader that must have been the strongest and bravest of the pack and demanded respect and loyalty from the weaker members. Qualities I had witnessed within my own tribe, qualities I wished to possess myself one day. The wolf was as admired and respected as it was feared. The wolves in our woods had tasted the flesh of our people before and hungered for more, but we loved them still, longing to be as courageous and as free as the wolf.

I was losing myself in the wilderness as I gazed deep into the eyes of the cub when I suddenly felt a shiver down my spine. 'They never abandon their young' I thought. That's when I turned around and my body turned to stone and I felt sick as the oxygen rushed from my lungs. My heart was beating faster than a rabbit's at springtime as it receives a sax to its throat at our *Eastre* festivities. I began to tremble.

A huge black demon with fur blowing in the gentle breeze was watching me from the shadows of the trees. My body's response was to stay and accept my *wyrd* and fight the monster, but my thoughts were to run into the dense woods and hide. Why wasn't my body moving?

Then the wolf began to slowly walk from the comfort of the shadows and into the light, one limb at a time, gently, as though it was afraid of upsetting the hollowed ground where the Gods dwelt.

Still holding the cub in my arms, I looked deep into the eyes of the approaching wolf. It had retreated from the shadows and I could see that the creature was as white as fresh snow, but it wasn't a wilderness that I could see in its eyes, but an abyss of terror.

The wolf was looking into my terrified and bewildered eyes showing me it's perfectly white, razor sharp fangs that it wished to devour me with. Finally my legs awoke and without calling to the Gods for help, I dropped the cub and found myself running to the nearest tree and I desperately tried to climb to safety. The wolf had begun chasing after me, snarling and hungry for blood. I scratched my already bloodied chest and legs against the harsh bark of the tree as I frantically used all my power and might to scurry up to safety. All the while I was having visions of my ankles being caught in the jaws of darkness and death.

As I reached a high point, I suddenly felt a rush of relief as I knew that I was too high to be captured. I was gasping for air as my heart was beating so fast that I thought it was going to burst out of my chest like a raging boar charging at a group of hunters. I clung to the tree like it was my father that I hadn't seen for as long as I could remember. And as I looked down I could see several wolves prancing impatiently around the base of the tree, irritated and hungry.

I began holding Thor's hammer in my hand hoping that the Gods would come to my safety and free me from the jaws of death that lurked below. I wasn't sure how long I had been in that tree when I finally found the courage to look down for a second time hoping to see them gone. They had not. The largest of the wolves, the one that had chased me, was sitting in the shade of the bushes watching me from a distance, panting in the heat, waiting…

Not taking my eyes off the wolf, I reached for my sax and pulled out my blade from its old tattered sheath, my only comfort in a moment of terror. As I began to look around I saw the wolf cub that I had been holding. It was limping as it was trying to catch up with the other infants as they played. I felt guilty for dropping and maiming the poor thing. I didn't realise it, but after some time clinging to the tree I had slowly lost my fear as I watched the other wolves playing and teasing each other. I watched with curiosity and wonder as I witnessed them play fighting, testing each others courage, chasing each other and biting each others tails.

I drifted into a dreamlike state as I imagined myself to be a wolf, a member of the pack, playing games with them, forgetting that I was to be their dinner. I wondered how such wild beasts could be capable of so much love and affection towards each other. I was fascinated.

I was suddenly startled and almost fell out of the tree when I heard the distant, frantic voice of a girl calling my name. I called out as loud as I could when I suddenly recognised the voice. It was my older sister Helgi: 'Come quick, its mother!' she bellowed, hearing my voice. The wolves began to stir, their ears popped up to listen to the strange unfamiliar sounds, they all rose looking in the direction of my sister's voice. Coming to my senses, I suddenly screamed: 'Wolf!' And there she was, appearing above the thorn bushes, her face peering out of the shadows, her blonde platted hair blowing in the breeze. She looked up at me in the tree, not noticing the wolves: 'Come down Aesc!' she ordered. I then yelled again: 'Wolf!', only this time with horror in my voice. And I'll never forget her screams as the beasts charged at her like *Fenrir* is fated to do against Woden at *Ragnarok*.

Helgi gave a chilling warlike scream as she pulled out her sax from her leather belt. The largest of the wolves, the white ghost, jumped at her, knocking her to the ground and sinking its razor-like teeth into her flesh, ruining her beauty forever. She had dropped her sax and more wolves tore at the flesh on her legs like starved creatures of the night.

I then heard the white ghost yelp as Helgi had managed to pull its front legs apart ripping its blackheart in two. She then grabbed her sax as I watched terrified, unable to move, she then used the sax to furiously stab one of the adults in its eye killing it instantly.

I was screaming in the tree as I watched my beautiful sister Helgi struggle for her life as a wolf bit into her face and others still ripped and torn at her legs whilst another tore out her throat. And I'll never forget the way her head rolled to the side; she was looking at me through the green blades of grass with her big blue eyes, empty, her face haunting me.

Helgi was dead and the wolves devoured her body before my very eyes. I was numb with terror and curiosity as I watched the wolves feed on the flesh of my blood kin. I watched as the wolves fought with each other furiously. They were deciding the new leader, deciding who would get the mating privileges and the finest parts of the carcass, the liver and the heart.

Finally two of the wolves surrendered and cowered to the new alpha male, a huge black beast I called the *Shadow*. I watched *Shadow* carefully as he devoured the heart of Helgi and I wondered how the *Norn* sisters would weave their webs and free me from the same *wyrd*.

Blood was everywhere, covering the forest floor and was all over the snarling teeth of the wolves. Helgi's intestines were torn out and fought over by two of the smaller wolves. Her entrails were stretched, pulled and eaten by the blood hungry beasts. I threw up all over the tree trunk.

As I was waiting for a sign from the *Fates*, still sitting high in the temples of the Gods with the leaves flapping above, I saw a raven sitting on a branch on an adjacent tree. It was a huge bird with a long black beak and the darkest of eyes. It was *Huginn*, one of Woden's ravens that watched over the lands and reported back anything strange to the Lord of Hosts. And I was afraid that *Huginn* might report to Woden that I wasn't worthy to one day being chosen by the *Valkyries* to dine in the great warrior-hall of *Valhalla*. My father once told me that a man's greatest honour is to join the war band of dead heroes and dine with the Gods in the hall of *Valhalla*. But I felt shame and dishonour as I sat hiding in the tree like a worm and watched as my own blood kin fell and I did nothing to help. How could I go back home and tell the queen that her son is a coward and has committed the greatest of sin?

I wiped the tears from my eyes, I wouldn't show weakness, not in front of Woden and I wouldn't sit and hide from the wolves anymore. With Woden's help I would find the courage to climb down and confront the wolves. I could hear them nearby resting their bellies after feasting on my sister's bloodied corpse. I had my sax in hand and my back to the tree. I was still shaking as I stood tall and proud, as tall and proud as a scrawny seven year old kid could be. I then looked up at the raven still watching me from the treetop and I was determined to make

Woden proud. I breathed in as much oxygen as possible and gave out a Jutisc war cry. I screamed as loud and as hard as possible and gave out a primal scream that echoed throughout the woods.

Suddenly *Shadow* walked slowly out of the bushes, snarling and showing me his bloodstained fangs. That was my blood dripping from his mouth, I thought, blood that I shared with Helgi. And I was going to avenge her death even if it meant sharing her *wyrd*. I was frightened, my heart was beating so fast, my mind telling me to climb back up that tree and wait for help. But I wouldn't listen, I couldn't go back home a coward. *Huginn* was watching me and I would never be allowed into Woden's feast-hall with the slain warriors if I was to die like a piece of gutless vermin. *Shadow* was coming closer and closer, seemingly savouring the moment, staring into my eyes, his fur erect and lusting after the kill. I called to him: 'Come and taste my blade'.

As I stood my ground waiting for whatever *wyrd* had been decided for me, I was suddenly shocked when I heard voices from behind the trees. I then briefly took my eyes off *Shadow* as I glanced over at a group of hunters that came into view. I would later learn they were Angles from King Hoc's tribe. Amongst them was Hnaef, the son of King Hoc. He was just a boy back then, maybe eleven years old, and the *Fates* had entangled our destinies together more so then Hnaef and I could ever had realised at that moment in time.

I noticed they were carrying swords, spears and bows and they had no armour. The wolf pack had been aroused by their sudden appearance and *Shadow* had stood to a halt assessing the new situation. I stood there with my sax in hand, still shaking. One of them called out to me in a strange foreign accent: 'Don't move kid, everything's alright!' He said in a reassuring voice.

I would later learn that his name was Hunlaf and he was a powerful tribal chieftain in England. He was a well built man with long red hair and a long well groomed beard. Next to him was his son Hunlafing, he looked about ten or eleven years old and he was the spitting image of his father, only without the beard. Many years from now Hunlafing would be forced to make a choice whether I lived or died. His decision would change the *wyrd* of my people forever.

'Thank you.' I whispered to Woden, noticing the raven had disappeared.

Hunlaf stood with his spear in hand: 'Who are you boy? speak up!'

'I am Aesc, son of King Whitgils' I said with pride. My skin was covered in the bloody scratch marks from the wolf cub and I was standing and holding my ground against *Shadow* as Hunlafing spoke: 'What kind of sorcery is this?'

'Wolf-Tamer!' Hnaef shouted out loud.

My people were at peace with the Englisc and so they wouldn't leave without helping the son of the Jutisc king. The wolves, sensing they were outnumbered, began to walk away. But the hunters hungered for the kill and started throwing their spears and pulling back on their bowstrings. One of the men pulled out his sword and began to slash at the wolves drawing blood. I can't remember what was going through my mind as I just panicked and finally saw my chance to run away. Then I did the craziest thing. I believe I must have been under the spell of the dwarves as I suddenly picked up the limping cub and

ran deep into the forest,
leaving my basket
of apples
behind.

"And since the sacrifice of many oxen to devils
is their custom, some other rite ought to be
solemnised in its place,
such as a day of dedication or festivities
for the holy martyrs whose relics
are there enshrined…
They must no longer sacrifice animals
to the Devil."

A letter from Pope Gregory
To Bishop Mellitus

Chapter Three:
The Darkness Consumes

Jutland 419 AD
(Northern Denmark)

I ran and ran, not daring to look back. I had run all the way home as the cub struggled and scratched at my bare flesh desperately trying to get free from my grip. I was exhausted as we approached the village. The sun was low in the sky, orange and red as if it was bleeding. It was becoming dark when I stopped to rest on an embankment overlooking the wooden fort. I could see dozens of huts and small fires as I waited for the God of the sky *Night* to ride round the heavens on his horse drawn chariot and chase away his sister *Day*. I was frightened to go inside, how could I tell my pregnant mother that her only daughter lay dead in the lands of the Angles as her cowardly son watched and did nothing? But that wasn't what frightened me the most.

It was dark before I finally found the courage to enter the village. I had hidden the wolf cub outside, concealing him inside the hollow arch of an old oak tree and covered the entrance with broken branches. I was protecting him from hunters and the dwarves, creatures that bred in the earth like maggots and dwelt in hills and rocks.

As I came to the entrance, the guards opened the great gates on the request of their prince. I was filthy, cold and hungry and as I entered the guard with brown shaggy hair, wearing a green long sleeved tunic and carrying a spear, grabbed my wrist: 'Come with me Aesc.' he said in an authoritarian voice as he pulled me towards my mother's hut. I struggled to free myself from his grip, I wanted to run and hide. I had denied myself to think such a thing, but deep down I wondered 'why did Helgi come looking for me?' Had the prophecy come true? Had my mother and my brother or sister been cruelly taken away? I had thought many times that I wanted a younger brother and I often had fantasies of the two of us riding horses as we travelled the lands together and the world bled at our feet. And I feared that my dream was over before it even began.

The guard held me tight as he dragged me to the queen's hut. Pulling away the bear skin, he threw me inside. I was screaming, begging him to let me go. I had tears rolling down my dirty face as everyone in the hut was looking at me with pain and sorrow in their eyes. My uncles and aunts, cousins and thralls, were all staring at me. 'No!' I screamed as I saw my mother lying on her back wrapped in a woollen blanket. The baby was by her side also wrapped up to the neck. Their eyes were closed, but they weren't sleeping. My aunt Ingeld gestured for me to walk closer, but I was frightened and refused. My body was weak, hungry and terrorised. I had been through an ordeal. I had witnessed the death of my sister Helgi, I had almost been killed myself and I had come home to discover my mother and new brother were dead. How could the Gods be so cruel? I couldn't take anymore and I just collapsed into the arms of Ingeld. I don't remember anything after that; perhaps I just fell asleep in her arms.

The next morning I remember running into the woods exited and desperate to discover if the wolf cub was still hiding in the oak tree. As I moved the branches out of the way, I looked into the darkness, but I couldn't see him. Then I saw something moving and suddenly a small black nose came out of the shadows, followed by a huge yawn showing me his razor-sharp fangs. Thankful to the Gods that he was still there, I picked him up and ran away deep into the Black Forest.

I hadn't told anyone about Helgi as I couldn't find the words and the thoughts were too painful. I had not eaten that day and suddenly my stomach began to growl like I had just swallowed a bear. I was hungry and so must the wolf, I thought. I had walked for several hours passing the great Swan Lake that reflected the beauty of *Sun*, the fair girl in the sky that's eternally being chased by the wolves that wish to devour her.

Before long I had found myself near the border of England. I placed the wolf cub down on the floor, hoping it would find its way home, as I didn't know how to look after such a creature. It began walking, but I noticed that it wouldn't put much weight on its front right leg and I felt guilty as I had been the one to maim it.

I had named the wolf Fenrir after the wolf that grew up in Asgard and grew so big and fierce that in the end only *Tiw*, the God of justice and law, had the balls to feed him. And guided by the wisdom of Woden, the dwarves forged a chain for him called *Gleipnir* made from the secret things of the world such as the roots of a mountain, the noise of a moving cat and the breath of a fish. It was only a thin cord, yet no force in *Asgard* could break it. The wolf Fenrir thought that it was safe enough, but he wouldn't allow it to be put on him unless one of the Gods placed a hand between his jaws as a hostage. *Tiw* stood up and volunteered as he showed everyone how brave he was and so the wolf was bound and the Gods laughed, all but *Tiw*, who lost a hand. 'It's a good thing it wasn't his dick' my father used to always say.

I watched as Fenrir sniffed at the air around him, perhaps tracking his family, if they still lived. I followed Fenrir unaware that he had taken me to the spot where I had first met him. He was still sniffing the air when he suddenly stopped and lowered his head. And as I slowly approached him, I looked over the top of him and I was mortified at what I saw. Fenrir was feasting on the rotting, stinking corpse of my once beautiful sister Helgi. 'Get off, Get off, you filthy beast!' I yelled as I was pulling him away.

The wolves had left little flesh on her body and the creatures of the night had enjoyed a feast. The smell was awful as her body had been torn apart and she no longer resembled the beautiful young women she once was.

I had picked up a stick and out of curiosity I began to poke at the mangled flesh and bone. How could I have allowed such a thing to happen? I was overcome with dishonour and shame. Fenrir had once again begun to take little bites out of what was left, but it no longer mattered, I allowed him to have his fill. I stood watching him pull and tug at the tough flesh and I felt bad for him as he had probably lost his family to hunters. We were alone; we only had each other now.

I pulled out my sax and began to cut several chunks of flesh off the body and fed it to the wolf. I didn't know what part of her body it was, I no longer recognised what was in front of me. As I sat in the grass with my sax in hand and blood on my fingers, my mind wondered to the Gods. I stared into the blue sky watching the white clouds slowly drift by when Fenrir came up to me and began to taste the black congealed blood on my fingers. I still held my sax in hand as I watched him lick and savour the taste, his teeth so perfectly white and sharp. '*Wolf-Fang!*' I said out loud. I shall name my sax *Wolf-Fang*. I couldn't have known it on that day, but the *Fates* had already decided that *Wolf-Fang* would one day save my life and secure the *wyrd* of my people.

I then placed my sax back in its leather sheath and tried to pick up the remains of Helgi. She deserved a funeral, but I couldn't hold the torn dismembered flesh and bone, it slipped out of my hands, it was hopeless, I needed help. I later made the long walk home through the Black Forest with Fenrir hobbling behind struggling to keep up. I placed him back in the hollow oak tree and made my way inside the fort and went to my mother's funeral. I told my aunt Ingeld about Helgi's *wyrd* and she had ordered the thralls to retrieve her remains and had them placed under the woollen blanket that was wrapped around my mother's body, concealed from the eye.

Later that evening the whole village had gathered round the heath on the hilltop outside of the fort overlooking the ocean. Farmers, soldiers, tanners, thralls and free men and women came to show their respects. My mother and brother were placed into a wooden casket and were slowly lowered into the ground by four men using ropes as pulleys. Before they were lowered, I had placed my mother's favourite silver-gilded brooch and her most valuable ivory comb inside. I had also retrieved Helgi's sax and placed it into the casket along with Thor's hammer that I had taken from around my neck and gave them as a gift for our brother that we had never met. I stood and watched as they buried my kin, wondering when my father would return, wondering if he would return. Fighting back the tears, I refused to cry that day. 'A soldier should never show weakness, not if he is one day to become king.' my father used to always say.

As the weeks and months passed, I spent most of my time away from the village leaving my friends behind, desperately trying to conceal my secret. I was afraid that if Fenrir was discovered that he would be hurt and I would be flogged for harbouring a wild animal so close to the village putting the children at risk. I had gone on many hunts with the villagers, always concealing a hare or two for Fenrir. If I was unable to steal a hare then I would sneak out late at night and jump over the farmer's fence and throttle the chickens, giving the wolf a juicy breakfast in the morning. He had grown well; big and strong, my only friend, tame and friendly, but still wild at heart. I had started giving him live chickens and enjoyed it as I watched him play with them, teasing them with his huge paws and I watched him as he devoured them.

As winter approached the land was cold and grey; the trees were lifeless like gravestones striking out at the night sky. The weather had turned bitterly cold, even turning the great Swan Lake to stone and hunting had become scarce. One morning as I approached the old oak tree, I noticed the bushes had blown away and Fenrir was gone. I was wrapped in my brown woollen cloak and I was shaking as I desperately looked for him. There was no mention of a wolf from the villagers. Fenrir was grown now and had been bringing back hares, rabbits and small birds on his own for a while. I knew he would be safe and I wished him luck against the dwarves, the hunters and the monster *Grendel* that stalked the night time woods.

Weeks had passed, but I had not seen Fenrir, he had gone forever, perhaps looking for his own kind. As I sulked around the village, I was thinking about Fenrir, my father, my mother, my sister and my baby brother. He should have been lying in his crib wrapped in linen sheets, but his crib was empty and silent and I was alone, truly alone. And I was angry with the world and with the Gods themselves. I hated my miserable life and my self and I often wished that I was never born. It was the first time that I truly felt hate and it was a feeling that would dominate the rest of my life.

Many of the queen's thralls had been given their freedom since the death of my mother and one of them had recently given birth to a healthy baby boy named Breca. I had wanted to see the baby, to hold him, comfort him, if just for a moment, but I was too afraid to ask. One night as everyone was sleeping; I sneaked out of my hut and entered the dwellings of the baby as his mother and father were sleeping. I was quiet as I stood wrapped in wool, still shivering as I watched the baby sleep. There was a small fire in the centre with smoke flying through the hole in the thatched roof. I quickly warmed up and the baby began to stir and soon he awoke. He looked at me with his big green eyes and I swear I saw him smile.

I remember picking him up and walking outside being careful not disturb his sleeping parents. He was wrapped well and didn't seem to mind the freezing temperatures. I looked at him, I was smiling and pulling funny faces, but he didn't seem to like it as he started crying. 'Shush!' I said, as I didn't want him to wake anybody up or disturb the guards that stood watching the woods from their watch towers. I rushed to the opening in the wall, a secret hole in the fort that only the children knew about. I then placed Breca at the other side of the fort before climbing through myself, scratching my face on the broken wood.

It was a bright night with the moon lighting the aluminous sky, the heavens were clear and the eyes of the giant *Thiazi* filled the sky with sparkles. I picked Breca up and began to rock him gently and he soon stopped crying, he seemed to like the natural noises of the forest with only the sounds of the owls and the whispers of the Gods in the night time wind. And he looked at me with his big green eyes and listened to my story with enchanted as though he was listening to the Gods themselves.

I told Breca how our ancestors came to these lands from the frozen north in Scandinavia. I told him how our harvests were terrible in the north and many men, women and children starved to death. And hundreds of our kind simply threw themselves off the cliffs to end the pain in their stomachs, sometimes with their babies still in their arms. I told Breca how we fought the natives for their country as we desperately needed better lands to feed our own people. There wasn't enough food for both our races to survive and the natives wanted us to leave and so blood was shed, lots of blood. And many good men and women died in that war, they sacrificed their blood for us so we can feed ourselves and our babies. And they should never be forgotten, no matter how long ago it was. I told Breca how the war continued until their entire race was wiped out and destroyed forever and the dust from their bones still blows in the winds to this very day.

I had noticed that the sounds in the woods had completely disappeared and not even a cricket could be heard. I had no recollection of how long I was out there as time seemed to have no meaning. Before turning round to go back inside, I suddenly became aware of an eerie figure watching me from across the field, watching me from the edge of the Black Forest.

I held Breca close to my chest to protect him as shivers ran down my spine, but somehow I didn't feel frightened. It was a white figure of a young girl draped in a long white gown that fell to the floor. She was standing perfectly still, not taking her eyes off me. The ghostly white girl had become the only light in the darkness of the woods. My eyes began to fill with tears as I witnessed her long white hair blowing in the cold breeze. Was it Freyja? I wondered, or some kind of ancient spirit of the woods? I walked closer and closer and the ghostly figure stood silent, seemingly unaffected by the blistering cold. I had forgotten about the guards as I walked closer and closer, still unafraid.

As I approached the figure I suddenly got a chill down my spine and my heart began to beat really fast. I couldn't see her face as whom ever it was suddenly turned with her long white hair blowing in the wind and walked into the dense woods. Tears were rolling down my face and as I still held Breca in my arms, I quickly began to run after her, yelling for her to wait. I became compelled to follow her into the deep untamed forest in the dead of night, not knowing who or what she was.

It was incredibly dark under the cover of the trees and tears blurred my vision further as I ran round bushes trying to spot the trodden path in the dark. I could see the figure walking in the distance, turning and looking over her shoulder to see if we were still following. I could hear bats flying above the trees and the strange sounds of the elves in the distance, but I wouldn't stop as I was determined to catch her up. And the trees slapped my face for the intrusion as I ran deep into the darkness. After running further and deeper into the woods, Breca had become startled and began crying. And suddenly the light disappeared and all became dark, leaving Breca and I alone deep in the woods with only the wolves and the elves for company.

I had heard stories from within those woods, stories of the monster *Grendel* that lived in a cave deep in the woods where wild animals and even wolves have been found half eaten by the beast. Fear had set in and I began to panic as I didn't know the way back home in the pitch dark. I could no longer see anything, not even my own hand in front of me. I was unarmed and terrified as I begged for Woden for help and I believe that he must have been present that night as no harm came to either of us. The monsters and the beasts were no match for the power of Woden.

Many hours had passed and daylight began to break. It had been snowing most of the night, but I had hardly noticed as I desperately tried to find the sloping muddy path that led us back home to safety. I had been wandering lost and confused for most of the night and both Breca and I were hungry and tired. As the sun became the dominant image in the sky, I had found the right path and we began to make the long journey home.

My feet were sore and my stomach ached when finally I saw the wooden towers standing high above the forest canopy. But suddenly my heart began to beat faster and faster as I noticed thick black smoke coming from inside the fort. It was common to see bonfires in the morning, but I knew something was wrong. Nobody was in the towers and there was an eerie, haunting silence. As I exited the woods and made my way across the frozen white field, I expected to see children playing, smithies collecting firewood and people everywhere going on about there daily lives. I saw nothing. It seemed deserted.

I walked to the main gate, but it was gone, smashed up and crumbled into splinters. And then I saw them. Bodies were everywhere. Men and women lay in the grass, cut and bloodied. Some had black marks across their necks and stomachs where the blades had cut. Some were lying with arrows in their backs. It was a massacre.

I rushed inside the fort following the trail of bodies and blood that coloured the snow a strange pinkish colour. I saw decapitated heads on stakes with their eyes missing, perhaps a tasty treat for the crows and ravens. And the birds that had been enjoying a feast flew away from fright as I rushed past searching for survivors. I was holding Breca tightly and he began to cry as he must have sensed my panic and desperation as I searched my home for anyone that was still alive. But they were all dead; they had spared no one, not even the dogs or the children.

Many of the people seemed to have been trapped inside the barns and everything had been burned, even the crops and fowl. The bodies looked like little children reduced to charcoal; I couldn't tell if they were men or women. I searched for my family, but they were all dead. I saw my aunt Ingeld; she died bravely with my long knife in her hand, she had been burned to death. There were death and destruction all around me, just like Modthryth had predicted.

As I paced around the village I came across one of my father's greatest lords known as an ealdorman. He had received a horrific and painful death known as a *Blood-Eagle*. His torso and ribs had been opened up allowing his lungs to be pulled out past the ribs to make it look like an eagle had spread its wings. This would have been done whilst he still lived; it was a clear warning to the neighbouring tribes.

It must have been the Scyldings, I thought. Our families had been at war with each other for generations, always fighting for Jutland. My country was a gateway for the Danes, the Geates and the Scyldings to trade with the rest of the world and they desperately needed new lands as theirs were prone to flooding and bad harvests. The king of the Scyldings was a powerful man whom my father respected and feared greatly. There had been many wars between our tribes and my father had killed many of the intruders. Perhaps this was their cowardly vengeance.

Breca was crying and I knew he was hungry, as was I. My stomach was in pain and there was nothing to eat but apples. I had thought about the wolves and how the alpha male had searched out the best bits to eat, the liver and the heart. I must have been under a spell by the dwarves as I began to locate the heart of my father's ealdorman, using my sax to cut the flesh. I cut hard and deep struggling to free the heart from the corpse. When I finally succeeded, I held it high in the sky like the kings of legend holding the heart of their greatest rival. It was covered in black sticky congealed blood as I then used *Wolf-Fang* that I had retrieved from my aunt's lifeless fingers, to cut it in two and I didn't hesitate to take a bite. I screwed up my face as I bit down hard on the chewy raw flesh and swallowed. It was disgusting and I suddenly felt faint as it didn't agree with me and it returned with a vengeance.

As I wiped the sick from my jaw, I was suddenly startled as a loud, deep voice shouted at me from behind: 'Get up boy!' a man said in a very commanding voice.

I then jumped to my feet wiping the blood from my hands onto my woollen cloak. The man walked towards me, he had a long brown beard and was wearing a red woollen cloak held together by a silver brooch over his chain-mail. I noticed a sax tucked into his belt and he held an axe and shield. Most of his face was hidden under a dirty, unpolished war helmet and I could tell that he was a thane, a fully trained soldier. But I didn't recognise this man and I thought that he might have been one of the attackers. 'Who are you boy?' the man asked with a very serious tone. I was tired, hungry and agitated and my body was shaking with hunger and fear. He was the one intruding into my lands and so I held out *Wolf-Fang*, showing that I was armed and prepared to fight. I then asked him a question: 'Who in the name of Thor's ginger testicles are you?'

The man looked at me puzzled whilst gaining speed as he walked towards me. He then smacked me in the face using his shield as a weapon knocking me to the ground. I stayed on the floor too frightened to get up. Breca screamed as he was lying wrapped in blankets on the grass. 'My name is Froda' he said, 'son of Froda.' And I suddenly felt a sense of relief as he told me that he was Jute from the northern coast. He was followed by a group of survivors from a separate attack. Amongst them were other thanes, women and children, all shivering in the blistering cold. There were dogs, goats and horses and other animals that had been saved from the slaughter. The *Fates* weaving their tangled webs must have been smiling that day as that's how I first met Dresden.

Dresden would become a favourite amongst the *Valkyries*, Woden's maidens from *Valhalla*, the choosers of the slain. The *Valkyries* live between life and death and are always present on the battlefield, choosing who was worthy to die and be taken to the feast-hall in the sky. It is said that sometimes the *Valkyries* choose to fight in the battle themselves by possessing the female spectators. Some of the women would find themselves picking up their yelling spears and go charging into battle, possessed and fearless. Dresden would come to know the *Valkyries* well, but on that day I didn't think much of her. She was maybe six years old and she had long matted, black hair and a dirty face, the daughter of a thrall. She was wearing torn and filthy rags and as our eyes met for the first time she stuck her tongue out at me. She had no front teeth, she was hideous.

'Who are you?!' Froda shouted, demanding an honest answer. And I didn't dare tell a lie: 'I am Aesc, son of King Whitgils.' I said loud enough for the others to hear as I wanted them to know that I was of high birth. Froda of course had heard of my famous father and had served under him over the years against the Scyldings, the Geates and the Danes. He knew that my father had many enemies, enemies that I had already inherited. I explained that I had been in the woods all night talking to elves and ravens and that I didn't know what had happened to my village. Froda had removed his war helmet, he had a sour look on his face and he looked angry. He was about twenty years old when I first met him and he didn't know it at the time, but we were destined to become close friends and he would one day become a loyal follower of mine. But on that day, I was a scruffy little kid born into power, spoiled and offensive and I could tell that he didn't like me.

Froda asked who the baby was, still wrapped in a woollen blanket on the floor. I picked Breca up and held him close to keep him warm and kissed him on the forehead. And after a long silence and a little thinking, I glanced over at the horses and I gave a cheeky smile as I answered the question: 'He is my brother,

his name is Horsa.'

The *Fates* were

laughing.

*"We don't bother much about dress
and manners in England,
because as a nation
we don't dress well
and we've no manners"*

*George Bernard Shaw
1856-1950*

Chapter Four: Wyrd!

Jutland to England 419 AD
(Northern Denmark to Southern Denmark)

Froda and his followers were survivors from several tribes that were scattered around the north-east coast of Jutland, they had survived the massacres. They were travelling south to England, the land of the Angles. As we travelled through the Black Forest, that I had become so familiar with, Froda began telling me his story. He told me how the leader of the Scyldings, King Folcwald, had invaded from across the northern sea, from Scandinavia. The combined forces of the Scyldings, the Geates and the Danes had attacked the Jutes across the coastal areas destroying everything they came across. The three tribes from across the *Swan Road*, from Geatland to Jutland, were often at war with each other, but now they were under the leadership of King Folcwald and they had surprised all of us with such a vicious attack.

Many people had managed to run away during the massacres and some had regrouped and started making their way south where they believed it would be safer. Froda had grouped together maybe a hundred Jutes, amongst them were many thanes and their families, homeless and pissed off. We didn't know the *wyrd* of the western tribes in Jutland and so Froda had decided to go south and across the border to the closest tribe that were led by King Hoc, the greatest king in all of England.

Froda was a quiet man and with him was his beautiful girlfriend Saxburga, she must have been only fifteen when I first met her, but she was a woman to my youthful eyes. She was tall and had long free flowing blonde hair with striking blue eyes and was well dressed. As the group marched forward, I saw her comforting the orphans making sure they weren't left behind. I watched as Dresden was shouting at the other children to hurry up, I felt bad for her as she too was an orphan. I couldn't see it looking at Dresden, but as I later got to know her, I learned that a fire burned deep inside and she longed for the day she could be avenged.

We had travelled long and far, we were tired and hungry and not many people were talking, perhaps remembering their loved ones. It began to rain and soon the snow began to melt as we made our way deep into the lands of the Angles. We were plodding along the beaten path, pushing the trees and the bushes out of our way when we were suddenly stopped and a band of warriors blocked our path in front and we found ourselves completely surrounded.

'Halt!' one man shouted from the path in front. And the Jutisc thanes held up their iron and steel as we prepared for a fight. We had maybe thirty or forty trained thanes with us and all of them pulled out their saxes or spears. The man that had stopped us was wearing chain-mail and wore a boar-crested war helmet and was armed with a sword and shield. He looked familiar to me and I later recognised him as the man that had spoken to me in the woods whilst I was being hounded by the wolves.

'Relax!' Froda shouted at the men and women behind. He could see that the thanes were Angles as one of them was holding the emblem of the Englisc, a picture of a magnificent white dragon on a red background. 'We are Jutes' Froda told the Englisc thanes. 'and we come looking for the protection of your king, my lord.' The thane spoke: 'More of you?' he asked in his strange accent. He offered us a guide that led us to the land of the Angles; he led us to England.

We were led to Hocsburh, Hoc's stronghold, a huge wooden fortress not far from the ocean. I loved living by the ocean, the smell of salt in the air, the cold breeze and the sounds of seagulls reminded me of home. We were taken inside and were greeted with stares and sniggers from the villagers as many of them didn't want us there. An old woman snarled at me, showing me her last two remaining yellow and rotten front teeth. Dogs were barking at us as we passed and I held Horsa tightly as I feared that some of the women might have lost their own babies. I feared they would take him from my arms and never give him back. He was all I had and I would kill to keep him.

Soon we were greeted by King Hoc and his wife Onola. The king was a tall man and was as wide as a tree, he had a long yellow beard and big blue eyes and his hair fell to his shoulders. He wore a grey long sleeved tunic made from linen and was wrapped in a green woollen cloak. His arms were decorated with golden rings showing off his power and wealth and I couldn't help but notice his sword sitting in its highly decorated scabbard. He had a friendly face and welcoming eyes and I couldn't help but stare at his huge gut sticking out like a pregnant woman.

Recognising him as the leader, King Hoc greeted Froda in the strange accent of the Angles and welcomed us all to his kingdom. He introduced himself as King Hoc Healfdene, son of Trojan Godwulf. He also introduced his beautiful wife to us; her name was Onola and she was a huge woman with a square jaw and long blonde hair to below her shoulders. She was dressed in a long blue satin gown and was wearing a blue headband encrusted with emeralds. Her eyes were as blue as the ocean, eyes you could drown in. She gave me a beautiful friendly smile as she leaned forward and asked me the baby's name. I was nervous as I told her his name is Horsa, son of King Whitgils. 'Ah', Hoc said, recognising my father's name, 'then you must be Aesc? also son of Whitgils?'

'Yes my lord', I replied. Onola reached out her arms and took Horsa away from my grip: 'Don't worry Aesc; I'll take good care of him'. There was something about her, I trusted her. Hoc spoke to me in a very warm tone: 'Aesc my boy' he said as he put his arm around my shoulders, 'Welcome to England.' He told me that he knew my father: 'He's the only man that I had ever had to look up to; he's the size of an oak tree and a great warrior.' Hoc continued: 'Tell me Aesc, how long has your father been away?'

'He's away fighting the Britons and the Romans and he's been gone for many months.' I replied. Hoc sighed, 'And your family now live on in *Asgard*, the other world?' I looked down and said nothing. 'Aesc, listen to me very carefully.' Hoc said as he raised my chin with his fat, hairy fingers. 'Whilst ever the sons of Whitgils live, then the Scyldings will continue to hunt them down and end the royal bloodline of the Jutes forever. Then of course they plan on taking over your father's lands and force the remaining Jutes to accept them as their masters.' I looked up at him with worried eyes. 'Keeping you and your brother here will bring the Scyldings to my lands and I can't risk that Aesc, you understand?'

'But where will we go?' I asked with tears rolling down my cheeks. 'To *Asgard*' Hoc replied. I was confused. 'You and your brother Horsa died in the attack on your village. Aesc and Horsa are dead. You and your brother are Englisc now and as long as no one finds out your true identities then you will be safe here in England under my personal protection.'

'He's not my brother.' I confessed. Hoc laughed. 'He's the son of a thrall, but she's dead now and so I pretended he was mine and named him Horsa after a horse that I liked.' Hoc was laughing as he told me: 'I appreciate your honesty Aesc and I like the name Horsa, but what are we going to call you my boy? We can't keep on calling you Aesc, son of Whitgils, can we?'

'My mother used to call me Hengest; she said that I was a little stallion.' Hoc smiled. 'Hengest and Horsa? The stallion and the horse. I like it. Come Hengest, my wife will take care of you; we won't have you living with the thralls with the rest of your people. A future king must be groomed well.'

'A future king?' I asked puzzled. 'Of course!' Hoc replied. 'I don't want the Scyldings ruling land that borders my own. I can never trust the bloody northerners. I promise Hengest that we Englisc will fight to the death for Jutland and when the time is right you will become their king. But first we need to put some muscle on those bones and teach you the way of the Englisc warrior.'

Over the years I would come to know Hoc very well and would learn that he was a very smart king and knew how to play politics very well. The Hocings lived in the north of England and the northern tribes didn't get on well with the southern tribes and King Hoc was the glue that held the Englisc lands together. Hoc knew that by allowing the Jutes to settle his lands that he was securing his own status as king, as well as securing his own territories by boosting the numbers of thanes that defended it. Hoc knew that the Jutes had no choice but to pledge their oaths to him in exchange for land and security. And all of the Jutisc children would grow up loyal and obedient to the Angles. A wise investment indeed. Hoc had taken care of me in my youth and would earn my loyalty and respect, regardless of the reasons for his generosity.

That night there was a feast in the king's mead-hall to welcome the Jutes to the home of the Angles. It was lit up by torches on the walls and had a fire in the centre. There were pigs roasting on spits, dogs roaming free and there were lots of singing and dancing and merry making. Hunlaf, the man I met in the woods with the red hair, had returned from the Black Forest and had invited me to share a room with his son Hunlafing. And that's when Hunlafing's best friend Hnaef introduced me to his father's famous mead. It was made with water and honey and tasted disgusting. Hnaef and Hunlafing always called me by the nickname Wolf-Tamer; it was a name that would stay with me for the rest of my life.

Hnaef was eleven years old when I met him; he had long blonde hair like his parents and was full of life and adventure. And the three of us would go on many adventures together, quenching the thirst of our swords and quenching our own thirst for ale and chaos.

That night became a blur to me and I only remember little parts here and there. But I still remember the taste of the mead, I remember feeling dizzy and I remember the taste of my own puke as I threw up all over the floor during the dancing and frolicking. I remember tripping over the dogs that were fighting for scraps of chicken and beef that had fallen to the floor. I saw things that night between the men and women that I had never seen before. I remember seeing the king laughing as I chucked the mead from my gut all over the hall floor and he gestured for me to come to him. 'Tell me Hengest; is it true that you eat a human heart?' He asked as he took a sip from his emerald encrusted bullhorn. 'Yes my lord, I did.' I replied whilst wiping my chin. Hoc burst with laughter, spitting chicken and mead all over my face. 'Bloody Nora! Whatever for boy?'

'I was copying the wolves my lord, I was hungry.'

'Hungry?' Hoc couldn't control his laughter as I was sprayed in the face. 'I know you Jutes are a bunch of savages, but you're something special Hengest.' We both laughed, until I turned to throw up again. Hoc nearly choked on his chicken as he laughed and laughed.

The next day Hoc ordered an army of forty thanes to go back to Jutland and give the dead a final farewell. Froda led the way and I and many of the Jutes followed. Hunlafing, Hnaef and his older sister Hildeburh also followed us without the knowledge of their father as they mingled in with the common folk and amongst them was Saxburga and Dresden. Princess Hildeburh was thirteen when I first met her and like her brother Hnaef, she had long yellow hair, only hers was naturally thick, curly and twisted and she too was full of life and adventure. Dresden had long black hair and didn't look like everyone else. It was rumoured that her mother was a Saxon thrall from southern Germany and her father was a Roman General. The Jutes and the Angles hated the Romans and so Dresden had no friends and was often bullied by the other kids.

On our way north, Hnaef and Hunlafing began to throw stones at Dresden, telling her to go away, calling her a filthy flea-bitten Roman thrall. Hildeburh didn't like what she saw and smacked her younger brother Hnaef on the back of his head. It was hilarious and Hunlafing and I laughed out loud and I noticed Dresden was laughing too as she ran to the side of Hildeburh.

As we made our way into my father's fort, a couple of thanes noticed the ravens and the wolves were having a feast and began to throw stones. As I came closer, I was shocked as I saw a white wolf running away through the burned fort walls, running with a slight limp. It was Fenrir and he wasn't alone, he must have found himself a girlfriend and some new friends, I was delighted.

We began to collect the frozen bodies, the dismembered limbs, the decapitated heads and the charcoal remains that were scattered around the fort. We tried to start a fire, but everything was wet and so we tried to dig a fresh grave, but the ground was too frozen, it was useless. We had no choice, but to take the bodies and throw them over the cliffs and feed them into the jaws of *Aegir*, the God of the sea.

It had been a long, cold winter day, but Froda insisted on going further north to lay his people to rest and no one argued with the young thane. We passed the mounted trees growing out at an angle above grey stones that littered the valley. We travelled past *Grendel's* cave, through forests, over rivers and across farm lands when we finally came to the last tribal settlement known to have been attacked by the

Scyldings. This village belonged to Froda and Saxburga and there were bodies everywhere, including many Scyldings as the Jutes had put up a great fight against their attackers.

As the men and women walked around the village collecting their dead, I heard a loud and horrific scream. It was Dresden, it was her home too and she had just discovered her mother's raped and brutalised corpse. Her screams echoed across the village, bouncing off the fort walls. She was clinging to the frozen body of her mother whilst Hildeburh was trying to console her. Dresden cried a small river that day like she had a thorn in her eye, collapsing into the arms of Hild. I watched with pain in my heart as I saw Froda walk towards her, he had been Dresden's master and her mother was his thrall. He comforted her and whispered something in her ear to help calm her down; I don't know what he said.

We then disposed of the bodies and said our farewells and began to make our way south and we were followed by many dogs that had been left behind during the massacres. We were all tired and hungry and had very little to eat and Dresden was carried home on the back of Froda. We were walking across a field in Jutland when suddenly the Scyldings came charging out of the woods in front. We were ambushed and panic swept through the people like fire blowing across the summer cornfields. The unarmed men, women and children rushed across the field to the safety of the trees. Hnaef and I stood still, mesmerised by all the horses and shiny weapons that dazzled our eyes. But Saxburga dragged us both by the scruff of our necks to the edge of the woods and told us to stay put and she meant it and we didn't dare move. Besides her was Dresden popping her head up, trying to get a good view. The Scyldings were on horseback and I could see their black bear banner being carried on a staff by a thane, flapping in the wind. My father once told me that if I ever saw the black bear emblem to run away and hide.

The Scyldings were armed with swords, spears and shields and were protected by chain-mail, breastplates and war helmets. The Angles and Jutes were on foot and were armed and ready for a fight. Hoc's thanes and most of the Jutisc thanes wore chain-mail and were all armed with spears or axes. Most had shields, but only the greatest warriors had swords as a sword was a token of honour. Froda was wearing his own boar-crested war helmet and was armed with a huge double edged war axe and the Scyldings would soon learn that he was a highly skilled warrior.

Three brave warriors from the Scyldings moved forward on their black and white war horses, they left their thanes behind them, patiently waiting. Froda and two other thanes, each carrying spears and shields, walked forward to greet the Scyldings to discuss the *wyrd* of us all. I couldn't hear what was said, but I soon realised what was happening as the two Scyldings trotted back on their horses leaving their chosen warrior behind. He was sitting on a black horse with white patches down the left hand side; he was a large and menacing man as he sat wielding his sword in the air preparing for single combat.

Froda sent his two companions back to the Jutes and Angles that were waiting by the woods as he had been the one to bravely accept the challenge for a duel. His opponent was wearing a silver and gold war helmet covering his face. He was covered in an impressive animal skin held together by two golden brooches, making him look like a bear and he wore iron chain-mail protecting him from even the mightiest blows. Froda looked serious as he stretched his neck and flexed his muscles. Hunlafing, Hnaef and I watched from the edge of the woods with anticipation as Froda stepped forward and prepared to fight to the death. The two men looked at each other from across the battlefield and both had every intention of killing each other. Froda stood still and waited for his opponent to make the first move.

The man in the bear skin sitting on top of his horse suddenly charged forwards wielding his sword towards Froda. Froda stood his ground as he lifted his wooden shield for protection. As the man came closer, Froda stepped out of the way and swung his great axe deep into the muscles of the horse's front leg. The horse squealed as the beast smashed to the ground throwing the Scylding across the frozen field. The horse was squirming on the floor; its leg had been dismembered by the axe and blood was everywhere. I could feel the touch of the Gods stroking the back of my neck causing a tingling sensation. I was filled with excitement as Saxburga, Hnaef, Hunlafing, Hild, Dresden and everyone else were cheering for Froda. But he wasn't listening as he was utterly consumed by the battle-fury as he charged at his opponent wailing his great axe.

The man in the bear skin had gotten to his feet and raised his shield to take the blow. The shield shattered into a thousand splinters as Froda swung with all his might. The man was dazed as he swung his sword at Froda, but Froda blocked it with his own shield and struck with a mighty blow. Froda left the Scylding in a bloodied mess on the battlefield. He had hit him in his neck, almost decapitating the intruder; his body was twitching and quivering as he lay in a puddle of his own blood. And then Froda satisfied some of his hunger for revenge as he heaved the axe above his head and struck the killer blow and decapitated his opponent.

'Fucking Hel! That's my fella.' Saxburga shouted with pride. We were all laughing and cheering as we had won the battle and Saxburga picked up Dresden and spun her around. Hild and Hnaef hugged and I rushed towards Froda as he slowly walked towards the dying horse. He raised his axe and sent the horse into the afterlife. I looked into his eyes as he gave the killer blow and I'll never forget what I saw, I liked it.

The two men from the Scyldings, each with long black bear skins, began to make there way towards Froda and I, and we were joined by our own thanes to help back us up. They were highly decorated soldiers, wearing gold and silver war helmets, each with a dragon mask covering their faces. They wore iron chain-mail, golden rings on their arms and each had a highly impressive long sword. The Scyldings both approached us slowly on their horses and as one took off his helmet, I noticed that he had a long wrinkled face, two chins, big blue eyes that were sunken into his skull and wore a series of small bones attached to his long black beard that clanged as he moved his head. They were obviously men of great courage and power. The older and larger man then leaned forward on his black and white horse and addressed Froda in a very polite and formal manner: 'You fight like a true champion, with courage and honour. What is your name young man?'

'My name is Froda, son of Froda.'

'Froda? I recognise that name. Is that the same Froda that fights alongside King Whitgils?'

'The one and the only, my lord.' Froda said with respect. 'And now please tell me, what is your name? And what business do you have here in Jutland?'

'My name is King Folcwald, the Lord of the Scyldings and this young man next to me is my son Finn.' I was standing in the mud and was straining my neck as I looked up at the two men on their horses. And I suddenly felt afraid and angry as they had been the ones to destroy my village and kill my aunts and uncles. 'You fucking bastards!' I shouted at them both, showing my grievance. 'Be quiet, boy!' Froda yelled at me as he smacked me at the back of my head.

Both Folcwald and Finn looked down at me from their horses. I couldn't see Finn's face as he was still wearing his face mask, but King Folcwald looked at me with a shocked expression. They probably weren't used to such disrespect, especially from a young scruffy kid that probably looked like the son of a thrall. Finn then removed his dragon mask revealing a very youthful face: 'How dare you talk to my father like that? You filthy little vermin. Apologise at once.' Finn demanded. 'Piss off, who are you calling vermin? you murdering bastard!' Finn's eyes widened in disbelief whilst his black hair blew in the chilly breeze. 'Be quiet Hengest!' Froda yelled for a second time. Whilst still sitting on his horse, Finn then pulled out his sword from its scabbard and pointed his blade at my face: 'I shall have your head on a stake boy, you filthy Jutisc rat.'

'Calm down, Finn!' His father ordered. 'I like a boy with spirit.' Folcwald said as he then leaned forward and asked me my name. 'You heard what my name is old man. My name is Hengest the Wolf-Tamer and I hope you remember it well, for it will be the very last name you'll ever hear, you fat bastard.' Folcwald laughed. 'I like you Hengest; you have the spirit of a wild boar. And I guess that you must have lost family in one of these villages, otherwise why else would you be so upset?' I was gritting my teeth as I stared into his blue eyes as Folcwald continued: 'I'm sorry if you have lost your loved ones, but all is fair in love and war.'

Folcwald then turned to Froda and the two thanes and told them that no more blood needed to be shed that day. Froda laughed at that comment, knowing full well that the reason the Scylding didn't want to fight was because they were outnumbered. Their allies were probably miles away scavenging for what they could find from the burnt out villages. But Froda didn't want a war with too many unarmed women and children as he felt responsible for their safety. Froda was an honourable man, an honest man and one of the bravest men that I had ever met and he earned my respect that day.

Finn was only fifteen years old when I first met him that afternoon, still just a boy, but under all that war gear he looked like a formidable warrior. I came to respect Finn over the years as I found him to be a great king and a worthy adversary. I believe that one day Finn and I will meet again in Woden's feast-hall and we will become friends telling stories of our past battles. But in this lifetime we were destined
to inherit the blood-feuds of our fathers
and destined to be enemies.
But for now we
went back to
England.

*"If anyone makes an offering
on trees or wells
or stones or railings or anywhere
except in the church of God…
this is sacrilege,
that is,
sacrifice to demons"*

*An Anonymous English Christian
7th Century*

Chapter Five: Return of the White Horse

England 420 AD
(Southern Denmark)

    Many months had passed and spring had arrived and Froda was enjoying his gift from the king, a huge shiny new axe for his bravery against the Scyldings. We had known peace for a while, although word had spread that the Scyldings had began to settle in my father's territories and my inheritance was fading. The Jutes had adjusted well in England and many had built their own homes around the edges of the fort made from woven branches and dried mud.

    I remember one morning when I was having breakfast with the king, his wife Onola, Hnaef and his daughter Hildeburh were also present. They were discussing Hild's future and talking of marriage as she would soon be old enough to marry and Hoc was worried that she would get too old and that nobody would want her. I was shocked to hear the king suggest that Hild should marry into the Saxons that lay to the south of England to secure the peace that the two tribes had enjoyed for generations. Hildeburh screamed in defiance and stormed out of the hall. Hoc laughed at his daughter's response and Hnaef joked that Hild was going to be an old wrinkly that not even the thralls would want. Onola belched out loudly and said nothing.

    They have a common custom in England; they hunt wild boar and eat its brains, intestines, blood and even its penis. They fry it all up in pig fat with bread and eggs and eat it for breakfast. As I was given a plate of pig guts, I picked up a long floppy meaty thing. I looked at it puzzled: 'Is this its nob?' I asked. Hoc and Queen Onola burst into laughter followed by Hnaef, all spraying food and ale across the table. 'It's a sausage' Onola said with amusement. 'I'm sure you've eaten worse things than a sausage Hengest.'

'So have you my dear.' Hoc said as he burst into laughter. And all three of them laughed and laughed. What did he mean? I wondered. Hoc began explaining to me that a king must learn how to fight and must teach his followers the way of the sword and spear. He told me that only practice brings skill and grace and the art of warfare must be taught at a young age. He warned me that my training must begin soon. I couldn't wait.

Whilst still sitting round the table Hoc asked me a question: 'Tell me Hengest, what is it that you think we fight for?'

'We fight for the honour of the Gods so we can go to *Valhalla* and be merry and fight some more, my lord.'

'You're right Hengest; I guess you Jutes aren't as worthless as they say you are. But don't forget, we fight for our lands, for our children, for our future and for our survival.' I was listening intently as Hoc continued. 'Our survival depends on our babies; we need them to grow up big, strong and healthy. The secret of success Hengest is babies and steel, lots of healthy babies and lots of steel. If we don't fight for our babies Hengest, then we fight for nothing.' That conversation would stay with me for the rest of my life.

I was sat eating my sausage and dried pigs blood when suddenly a messenger came into the hall: 'Sorry to interrupt my lord, but they're here, the *White Horse* has arrived.' Hoc stood up and told his servants to go and fetch the men and pass him his sword and armour: 'Come with me Hengest, you stay here Hnaef'. I was taken outside where the thanes were waiting on their horses dressed in their golden bridles. The horses were draped in flags that were decorated with pictures of dancing wolves and some of the men were carrying the white dragon emblem of the Englisc.

We then rode to the beach; I was on the back of a brown and greyish horse clinging onto the armour of a thane as we bounced up and down and over the hills and through the short woods that led to the shore. The beach was close and there I could see below the cliffs, the red sail of a ship with the white horse emblem of the Jutes, it was my father's Viking ship.

It had come from the north, passed the east coast of Jutland and had made its way into the waters of England. The men were heaving the ship onto dry land as we watched from across the beach. And then they cautiously walked towards King Hoc and his men that were waiting for them, still sitting on their horses with their Englisc emblem of a white dragon held up high.

About thirty thanes walked up the beach, they were fully armed with swords, spears, axes, shields and javelins and some of them were carrying treasure chests that were heavy with the spoils of war. They were all Vikings and were obviously very rich from a year's worth of raiding the coasts of Britain and Gaul. I then jumped off the back of the horse and rushed past the king's men and ran towards the Jutes shouting for my father. A man then approached me, he was wearing a black leather tunic and he had golden rings round his arms and I then recognised his face as he removed his dented boar-crested war helmet. He was bold headed and had a long scruffy blonde platted beard and a distinctive scar down his left cheek. His name was Wipped the Skull Crusher and he was one of my father's greatest thanes and advisors. He knelt down to me and told me that my father died well and had entered the hall of the warriors in the sky. The Vikings looked at me with sympathy from under their helmets as Hoc's men looked on from across the beach.

They had brought my father home for a king's farewell, he was at the back of the *White Horse* still wrapped in blankets, rotting and stinking and covered in black coagulated blood. Wipped and his men offered tunics of iron chain-mail, shields made of the toughest hardwood, jewel-studded drinking vessels, cheek-hinged war helmets and silver and gold coins to King Hoc in exchange for land and hospitality. Hoc accepted.

My father's body was laid to rest that morning on his favourite ship the *White Horse* and was surrounded by all the Jutes of England. The Angles built a pyre for my father that was stacked and decked in abundance with his share of the booty. The ship was hung with war helmets and emblems and by his side were boar-headed spears, war shields, shining armour and coins made of silver and gold. 'What the Gods give you in life, you give back in death.' my father once told me.

The ship was sent out to sea as archers sent their flaming boar-headed arrows from above the cliff tops and I watched, waiting for my last remaining blood kin to disappear beneath the waves in a haze of fire. They let him drift to the tide alone, except for his hoards of treasure and his sword, a jewel-studded pattern-welded sword that had been given to him by his father before him. And it was placed into his hands, snapped in two so that it can be forged again in the afterlife.

Wipped and the Vikings had brought back fifteen thralls hoping to sell them to the Jutes and Angles. He told one of them, a young boy with short black hair named Derfel, to bring me a gift that was tightly wrapped in linen. The boy handed me the gift, it was long and heavy and I was amazed as I slowly unwrapped it. It was a beautifully decorated long sword with runes carved into the blade, spelling the words '*Dances with Corpses*'. It had a broad steel blade and a silver decorated hilt. The sword was inlaid with worm-looped-patterned steel and swastika runes engraved down each side of the lethal blades. The hilt was engraved all over and showed how war first came into the world and told a story of a flood that destroyed an ancient tribe of giants. The inlaid hilt was embossed with red, orange and purple jewels and was a sword that even a great king would envy. 'It was your father's' Wipped told me. 'He slaughtered many Christians for that and it's worth the value of many ships.' It came with a leather scabbard and belt decorated with runes, the language of the Gods. Wipped explained to me that it was a Frankish sword as the craftsmanship was exceptional and the Celts must have taken it in battle. 'It had drunk much blood.' Wipped added.

Later that night Wipped approached me in the mead-hall and took me to one side for a private word. He told me that he had made an oath to my father and promised to go back home and protect his son. Wipped whispered as he spoke: 'We'll stay here with the Angles and live under their protection until you are strong enough to name yourself King of all Jutes without fear of an uprising. And one day when the time is right we shall name you King of all Angles too.' I was now scared and confused as I liked the Angles, they had been kind to me, but the Skull Crusher, my father's greatest advisor, wanted me to use the Angles and then stab them in the back for land and power.

Wipped was an ambitious man and dare I say he was a terrible influence on my impressionable young mind. Wipped and his men had not given their oaths to King Hoc making them free men. Wipped warned me to deny the king my oath, otherwise Hoc would own me and use me however he wished. I was only young, but I was wise enough to know that if I gave my oath to Hoc then I would be forever tied to him. And Wipped didn't want that as he had pledged an oath to my father promising to protect me until his death. And so Wipped was now destined to share the same *wyrd* as the Wolf-Tamer, otherwise he would lose his honour and risk being rejected at the doors of *Valhalla*.

The Skull Crusher and his thanes spent most of their summers raiding the coasts of Britain and Gaul looking for thralls and booty and they only resided in Jutland during the harsh winter months. But that night Wipped promised to spend much of his time taking vengeance on the Scyldings in the name of the Jutes and in the name of my father. If I can only say one thing about Wipped, it would be that he lived for war.

The following morning Wipped had displayed his thralls in a straight line, shoulder to shoulder and bartered with the free men and women for a price. He had told me the night before that if any of the thralls were unwanted then I could pick a thrall for myself free of charge. Wipped was always good to me in that way, he had been my father's closest friend and after his death he became like an uncle to me.

The richest of the villagers and many of the Englisc thanes inspected the thralls, looking at them, touching them, smelling them and spitting on them. Most were sold and immediately dragged away to work in the fields, but some were left behind, unwanted. Looking at the thralls, I noticed several wooden crosses around some of their necks and I knew what it meant, as my father had once explained to me what a Christian was. He told me that the British killed our people, burning us alive, calling us devils and infidels as they spat on us and they even called our children 'the Devil's litter'.

My father explained to me that the Christians worshipped a strange sand god named '*Jehovah*' and they believed that all things pleasurable in life are evil and their god burns them just for having fun. 'Christianity is a disease of the mind. Their cult is an effeminate way of life. They follow the god of slaves, the god of women and the god of wimps, they are vermin.' I remembered my father once telling me as he gritted his teeth in disgust.

Wipped told me that children like me and Hnaef and even little Dresden would be beaten until we were bloody and close to death unless we screamed in horror that we believed in their lies. And we would be forced to work for some kind of shaman called a 'monk' and be forced to give all our money to their sacred churches where their god lived even if we were starving. I looked at Horsa in the arms of Onola and I looked at Dresden watching the other kids play. I imagined them beating her, putting their filthy foreign hands on her. It was now time for me to choose a British thrall and I was furious and I had worked myself up into frenzy, just like the famous Vikings.

I screamed out loud in the centre of the village like a *Berserkir* as I walked over to the thralls with *Wolf-Fang* in hand. All the villagers were staring at me in amazement as I was screaming in the faces of the Christians. All the men and women had been sold, but several of the children were left. Some were older than me and some were younger, but they all feared me as I waved my sax in their faces screaming like a rabid beast.

I walked over to the tallest of the boys, he was maybe twelve years old and had short black hair and was wearing a long robe. He was much bigger than me and I screamed at him, calling him a murderer, vermin, scum, a piece of rat turd. I knew he didn't understand a word I said, but he was scared and was shaking. The king and queen, Hnaef, Hild, Wipped and many others were watching with anticipation as I showed the boy my blade. And I screamed in his face before plunging *Wolf-Fang* deep into his rotten guts. I twisted the knife relishing in his pain as he fell to the floor in agony and blood gushed from his open wound whilst he was waiting for his god to claim his latest thrall.

Some of the thralls were screaming but didn't dare try to escape as they had been told to stand still during inspection; otherwise the Vikings would cut off their feet. One of them did a strange sign across his chest; it was some kind of foreign Christian magic and I didn't like it. As the boy was writhing in agony on the floor, slowly dying, I knelt down and took the cross from around his neck. It was a cast of his god nailed to a piece of wood, similar to the way we sacrifice to Woden. I stared at it and making sure the other thralls were watching, I then spat on it and threw it to the floor. 'Pick that up vermin.' I said, pointing to the cross. A boy much smaller then I knelt down to pick it up and as he did so I raised *Wolf-Fang* in the air and struck down hard into the neck of the waelisc scum. 'That's my boy Hengest.' Onola shouted with words of encouragement.

Blood began squirting from the thrall's neck as I got a cheer from the crowd of villages and Vikings. I noticed Wipped was watching me with his arms folded and had a smile on his face. I told the thrall next to him to pick up the cross; she was a little girl about the same age as me. She looked terrified and didn't move as I gave her an order. I howled in her face like a wolf, telling her to pick it up, but she was too frightened to move, so I sliced my blade across her delicate skin that held in her throat. She quickly bled to death.

I was now soaked as the blood of the waelisc was dripping down my face. I then came to Derfel, the boy I met on the beach; he was about twelve years old when I first met him. He was five years older then me, but yet I was much bigger then that little waelisc weasel. I laughed and pointed as I noticed he had pissed himself from fear and the crowd laughed with me. I got in his face looking down on him: 'Pick it up' I said gritting my teeth, pointing to the cross on the floor. He was crying and shaking as he slowly knelt down and with his dark eyes closed, he gripped the cross with his hand. I then raised my blade into the air and swung it towards the boy's skull. Derfel didn't move, he was frozen with terror and the crowd cheered as I only pretended to kill him. 'Good boy' I said. 'You are obedient; you will make a good thrall.' He didn't understand my words, but I'm sure he understood what was happening. I then used the bone handle of *Wolf-Fang* to smack Derfel in the face and the crowd laughed as he fell to the floor and I noticed that even Dresden managed to crack a smile.

Derfel was a bright boy and was very good with words and numbers. I would later learn that Derfel could even speak in the strange Roman letters. He was a fast learner and understood the Englisc words well in only a short time. I didn't know it back then, but I now believe that the Gods had sent Derfel to me. Much later in my life Derfel would become invaluable with my dealings with the British King, Vortigern, as I didn't understand a word of the Celtic dribble that they spoke.

Derfel is the one that is writing my sagas for me, which you are currently reading, or at least getting your worthless Christian thrall to read it for you. I wanted my sagas and tales to be recorded for all time so even long after my death and my bones have turned to ashes or buried under a burial mound, the children of my children will remember the deeds of their long dead ancestor and remember. I believe it's important to remember, to know the truth, to know where you came from.

I asked Wipped what he was going to do with the remaining unwanted thralls. 'Chuck them off the cliffs.' he answered without care. I was horrified at his laziness. 'If they burn us then why can't we burn them?' I asked, wanting to make the Christians suffer. 'You have such an evil mind.' Onola said as she smiled. 'Burn a couple of them for fun.' Hoc said as he walked away. Wipped looked at Hoc with a surprised expression as the king left, and then Wipped turned to me and raised his eyebrows and pulled a funny face making me laugh. Hoc then turned back round and said: 'We'll nail the rest of them to trees as a sacrifice to Woden.

If we're going to attack the Scyldings,
then we'll need all the help
we can get.'

*'Close by them are their nearest and dearest,
so that they can hear the shrieks of their women and wailing
of their children. These are the witnesses
whom each man reverences most highly,
whose praise he most desires.
It is to their mothers
and wives that they go
to have their wounds treated,
and the women are not afraid
to compare gashes.'*

Roman Historian 'Tacitus'
1st Century AD

Chapter Six:
The Children of Woden

England 427AD
(Southern Denmark)

    Seven summers had passed since Horsa and I had joined the Angles. Wipped had told me to never forget my roots and I still thought of myself as a Jute, but after seven years at Hocsburh I now had a great sense of being an Angle, I was now Englisc as well as a Jute. Dresden was now thirteen years old and had begun dabbling into magic as she had become interested in the shamans and priestesses. She had long since been released by Froda and was now a free woman making her living the same as Saxburga, as a weaver, even though her real passion was learning how to fight with the men and cast spells on people she didn't like.

    Hild and I had become close over the years and we were now in love and were secretly betrothed. She had turned twenty and was deeply worried that she was becoming too old to marry. Her father had always tried to push her into marriage with the sons of many chieftains, but she had always run away, waiting for me to come of age. Over the last few years I had seen a change in Hild; she had become quieter and sometimes seemed hopelessly depressed as she stared at the walls, looking right through them. I knew she desperately wanted children and was worried that she would die one day without bearing a soul. It was common for our people to die before their twenty fifth birthday as life was often short and brutal. I guess that made it more special in a way as the tribes didn't like to waste time on the little things and enjoyed a full life of fighting, frolicking and being merry. But I couldn't help think that there was something else on her mind, something she wasn't telling me.

Hnaef and Hunlafing were now both eighteen years old and had been fighting the Scyldings for the past four years. I had watched Hnaef many times in battle and admired his courage as he charged like a champion into the mix of flesh, bone and steel. He always fought with his sword *Battle-Flame* and I often listened to it singing as it whistled through the air, cutting his enemies down like trees. I, Hild, Dresden, Saxburga and Horsa were always watching from a distance cheering Hnaef and the others on. I often took my sword with me *Dances with Corpses* hoping to go into battle and get my blade wet for the very first time, but I was forbidden until I came of age.

Wipped spent most of his summers raiding the coasts of Britain and Gaul collecting thralls and treasures and trading them in the Frisian markets. The Skull Crusher promised me that he would take me there one day. He tells me that a man can buy anything there, including the finest Frankish weapons, meat and fish, and the women are as cheap as a loaf of bread. When he wasn't away over seas, Wipped enjoyed fighting the Scyldings as he had done so for the last seven years hoping to reclaim the lost territory of the Jutes and restore the honour of my father.

Over the years the Angles and Jutes had made their way north and we slowly fought our way westwards taking one village at a time. We had cut off King Folcwald's supply route to his homelands across the seas in Geatland, leaving him and his troops to fight alone. Many of the western tribes, led by the Jutisc chieftain Gefwulf, a great friend of my father, had managed to keep their independence from King Folcwald's men over the years. But they were small and weak and had lost most of their territories and wooden forts to the invaders. But together with the Angles, we helped overwhelm the Scyldings and attack them from both sides.

I would like to claim that we slaughtered the Scyldings year after year, but the truth is that in the first five years we had lost almost as many battles as we had won. Many times the Scyldings, Geates and the

Danes had fought their way from Geatland and simply overwhelmed the combined forces of the Angles and Jutes. We were plagued by them, hacking and slashing their way through our ranks. And we often lost the forts that had been taken with so much might and with so much blood.

We had fought them on land and sea. I witnessed battles across fields, in woods and by lakes. I watched with a smile as men were butchered, trampled on and drown in the frozen seas. Many men died on both sides and it often seemed like no one really won anything. After a fort was taken it took such effort and logistics to keep it that our forces were often overstretched and it would become a matter of time before we lost it again. I witnessed horrific injuries as I saw Dresden, Saxburga, Hild and many other women and thralls helping the wounded. I saw them snapping bones back into place and sewing up nasty gashes. I saw Dresden cutting off rotten limbs and using her magic to cure the wounded.

From my youthful eyes I was witnessing an epic as I watched the tribes go to war. There were maybe two or three hundred thanes on each side at any one time. But now looking back, having heard the ground shake with the thunder of thousands of men under my command as we charged across the lands of the Britons, I now see that the battles with the Scyldings were small skirmishes compared to what was to come.

It had become common between the warring tribes to settle things with duels as an attempt to save many valuable lives and witness whom the God's favoured the most. Men were needed for the autumn harvests and for hunting and to repair the forts, not just from each other, but also from the other tribes of the world. King Hoc of the Angles and King Folcwald of the Scyldings, as well as Wipped and Froda, had earned themselves a great reputation for single combat and had become feared in all the lands.

Folcwald's son Finn was a brave and skilled fighter that I had grown up watching in battle. And over countless encounters with the Scyldings I had come to idolise Finn and wished to emulate him in battle. I had watched Finn since he was only fifteen years old and he had now grown into a menacing and greatly feared twenty two year old man. He had long black hair and wore an impressive silver and gold war helmet and was often riding high on his favourite black and white horse. I had witnessed him in many battles slaughtering the Angles and the Jutes. He had competed in many duels and fought to the death and lived to tell the tales.

I had come to admire the courage and skill of both King Folcwald and Finn, but they were both responsible for the death and destruction of my village. And if I didn't exact my revenge and continue the blood-feud then I would lose the honour of my father, my people and my self. And over the last seven years I had been training to fight, training to survive and training to kill. *Dances with Corpses* were thirsting for blood and I had become consumed with a thirst for vengeance.

Each week since the age of seven, I and all the youngsters from across the villages gathered at Hocsburh for our weekly training sessions. All free men and women were welcome and we were joined by many thanes, ealdormans and chieftains. Dresden was amongst the few females wishing to learn how to fight guided by the spirits of the *Valkyries*.

The youngsters were paired up with the much older and bigger kids as we practiced the art of warfare. The older kids were always eager to impress their chieftains and would be tough and aggressive with their smaller opponents. The thanes and ealdormans encouraged this behaviour as soon the older kids would be going into battle and they needed to become aggressive and mean. I was told by Hoc that it was good for me to get my arse kicked by the older kids as I would soon become used to a bigger opponent and when I fought for real, I would fear nobody.

I remember watching Hunlafing and Hnaef in training a few years earlier and when Hnaef was knocked down by large well built thane he started crying. And so his father ordered him to be flogged in front of the whole village. 'Men don't cry, especially the son of the king.' Hoc shouted at a terrified Hnaef. I never saw Hnaef cry ever again.

I remember the time when I was first introduced to my instructor Siegeferth. He was wearing a boar-crested silver war helmet, a iron breastplate held together with leather thongs and he had a glittering jewel-studded pattern-welded sword. He was also wearing a wolf skin cloak that was pinned to his tunic with decorated brooches made from gold and inlaid with gems. Siegeferth was a huge man with long brown hair that fell to his shoulders. He had small beady eyes, a long pointy noise and the loudest and most vile voice that I had ever heard and he enjoyed nothing more than to give us all a beasting. He was from Northern Germany in the Saxon lands and he spoke with an accent that irritated me. Siegeferth was the chieftain of the *Secgan*, originally from Germany, but now live in southern England.

On the day we met him he told us all to line up shoulder to shoulder and fall back into three ranks. And as he walked slowly down the front line he was yelling to us: 'Until you prove otherwise, you are all worthless Englisc scum. And I have a higher opinion of what has fallen out of a Christian's arse then I do of any of you. Is that understood?'

'Yes lord!' we all yelled with smirks on our faces. 'I'm here to teach lazy, fat, disgusting vermin like you how to become warriors that your country can become proud of. Do you wish to be vermin all your lives?'

'No lord!' we yelled. Siegeferth then looked at us all and shouted out: 'I don't accept puffs in my squadrons. So if you think you might be a little funny, if you look down at another man's sausage and think to yourself 'I definitely would'. Then put your hand up now and I'll cut off your balls and send you to do women's tasks such as milking the cows. I'm sure you'll love playing with the udders of a cow you filthy, dirty bastards!'

I, Dresden, Hunlafing and Hnaef were laughing hysterically and had tears rolling down our cheeks. I then grabbed Hunlafing's arm and held it in the air for Siegeferth to see. Everyone began laughing as Siegeferth came rushing over to us just as I let go of Hunlafing's arm. 'What's this?' he asked. 'Do I have a pair of cock munchers in my ranks?' I burst with laughter as I told him that Hunlafing was gay. 'No I'm not!' Hunlafing reassured us all. 'Silence!' Siegeferth screamed at me as his spittle hit me in the face. Hnaef and Dresden were holding their breath and dying not to laugh. 'You speak only when spoken to, do you understand?'

'Yes lord!' I replied. 'And stop fucking fidgeting, the pair of you. You only move when I say you can move.'

'But what if we need to scratch our balls my lord?' I asked as I dribbled from my mouth as I couldn't contain my laughter. Siegeferth then punched me with all his might in my stomach and winded me severely. And that took the smile right off my face. Hunlafing burst with laughter right in front of Siegeferth and he too got a punch to the stomach for laughing at me. And we were laid on the floor in agony as Siegeferth then turned to Dresden: 'No special treatment for girls either, if you want to act like men, then I shall treat you like men, is that understood you piece of vermin?'

'Yes lord!' Dresden shouted. 'If at any point I hurt your delicate feelings, then don't fucking tell me, because I don't fucking care. Is that understood?'

'Yes lord!' Dresden screamed. 'Good, good, then let's get on with the training shall we?'

We were all encouraged to be tough and every time we got knocked down we were told to go and join the women, the old and the lame. Joining the weak was a *wyrd* worse than death for any man. I remember one time when I was knocked to the ground and I was writhing in agony and holding my ribs and I was told to go and polish the chain-mail of the visiting thanes. 'Your mothers are the whores of trolls.' I shouted at the laughing thanes. I got to my feet, my ribs still sore, and charged at my larger opponent knocking him to the ground with a shoulder charge using my shield as a battering ram. The thanes watched and applauded.

As the years passed, I began to enjoy my weekly training sessions and had become a favourite amongst the thanes. Hunlafing, Hnaef and Dresden and I received private training from Hoc's men, and Froda, Wipped and most my father's Vikings helped too. 'Its all in the wrist', Froda shouted as he was showing me how to throw the javelins and spears. We were taught how to use a throwing axe, bows, axes and of course swords. We would have to stand on a field and use our shields and learn how to dodge the blunt swords and throwing axes that the Froda and Wipped were trying to hit us with. I had many bruises and broken bones from that sort of training. I remember seeing Dresden's face as she was once hit in the head by a throwing axe and it knocked her to the ground. She laughed as she sat in the grass rubbing her bruised forehead.

Over the years we all learned how to dance amongst swords, arrows and spears that were levelled at us. We were trained well. When we reached the age of ten we were each sent to live in the woods for a week alone, armed with only our saxes. And we were told to use our wits and courage to survive to prove that we were worthy of being Woden's warriors. And from the age of twelve we were trained how to ride horses and we weren't allowed to show any fear, even though we had all witnessed many older kids fall off and get trampled to death by the horses. And the ones that survived were kept alive until it was time for war and then they were mercifully sacrificed to Woden. 'They were sacrificed with honour, it was better than dying needlessly.' Siegeferth told us.

I was forced to swing a sword and axe that was too heavy for me to build strong arms and confidence. And when I was given a lighter sword or axe, I could swing faster than the eye could see, slaying all that stood before me. My training was hard and intense, but as I grew stronger *Dances with Corpses* had become lighter and I could now use my father's sword much better than before. I was now fourteen years old and I had grown to the size of a man. I had become a thane and I was ready for war. The Gods held their breath.

Once we had completed our initial training, Dresden and I joined the other kids as Siegeferth made us stand and salute the Englisc flag. And as many of us were also Jutes, he allowed us to salute the flag of our own tribe as well. Siegeferth spoke: 'Live thou for England, for many have died for thee.' We were made to stand and salute the white horse flag of the Jutes and the white dragon flag of the Englisc. And with our right arms held out straight we were told to chant the words: 'Hail England! Hail England!' We had done that for years, we were made to say it over and over again, day after day and month after month and each time we said it with more intensity and pride. And we said it every week after training and we weren't allowed to stop until Siegeferth was satisfied that we meant what we were saying.

The flags were covered in the blood of our people and the blood of our enemies from various wars. And it was a powerful feeling to salute the flags of my people as it gave me a sense of identity, a feeling of belonging and a purpose in life. I had been an outcast for must of my life, but not anymore as the people of England were my family now. The rest of the lads were screaming and yelling with pride on the day we finally passed out as fully trained thanes, but I didn't say a word, I just stood there in silence and saluted the flags of my forefathers.

In the last two years the Angles and Jutes had conquered all of the eastern forts in Jutland and now ruled the seas with dozens of warships that had successfully blocked the Scyldings passage from Jutland to Geatland. We had starved out many forts and simply destroyed others. Gefwulf, the chieftain of the western Jutes, had invaded from the west and along with his allies, the Angles and Jutes, we had now surrounded the final wooden fortress held by the Scyldings and we knew both Folcwald and Finn were inside.

The estimated numbers for Folcwald's men were four hundred and the numbers of Jutes and Angles combined were over nine hundred. The final battle for Jutland was about to begin. I was now a fully trained thane and was ready to make Woden proud, I was ready for war. But the *Fates* were once again playing games with me as tragedy struck.

Hoc was away in battle as Onola suddenly fell ill and was dying. It was a cold, bitter autumn and many of the villagers had fallen ill from the coughing disease. Hild was by her mother's side as was her brother Hnaef. Onola had been like a mother to me and Horsa and so I had declined my invitation to go into my very first battle, choosing to stay with my queen in her final hours. Dresden was too young to go into battle and she was in the room too, slumped on the dirty floor with Horsa, not knowing what to say.

We had all slept on the floor that night, keeping the small fire lit the best we could as the queen tried to sleep. She was sweating, coughing, tossing and turning all night. I don't think many of us slept well that night and I was horrified as I looked at Onola trying to remember the day I first met her. Remembering how beautiful she was with her big blue eyes and long blonde hair and welcoming smile. Her smile reminded me of my mother's and I had grown to love Onola like a mother. But looking at her that night she seemed a shell of her former self, she looked old and tired.

That morning the fire had gone out and Hild was inconsolable as Onola had passed away during the night. Hild and Horsa cried like babies as Hnaef, Dresden and I looked on with heartache. Hnaef and I told the others to stay in England and we told our thralls to fetch our polished war gear. We were preparing to go to Gefwulfsburh,

the last fort held by the Scyldings,
to tell the king that
his queen was
dead.

'The light-haired races place great value
on freedom. They are bold and undaunted
in battle. Daring and impetuous as they are,
they consider any timidity
and even a short retreat as a disgrace.
They calmly despise death as they fight violently
in hand to hand combat,
either on horseback
or foot.'

The Strategikon,
A 6th century
Roman military manual

Chapter Seven:
Under the Boar-Crest

England 427AD
(Southern Denmark)

    I laced up my leather and wolf skin boots as Derfel placed my silver, newly polished, boar-crested war helmet over my long brown hair that fell just below my shoulders. Boars are a sign of Freyja and bring luck to the bearer when worn in battle and they were very popular amongst the thanes. The helmet was a gift from Hoc as well as my spiked-boss shield that was made from the best hardwood and decorated with a picture of a bird and of course I was armed with my father's sword. I smiled as I placed *Dances with Corpses* into my leather scabbard and tucked *Wolf-Fang* into my leather belt. Hnaef and I were dressed for war. Hnaef looked like a young king covered in shiny new chain-mail and breastplates. But even Hnaef admitted that I had the better sword.

    As Hnaef and I were preparing to leave, Dresden came into the room and told us that she was coming too. She was wearing war gear and had on a rusty, dented old war helmet with a broken boar-crest that was too big for her head. Hnaef and I burst with laughter. 'Don't laugh at me, you bastards! I'm coming with you.' She had brought three rabbits with her and smiled. Hnaef, Dresden and I then held the rabbits tightly by their ears as we slit their throats with our saxes to help quench the thirst of Woden and secure us a safe passage into Jutland.

It was cold and dark as we marched northwards and up the east coastline of Jutland, our armour was heavy and it clanged loudly as we ran. We had travelled for hours and as the night finally closed in on the day, we decided to settle down for the night, still deep in the Black Forest, miles from any settlements. Dresden had only an old rusty axe with her that she had found discarded. 'Here, take *Wolf-Fang* and don't lose it or I'll bury you in the woods somewhere.'

I tried to make myself comfortable on the cold forest floor with only an itchy woollen blanket with holes in it for comfort. It stunk like a horses arse, but I didn't mind as the cold was so bitter. I was shivering when Dresden came and threw some rags over me and snuggled up to try and keep warm. Hnaef then sat up and did the same, squashing Dresden in the middle of us both.

I didn't sleep well that night as I was nervous and exited about the battle to come and was terrified about telling the king of his wife's death. We slept in a small clearing in the woods at the bottom of a banking. It was a clear night and I could see the moon and stars brightening up the night sky. In the distance I could hear owls, bats and other creatures moving around in the dark and the trees were moving in the night time breeze making a sound like fire crackling in the wind. I kept a look out that night as I was unable to sleep, listening for wolves, elves, dwarves and the monster *Grendel*. And I was wondering if I would ever see the ghost again that had saved me from disaster as a youngster. I thought a lot about Onola that night and I'm not ashamed to admit that I cried myself to the sleep in silence. I think we all did.

The next morning I awoke to a moment of terror. As I opened my eyes, I was face to face with a big white and grey wolf. My body froze unable to move, the wolf was licking my chapped lips tasting the dried salted mutton and bread that I had eaten for supper the night before. I stayed deadly still as I didn't want to startle the wolf, when I suddenly felt a sense of familiarity. As the wolf began to sniff around the burned out campfire, I noticed it was not alone. There were a pack of wolves trying to get at our rations of food that had been wrapped in leaves hidden in Dresden's gear. I slowly lifted my head and noticed that the white and grey wolf walked with a slight limp. It was *Fenrir*, my old pet. But he was old now and wasn't the same wolf that I had raised as a child, he had become wild and dangerous.

I stayed patiently still and waited for the wolves to finish off our rations and leave. But then a grey wolf with a striking white tail walked over to Dresden and began searching her for food. She woke up. And screamed! She frightened the wolves and fearing for their yearlings the wolves suddenly turned aggressive. The three of us jumped up from underneath our flea infested blankets and raised our swords. Hnaef and Dresden began hacking and slashing at the wolves, screaming for their lives. The wolves yelped and backed away and began to retreat. Then Dresden moved forward and slashed at the wolf with the white tail, killing it instantly. Then suddenly out of nowhere she was attacked, it was *Fenrir*. Perhaps he was protecting his girlfriend, I thought, as he jumped at Dresden knocking her to the ground. I suddenly had a flashback of when my sister Helgi was killed and how I had watched her death from the trees, too cowardly to help. As Dresden was laying on the floor fearing for her life, I raised *Dances with Corpses* in the air and slashed down hard, killing the wolf I once loved.

We continued our march north that morning, not speaking much, having death on our minds, when we suddenly walked past the cave of the monster *Grendel*. 'Let's go inside and say hello.' Dresden joked. 'Don't be bloody stupid woman, I'm not going in there, its dark and we don't have a torch and besides, I don't fancy getting eaten today.' Hnaef grumbled.

Dresden spoke: 'You big puff. You're going to be king one day. Aren't kings meant to have hair on their balls and show no fear?' Hnaef frowned: 'I'm not scared, I've already had a fight with wolves this morning and I can't be arsed killing another monster in the same day.' Dresden and I laughed. 'Chicken shit!' Dresden said as she taunted the prince. 'Come on Hengest, I know you wont let me down.' Dresden said as she tugged at my arm. But I was more frightened than Hnaef. I had grown up with horror stories about *Grendel* breaking into villages at night and running away with the children.

As a small child sitting around the camp fire, I was told how he would bite into the skulls of the children and chomp them down. And then *Grendel* would rip open their stomachs and empty the shite from their intestines before eating out their innards. I remember the children crying and shitting themselves before they went to bed. And I remember waking up in the middle of the night to the sounds of children screaming in their nightmares, having pissed themselves. And now Dresden was encouraging me to enter the lair of *Grendel* and I was bricking it. But just like Dresden had said: 'kings are meant to show no fear.' And I had hoped to one day become King of Jutland and so I pulled out *Dances with Corpses*, took a deep breath, clenched my arse and followed Dresden through the bushes and towards the opening of the cave.

Dresden pulled out *Wolf-Fang* and crouched slightly as she slowly entered the lair of the child-munching monster *Grendel*. I turned round and looked at Hnaef as I pulled a funny face showing him my concerns, he laughed as he stood outside, alone, still shitting himself. It was dark in that cave and I could barely see anything. I kept bumping into Dresden whom told me off for holding my sword out in her direction. I then held onto the bottom of her tunic as she led us both slowly into the darkness of *Grendel's* lair. I began to sniff the air around me and I could smell something awful. 'Is that you Dresden?' I whispered as I still held onto her tunic. 'Piss off!' she muttered. 'I've only just had a wash last week.'

We had now walked quite far into the cave, when suddenly Dresden raised her voice and asked: 'What-in the name of Woden's hairy arse-is that fucking smell?' and then suddenly we heard a loud noise coming from in front of us. It was a loud groan, almost like a yawn. I stumbled to the side and trampled on what seemed like bones, probably the bones of children. We then heard something move, but it was so dark that we could barely see anything. Our eyes had adjusted well in the dark, but there was little light in that cave and we could barely make out shadows. We then held out our weapons as something big moved around the floor of the cave.

I hung onto the back of Dresden, making sure that she was stood in front of me, when suddenly a huge shadow stood up in front of us. We both screamed! The shadow was huge, at least ten feet tall and I could just see the outline of it. It was definitely hairy and had two huge claws and it roared at us with a mighty wide jaw. 'Fucking move!' Dresden yelled as she turned to run, pushing me out of the way. I tripped over the bones that scattered the floor and dropped my sword as Dresden ran for the exit. 'Don't leave me.' I begged.

Dresden had gone and left me all alone with the monster *Grendel*. I could feel the bones of children all around me as I desperately tried to feel for my sword in the pitch dark. *Grendel* was now crawling on all fours as he sniffed the air and tried to find me, perhaps he was hungry. I then picked up something that I thought was my sword. But it wasn't, it was a bone, it probably belonged to a child like me, I thought. I then threw the bone as far away as I could. And I could hear *Grendel* rush towards the area where the bone had hit the wall.

Finally I found my sword *Dances with Corpses* and I could hear both Hnaef and Dresden shouting for me to run from outside of the cave. The monster then heard me as I got to my feet and he stood back up on two legs and roared at me in the pitch dark. I then turned and ran as fast as possible. I was holding out my sword with two hands, making sure that I wasn't running into walls as I could barely see anything inside *Grendel's* lair. I rushed as fast I could, feeling my way along the walls of the cave, shitting and pissing myself every step of the way. And as I was holding out *Dances with Corpses*, I could feel my belt loosen and my kegs began to slowly fall down my legs. And finally I could see daylight at the end of the tunnel and I saw two small figures of my friends screaming for me to hurry up. And I didn't stop as I exited the cave, even with my pants around my ankles and my man-bits hanging out. I then ran straight into Hnaef and Dresden and the three of us fell down the small banking that led to *Grendel's* cave.

The three of us were lying in the grass, my legs felt weak and my heart was beating fast, but we felt safe outside in the daylight and the three of us began to laugh. 'Thanks for leaving me Dresden.' I said as I desperately tried to catch my breath and pull up my trousers. 'Your welcome.' She said sarcastically. 'And what's that between your legs, it's tiny.' She said as she pointed and laughed. 'Fuck off bitch, its cold.' I laughed.

As we exited the woods, I could see my father's old fort; I noticed it had been repaired. And there were armed guards in the watchtowers equipped with bows and arrows, watching over the lands. It was now ruled by the Angles and Jutes and I had hoped that one day I would be able to reclaim my sovereignty over the fort and the Jutisc race, but for now it belonged to King Hoc. We were given water and other supplies; they then gave us directions towards Gefwulfsburh where the final battle for Jutland was taking place.

After almost two days of travelling, Hnaef, I and Dresden had found the old fort. The design was almost identical to my father's with huge watchtowers guarded by thanes with bows and arrows. I saw the Scylding banner of a black bear flapping in the breeze as it was attached to poles surrounding the fort. The Scyldings were watching the Angles and Jutes that were camped outside of the fort in their hundreds. I recognised King Hoc from a distance; he was recognisable from his war gear and always stood out from a crowd, standing tall, high above the rest and holding the white dragon emblem of the Englisc. He was with his right hand man Hunlaf and with him was his son Hunlafing. I also noticed Wipped as he was holding the white horse emblem of the Jutes attached to a long pole as he wanted the Scyldings to know that the Jutes had come for their lands back.

Dresden and I stood back as Hnaef walked slowly towards his father to tell him the *wyrd* of Onola. Moments later Hnaef returned to Dresden and I and told us to go and join the thanes across the back ranks whilst he returned to his father. Dresden and I were trained thanes, but neither of us had competed in a real battle before and Dresden was still underage. But nobody seemed to realise as she kept her face hidden under her helmet, determined to fight. This was mine and Dresden's last chance of revenge against the Scyldings for what they did to our people seven years earlier. There was no doubt that the Scyldings would fall at Gefwulfsburh and Dresden and I hungered for our last chance of vengeance.

Hours seemed to go past slowly as we waited and waited, hoping the Scyldings would come out and fight. Dresden and I nearly died of boredom hoping for some action. None of us knew what was happening as we could see King Hoc pacing around the outside of the fort on his white horse with the Englisc ealdorman Hunlaf, and the Jutisc chieftain Gefwulf was also present. Dresden and I fell asleep. 'Wake up! Wake up! you lazy bastards!' Siegeferth shouted as he kicked us in the leg. 'Get ready to fight; you little shits.' He said with authority. Finally I found someone who knew what was happening. 'My lord', I said showing my respect. 'What's happening? Why haven't we destroyed the fort already? What are we waiting for?'

Siegeferth told me that Hoc had been negotiating with the Scyldings for their surrender for almost a week now. Hoc had promised the Scyldings that his men would smash into the wooden fort with battering rams and slaughter everyone inside unless they surrendered. But of course surrendering is considered an absolute disgrace and so we had prepared ourselves for an all out war. It began raining gently as Siegeferth continued: 'But now the Scyldings are preparing to surrender, but be ready for a fight. These foreign bastards aren't trustworthy and will probably attack us as soon as the gates are opened as a last effort to save their miserable lives. Get your weapons ready.' And with her dark eyes hiding underneath her helmet, slowly drawing *Wolf-Fang* from its leather sheath, Dresden smiled.

'Are you scared Hengest?' she asked. 'Don't be bloody stupid woman! I don't get scared.' I said with a grin. But the truth was my bowels felt loose and I thought I was going to be sick. 'Me neither.' Dresden replied, just before she took off her helmet, allowing her long black hair to fall loosely and then threw up all over the grass. 'You dirty bitch!' I said with humour. It stank! 'Bollocks!' she said, laughing as she wiped her dirty gob.

As I looked at the front ranks I could see Froda and Wipped together with a group of ealdorman and thanes that I assumed were discussing tactics with the king. Then a man shouted something from inside the fort and everything went quiet as the gates slowly opened and the Scyldings were waiting inside, all of them armed and many of them on horseback. I could see King Folcwald and his son Finn sitting at the front on their trademark black and white horses. I reached to touch the hilt of my sword: 'It won't be long now.' I said, speaking to *Dances with Corpses*.

I looked at Dresden, her eyes were fixed on Folcwald and her right foot was tapping the floor with anticipation. She had waited for this moment since she was six years old, for a chance to kill the man responsible for her mother's murder. She was only thirteen and she wasn't very big, but she didn't care as she already was holding *Wolf-Fang* in her hands, freshly sharpened by Derfel, thirsty for blood.

King Hoc moved forward on his white horse armed with a sword and shield. He was speaking to the Scyldings, but I was too far back to hear what was said. 'Do you think they're going to surrender Dres?' I asked as she looked at me with disgust. 'Cowards!' she shouted across the field. Some of the thanes looked back, perhaps wondering where that soft voice came from. 'They had better not.' she said quietly with tears in her eyes. 'War!' a man screamed from the middle ranks and he was soon followed with more chants for war. There were many Jutes amongst the hundreds of thanes that had fully surrounded the fort; they had also lost their homes, lands and their families. The war with the Scyldings had escalated into hatred in the last seven years and many of the Angles had also lost loved ones in the blood-feuds and suddenly the whole army seemed to be chanting for war.

Dresden and I joined in the chanting and I saw Wipped looking back at the men, waving the white horse banner, reminding the soldiers what they're fighting for. Suddenly the King of the Scyldings charged his horse forwards and stroked down hard with his blade onto the shoulder of King Hoc. War had erupted. The Scyldings all charged forwards on their horses having no choice, but to run their horses into the front ranks of the infantry. It was chaos. Dresden and I were held back by the hundreds of thanes in front, but we were screaming as we desperately wanted to get to the front. The front ranks began to fall apart as about one hundred Scyldings on horseback charged at them with swords and axes. They were immediately followed by about three hundred infantry, also wearing chain-mail, helmets and were armed with spears, swords and axes.

As I was watching from the back, I saw that King Folcwald's horse had been stabbed in its stomach and its guts spewed out all over the battlefield. 'Come on Dres!' I shouted over the screaming and yelling as we desperately pushed our way through the thanes trying to reach the king before someone else beat us to it. I found myself tripping over bodies that began to quickly fill the battlefield as I screamed and shouted. My fear had disappeared and I was now enraged like a *Berserker* and I could feel the battle-fury that I had heard about so many times during training. I was coming for Folcwald's blood.

I saw boar-shapes flashing on the battlefield, the brightly forged work of goldsmiths, as I pushed my way through the mass of steel and flesh. Dresden was clinging to the bottom of my tunic not wanting to lose me. And then we saw him in the middle of all the chaos being challenged by two of our men. Folcwald had been injured and was favouring his left arm, but he was still dangerous as he swung his sword taking the head off one of our thanes. Folcwald pointed his sword at the other man that was now standing in front of me: 'You're coming to *Valhalla* with me tonight boy.'

The king knew he wasn't going to survive the battle and seemed happy to be going to Woden's feast-hall in the sky. He was feeling the battle-fury and was determined to take as many Jutes and Angles with him as possible. I had become obsessed with killing Folcwald that I did something crazy. I had not planned it and I didn't give it a moments thought as I suddenly plunged my blade deep into the back of one of my own men. Now nothing and no one stood between me and King Folcwald.

Folcwald was a tall man and even though I was only fourteen, I was able to look the king square in his blue eyes. I was very tall for my age, but I wasn't as strong or as skilled as Folcwald. He was a well built man and very strong with huge round shoulders and powerful arms that were decorated with golden rings. He was dressed much like the same day I first met him all those years ago when Froda killed one of his chosen men. He wore a silver and gold war helmet; his face covered with a dragon mask and had his impressive long sword. He carried a shield and his chain-mail was covered in the same black bear skin that I had seen before.

After stabbing one of my own men, I walked forwards challenging Folcwald, my hands were shaking as I held up *Dances with Corpses*. Folcwald looked at me with a surprised look on his face. 'Who are you boy? He asked waving his sword at me. There were banging and screaming all around me as I shouted: 'I am Aesc, son of Whitgils!' Folcwald laughed. 'I thought you would be a bag of bones by now, long dead and buried. You look well.' he said with amusement. 'Don't you recognise me? We've met before. I told you my name was Hengest, do you remember old man?'

'The cheeky little tramp from Jutland? I remember you boy.' Folcwald said as he laughed to himself. 'You're a very brave young man, but stupid like that over grown tree stump Whitgils. I guess it's your wish to go to *Valhalla* and be with your miserable father?'

I then yelled a battle-cry as I charged forward forgetting all of my training and discipline. I raised *Dances with Corpses* into the air and tried to run through the king, but I was young, arrogant and clumsy. I believed that Woden was protecting me in battle and that made me hopelessly reckless, but it also made me brave and extremely dangerous.

I was well trained by Hoc's men, but my youth and inexperience proved almost deadly on that rainy afternoon.

As I charged at the king, he raised his shield to block my attack and used my own enthusiasm against me knocking me to the ground. 'Get up boy! You're making this too easy.' I struggled to my feet; my armour was heavy making me slow and tired. I was angry and frustrated; I began doubting myself, doubting if I, a boy, could actually kill a great and powerful king. I was frightened and my hands were shaking, but I could still feel the battle-fury running through my veins. I got back to my feet, the rain dripping down my helmet, I looked at Folcwald and pointed at him with my blade: 'I want your blood, you worthless piece of baby shit.' King Folcwald looked furious. No more words were said. And we fought to the death.

It was raining hard as I walked over to him slowly, keeping my calm, and holding my shield high. He struck me with his sword sending a streak of pain down my left arm. My hand released the shield, but I didn't drop it as it was attached to my forearm with leather straps. I ignored the pain and struck him with a blow from my own sword. He easily blocked it with his beautifully decorated snake-looped shield. We both had bodies banging into us as the battle was being furiously fought around us. Men were bleeding, men were screaming and men were dying. But I almost became oblivious to the hundreds of warriors around me. And at that particular moment all I cared about was thrusting my blade into the guts of the man that had stolen my land and inheritance.

I swung my sword with fury and I could hear *Dances with Corpses* begin to sing in the wind, it was singing the sweat song of death as I danced and danced forcing Folcwald backwards. I screamed out loudly as I saw a weak spot in his armour. His chain-mail was too small to fit around his huge gut and as he raised his arms into the air with his sword his belly popped out leaving him exposed, unprotected and vulnerable. I planned to swing my sword again, hoping for him to block it with his shield and then wait for him to strike at me. And then with lightening speed, I planned to ram my huge sword into his fat belly and spew his guts all over the battlefield.

As planned, I had hit him with my sword and I waited for him to attack. And as he raised his sword up, I tried to slice him open, but my arms were too weak and slow. My sword was heavy and I didn't move as fast as I needed too. I had over estimated my own abilities and Folcwald slashed his sword down my left ribs. The pain was horrific and there was blood dripping out of my side as his sword had pierced my flesh. I screamed out loud as I lay on the floor gasping for air struggling to breathe. My heart was beating so incredibly fast that I thought I was going to die. I laid flat on my back and held my shield up for protection as I didn't know what else to do and I knew Folcwald wouldn't allow me to get to my feet again.

Then all of a sudden, I heard a huge death cry come from the lungs of Folcwald. And as I moved my shield to the side, I could see what was happening. And I was astonished to discover Folcwald lying face first in the grass. It was Dresden, she had saved me. She had stabbed Folcwald in the kidneys as he raised his sword to inflict the killer blow. I was still lying on the floor favouring my ribs as I saw Dresden jump at Folcwald and repeatedly stab him again and again with furious anger as Folcwald lay helpless in a puddle of his own blood.

Folcwald was dead and I'll never forget the ecstasy that I felt as I witnessed Dresden stand up covered in blood and with the rain pouring down on her she held up *Wolf-Fang* and licked the blood off the blade. That image had become distorted in my mind over the years, but I swear I saw her long black hair turn white, her eyes rolled into the back of her head and her face aged a thousand years. She was possessed by the *Valkyries,* if only for a moment. Dresden looked at me with her dark eyes shining through her old, rusty war helmet and smiled. We had finally avenged our village and our kin. I smiled back.

Dresden helped me to my feet; my left hand side had become numb with pain as she helped me walk over to the edge of the forest with the rest of the wounded. She dropped me on the wet floor under the trees, my armour was heavy and I landed hard, 'Whoops, sorry!' she said with a smile on her face. Dresden helped me undress and I could see that my skin was split all the way down my ribs. Dresden began to wrap bandages around me: 'Bloody *Hel* woman, be gentle.' I cried. 'Shut your fucking whinging' she said: 'It's for your own good.'

The battle continued for hours, both sides fighting furiously in the rain and sludge that had become the battlefield. There were bodies everywhere lying in the grass being trampled on by the thanes. Dresden and I watched on from the edge of the woods surrounded by Wiccas, priests and the flies that were gathered around the dead animals that had been sacrificed before the battle had begun. I could hear the screams and cries of dying men all around me that were been attended to by their loved ones. And I could hear the sounds of children wailing in agony of their father's deaths. I could see Froda fighting the Scyldings and was happy that he still lived. I wanted to shout encouragement, but I was unable to fill my lungs with enough air and I just couldn't find the strength.

I laid in the wet grass for a long time, nursing my wound, when I noticed that the fighting had stopped. I saw that a small band of Scyldings had grouped together in the middle of the field and were surrounded by hundreds of Angles and Jutes and in the centre was Finn. He was standing tall and proud with his sword held high, daring anyone to challenge him. His long black hair fell below his shoulders; his armour glistened in the sunlight. He was shouting something to the thanes, but I was too far away to hear. Then I saw King Hoc approach the Scyldings. I could see that Finn and Hoc were having a conversation. 'What the *Hel* do they have to say to each other?' I asked as I painfully rose to my feet. 'I don't know.' Dresden replied, looking worried and confused.

I began to push my way through the thanes, my body racked with pain, as I walked slowly towards the king wanting to hear what was being said. 'I will not surrender and disgrace my family.' I heard Finn say out loud. 'I'm not asking for you to surrender.' Hoc shouted. 'All I want is to discuss peace between the Angles and Scyldings.' Dresden had followed me into the crowd and asked me why Hoc didn't just defeat the Scyldings then and there. 'Because there's more of them.' I said, 'Thousands still live in the northern lands and if we kill Finn, the rightful king, then they will elect a new king and they will keep coming back.'

Hoc told the Scyldings that their king was dead and that he was willing to accept Finn as the new Lord of the Scyldings and negotiate their release. I stood close enough to hear every word being spoken and I heard Hoc agree to let King Finn and his men leave as long as Finn agreed to his offer and swore an oath to honour their agreement. Finn's lands had become more and more inhospitable and the Scyldings were often plagued with famines and even worse floods than us and were unable to feed themselves. That was the main reason behind the invasion and so Hoc and Finn agreed that the Scyldings would stay away in their own territories across the northern sea. And Hoc gave his word that his men would help supply Finn's people with salted fish, mutton and fresh crops throughout the frequent famines. Both men had reached an agreement and both swore oaths to honour that agreement.

There was quiet amongst the thanes as Hoc announced himself as both King of England and King of Jutland. I immediately turned my head to look at Wipped. I was the rightful King of Jutland and Hoc had promised it to me when the time was right. I was furious. The Skull Crusher sensing that I was going to say something gestured for me to keep quiet and gave me an ominous grin. Hoc told everyone that he and Finn were equals and that the wars with the Scyldings had officially come to an end.

On the way home, as we marched through the Black Forest, I approached King Hoc and asked him why he had made himself the King of Jutland and not me. He took a deep breath and explained to me that he had heard rumours that Gefwulf, the chieftain of the western tribes, had planned on using the Angles to take back Jutland. Hoc explained that Gefwulf had planned on killing whoever the new king was and would make himself king instead. Hoc explained that he was protecting me and my fellow Jutes. If I had been killed by Gefwulf's men then Hoc would have had no choice, but to go to war with the Jutes and leave both tribes vulnerable to an already fragile relationship with the Scyldings.

Hoc promised me that all the Jutes would be given back their lands and that he would provide security for both our people by not splitting the two tribes up again as we had strength in numbers. What Hoc said did make sense, now my father was dead the Jutisc chieftains would battle and play politics to determine the new king and my life would have been in constant danger. But if Hoc was king then both tribes would have a stable leadership and Hoc would be safe in England surrounded by his most trusted ealdormans. But I couldn't help but feel betrayed.

After my conversation with Hoc, the Skull Crusher approached me asking what the king had said. I told Wipped everything and he nodded his head approvingly: 'That's exactly what I was hoping to hear.' he said. Wipped explained that Hoc was right and that Gefwulf was not to be trusted. 'But I wanted to be king, it's my birthright.' I said with a deflated voice. 'Keep your voice down Hengest, don't you see, you aren't destined to be King of Jutland.' Wipped was whispering: 'You're going to be the King of Kings; your *wyrd* is to be King of Jutland, England and Geatland.' Wipped had confused me. 'How am I supposed to do that?' I asked, holding my sore ribs. 'Its pretty simple really, you need to allow Hoc to remain King of both England and Jutland and allow him to consolidate the two lands over a period of time. And make sure that you never offer him your oath like that fool Froda. And in the meantime you need to marry that daughter of his.' He was of course was referring to Hild, the woman that had promised herself to me. 'You need to plough that field until she bears you a son then you have a claim over the entire kingdom. And when the time is right we invade Geatland.'

I liked that idea, but there was a problem. 'What about Hnaef, he's heir to the throne?' Wipped sighed and he made sure no one was listening as he whispered: 'When the time is right, we need to kill him!' Hnaef was my best friend. And I suddenly felt faint
    and the marching thanes behind me cheered
    as I threw up all over the
    forest floor.

*'Many noble youths,
if the land of their birth
is stagnating in a long period of peace
and inactivity,
deliberately seek out
other tribes
which have some
war in hand.'*

*Roman Historian 'Tacitus'
1st Century AD*

Chapter Eight:
The Whale Road

England to Saxony 427AD
(Southern Denmark to Northern Germany)

Weeks had passed and Hoc and Finn had honoured their agreement and there had been peace for a while. The wars were truly over and Finn had even offered blood-money to the Jutes that had lost their loved ones in the Scylding attacks done by King Folcwald. I reluctantly received my share of the *wergild* as Finn still had no idea that I Aesc still lived and I had the blood of his father on my hands. There is no honour in blood-money and the death of my village sat deep in my pockets weighing down my conscience.

King Hoc had kept his word and had given the Jutes back their lands. Later, I learned that Gefwulf had been murdered and Wipped told me that Hoc had been the one to order the killing as he had feared a rebellion from the Jutes. And many of Gefwulf's followers, including his son Garulf, had been forced into exile and banished from Jutland. It was a decision that I took no part in, yet I would meet Garulf and his men again one day in the most unlikely of places and I would learn that they had blamed me for their exile and named me as a traitor to the Jutes and hungered for my blood.

Hild and I had planned to marry soon and I had taken the Skull Crusher's advice and ploughed that field well, but we now needed the consent of the king to marry. We both knew that Hoc had nothing to gain from his daughter's marriage to a common thane even though I was of high birth and the rightful heir to the Jutisc throne. It seemed that Hild's happiness wasn't very high on Hoc's list of priorities. Hild had been unhappy for a long time, but I didn't know what was wrong with her. I once saw her cutting her arms and crying as she shook with the pain. I asked her what was wrong and I wanted to know why she was hurting herself. But she just told me that she liked the way it felt as the pain made her feel alive. Hild was no longer allowed outside of the fort as her father had become more protective of her and he didn't like the fact that I visited her every night.

Wipped still planned on helping me take over all the lands of England, Jutland and across the *Swan Road* to Geatland, including the Danish mainland. The Skull Crusher told me that if I was to become a great king then I needed to attract followers and make a reputation for my self and I needed to have silver and gold in order to pay for an army. Wipped told me that the number of Romans that protected the British coast had been dwindling for years and the raids had become easier and easier and often he returned to England having not lost one man. 'Let's go and get gold Hengest!' Wipped said with a funny grin as he ran his fingers through his long platted beard.

I was eager to spread my wings and earn some silver and so I went to Britain on a slave trading mission and lived the life of a Viking.

Looking back, I had yet to grow any facial hair, I was still just a child and my voice was only just breaking, making me sound like something that had crawled out of the underworld and slithered past *Hel* herself. But I was a trained thane, young and arrogant and as big as a man and I longed to be a Viking warrior.

Before making our way to Britain, Wipped and I had to stop by in Saxony between the river *Elbe* and the river *Wesser*. So we loaded up a Viking ship with freshly salted fish and meat and lots of fresh crops to be delivered to the Saxon lords. The Angles had an agreement with the Saxons that had lasted for many generations, promising to deliver food and ships in exchange for the Saxons keeping the Angles safe from the Roman advances. The Saxons were known to be the most aggressive tribes in all the lands and had a fierce reputation and were greatly feared. The Skull Crusher warned me before our journey to be extremely respectful to the Saxons, as they enjoyed nothing more then to disembowel people that they didn't like and were well known for their extreme violence.

Many new ships had been built over the years to be used as trading vessels, Viking ships and to be delivered to our allies. Wipped had built a very special sea-worthy ship to be used to plunder the British coast. He called it *Ocean-Mare* and it was an exact copy of my father's *White Horse* ship that had sunk to the bottom of the ocean as it burned to ashes. The sail was red with my father's white horse emblem in the centre, the emblem of the Jutes. Wipped had a thrall sew two lightening bolts beneath the horse to indicate that it was the second Viking ship with the white horse emblem. The two lightening bolts were also a symbol of the God 'Thor', the God of thunder. We needed the protection of Thor if we were to cross the hazardous seas, and so we sacrificed several worthy war horses to quench his thirst. I would later learn that Thor was a powerful God.

Weeks after returning from the battle at Gefwulfsburh, both Hnaef and Dresden shocked me with a surprised gift. It was Fenrir; he had been skinned and turned into a cloak by one of the tanners. It was a beautiful gift that I have cherished ever since. I wore the fur of Fenrir over my war helmet and his body draped over my back, hanging loose. 'You look like a real warlord now Hengest.' Dresden said grinning at me. I wore Fenrir with the utmost respect and absolute honour, embracing the fighting spirit of the primeval wolf. And now with my viking trip to Britain, I had a chance to finally show it off.

I awoke to the salty scent of the sea before the waking of the world. And I, Wipped and the other Vikings were loading up the four ships in the cold morning dew when Dresden surprised me as she came over and jumped inside *Ocean-Mare* dressed for war. She looked at me with an irremovable smile that light up the morning glum. 'Let's go viking!' she said with enthusiasm. Dresden wasn't yet old enough to go into any battle, but Wipped didn't care, he needed someone to throw out all the seawater that would come over the side of the ship and Dresden had volunteered. We travelled to Saxony in four ships carrying forty trained warriors between us and each were loaded with food, steel and barrels of ale. And there was only one rule Wipped told me: 'Don't piss into the wind.'

We set sail due-north up past the eastern coast of England. I could see Geatland in the distance as we turned west and passed my former kingdom home of Jutland. As we passed northern Jutland, it was covered in dense woodland with an occasional manmade clearing with a village in the centre and I could see the small children waving at us. 'Wave back at them Dresden.' I told her. 'No! I don't like kids, they smell.'

We saw thousands of seagulls surrounding the seals, dolphins and whales as they came right up to the keel. Dresden and I even managed to touch one of them; its skin was all wet and strange. 'Get rowing you lazy bastards! this isn't a free ride.' Screamed Wipped with his bold head reflecting the sun into my eyes. A day after setting sail we had stopped on the western coast of England. We stayed overnight by the invitation of a local chieftain named Halga that Wipped and I had met during the Scylding wars. The landscape was beautiful, the ocean was mesmerising, the woods, hills and the skies felt alive and were greatly blessed by Freyja. Dresden and I slept on the hilltops that night overlooking the world, just staring at the stars. Dresden pointed at the sky: 'Look! a flying dragon.' she yelled as we witnessed our first dragon soaring beneath the heavens in a haze of fire. 'Make a wish.' I said. She never told me what she had wished for.

The following morning we travelled south to the river *Elbe* towards the Saxon stronghold. Once we had reached the mouth of the river, I could see dozens of thanes on lookout camped by the riverbed close to their own ships. Some of them were standing watching us and one of them lit his arrow and it looked as if he was about to fire at us and attempt to burn our ships down. He pulled back his bow and then froze as another man approached him and then he suddenly lowered the bow. Obviously they had recognised the white horse emblem on the sail as Wipped had been there many times before. And so we were waved through.

As we drifted further down river, we came to a wooden fort that was heavily guarded. A man approached us dressed in war gear and carrying an axe and shield, it was Siegeferth. 'Glad to see you've made it Wipped.' He said whilst inspecting our boats and admiring the carved dragon-headed prow. 'Oh no!' Siegeferth cried as he laid his beady eyes on Dresden and I. 'Why have you brought the two biggest pains in the arse that I have ever known?'

'Nice to see you too, my lord.' Dresden replied as we jumped overboard into the marshy, wet sludge. It was obvious that the Saxons weren't immune to the coastal flooding that had plagued the Jutes and the Englisc villages for so long.

This had been my first journey in a Viking ship and I didn't feel well for most of the trip. I had what Wipped called 'sea poison' and I threw up all the way to Saxony and I was relieved to be back on land, even if it was wet and sludgy. All forty of us were taken inside the main hall by Siegeferth and the first thing I noticed was the smell, it smelled like sweat and piss mixed with death and maggots. At the end of the darkened hall I could see a group of about twenty men hunched over a wooden table enjoying their evening meal. Amongst them, sitting at the head of the table, was Eadward the Saxon King.

Wipped once told me that Eadward had been taken as a child from his tribe in southern Germany and raised as a legionnaire in the Roman Federati. He had been trained in Roman military tactics and served over ten years in Britain and Gaul until the German rebellion that had left him and his fellow Saxons unemployed. And so Eadward and the Saxons had hired themselves out as mercenaries to all the warring tribes. Over the years Eadward had made an impressive name for himself and the Saxons now called him 'King'.

Eadward had long greasy yellow hair and had bits of food in his long scruffy beard that was hiding his three chins. He was a fat king, his arms, his legs; his guts and his arse were fat. Basically everything reminded me of the whales that I had seen on my journey down the coastline. And Eadward loved to drink; he always seemed drunk to me whenever I had met him in the years that followed. Dresden named him 'the drunken king'.

Eadward told us to sit down and help ourselves to some grub. Dresden and I followed Wipped and sat at the front table with some of the top ranking thanes and ealdormans. The rest of the thanes spread out across the tables behind us and were treated to a feast that had been brought in by the thralls.

Sitting next to the drunken king was his young son Aelle. He was only about ten summers old when I first met him and like me, he too was a favourite amongst the Gods. He had long shaggy blonde hair like his father's and the bluest eyes. He was a bright little kid, always listening to the older thanes and learning, always learning. He had been on slave raids before and would be coming with us to Britain.

'So Whipped, is this the best men you've got?' Eadward asked. But before Wipped could answer Eadward interrupted him and whilst staring at Dresden he asked: 'Is that a girlie hiding under that old tin bucket on her head?' Dresden removed her helmet and said: 'I'm not a girl, I'm thirteen and I'm a thane.' Eadward and his men laughed out loud, spitting food across the table. 'A thane?' Eadward asked still laughing. 'Is she one of yours?' Eadward asked as he turned to Siegeferth. 'She's pretty tough; don't be fooled by her pretty little face. She's as tough as any of the men.' Eadward then leaned forward and asked Dresden: 'And who's this kid sitting next to you? Is he your fella?' Dresden laughed, but I answered for myself. 'My name is Hengest the Wolf-Tamer and slayer of Folcwald.'

Just then the doors swung open and in came about twenty other Saxons accompanied by yet more thralls. They filled up the remaining tables in the hall and two of them walked over to the top table and sat down with us. One of them was called Hrothgar, he was maybe twenty five and he was King Eadward's ealdorman, only second to the king himself. He was a tall man with long blonde platted hair that fell to his waist; he had a shaved chin and had menacing blue eyes. And he too had once been in the Roman Federati with the drunken king and had served in Gaul. As he sat next to me, I noticed that he was wearing an amulet around his neck, it was the same amulet that I had owned as a child, it was Thor's hammer and it made me think of my baby brother that had never lived.

Hrothgar had huge shoulders that were forcing me to budge up next to Dresden. He stunk of ale and sweat and I was pissed off as he took a chicken leg off my plate even though there was a plateful within arms reach. I was shocked and angry as I looked at Wipped from across the table and felt for the bone handle on *Wolf-Fang*. Wipped looked at me and gingerly shook his head, encouraging me to think twice. And so I allowed the insult to pass. Then Dresden took the piss as she too grabbed a chicken leg off my plate and smiled at me with her cheeky grin.

The other man that had joined us was named Aelfred; he was eighteen and was a skinhead. He was a Frankish exile from the western side of the river *Rhine*. Frankia was a part of Gaul and was still ruled by the Romans, but the Romans had just lost a major battle against the Franks and the future of Roman rule seemed to be crumbling everywhere. Aelfred was a murderer and a thief and if he ever went back to Frankia then he would have to pay the *wergild* that he owed and have his hands chopped off for his theft. And so he had joined the Saxons and became a Viking. He spoke with the strangest accent.

King Eadward introduced Dresden and I to the two warriors: 'And this guy…' Eadward said, waving his fork at me with fat and gristle hanging from it. 'this guy killed King Folcwald.' Hrothgar stuffed his mouth full of meat and said: 'So fucking what? Folcwald was a pussy; even a woman could have killed him.' Dresden shouted out loud: 'I fucking killed him, I stabbed him in the kidneys and the fat bastard fell to the floor dead.' Everyone in the first three rows of tables went quiet. 'You killed Folcwald?' Aelfred asked. 'Both me and Hengest did, but I stabbed the cunt.' The men burst with laughter. Siegeferth walked over to Dresden and told her to climb on his shoulders as he paraded her in front of the thanes. And they all cheered and shouted: 'Folcwald's a cunt! Folcwald's a cunt!' Dresden was laughing hysterically.

As Dresden sat back down, Hrothgar asked how old she was and as she answered 'thirteen', he said: 'Nearly a woman then, that's old enough for me.' Dresden suddenly looked down at her plate and said nothing. Then Hrothgar stood up: 'What's the matter love? I'll be gentle.' I didn't think for a moment when I stood up next to Hrothgar and touched *Wolf-Fang* by the handle. My heart was pounding inside my rib cage as I looked eye to eye with the menacing blonde. Hrothgar asked me: 'What's this? Do you actually think you can kill Hrothgar? And I remained stone faced as I told him: 'I can fucking try mate!'

Siegeferth and Wipped looked on as the atmosphere suddenly got intense and everyone in the building was listening as Hrothgar asked me my age. 'I'm fourteen and I'm old enough and big enough to take you out.' Aelfred and the drunken king both spat out their food in disbelief and shouted: 'Fourteen? Look at the bloody size of him, fourteen?'

'I think so.' I replied. Hrothgar then placed his hand on my shoulder and said: 'I like you kid; you remind me of myself when I was young, only I'm better looking.' He then laughed as he shook my hand and turned to Wipped: 'He's a tough little bastard this one, isn't he? Nobody has ever had the guts to talk to me like that.' Wipped just smiled and said: 'I don't work with faggots mate.' Hrothgar then poured me some more ale. 'You've got balls kid, we're going to be good friends you and me.' I smiled. What Wipped hadn't told me was that Hrothgar was also coming viking in Britain with us. Dresden smiled as she sipped her mead.

That night as the mead-pot ran dry, a thrall came over with some Roman wine and Dresden asked the strange looking dark skinned thrall for some more gruel. But he didn't answer her and so she stood up and screamed at him spitting in his face: 'Get me some fucking gruel, you twat.' Hrothgar and the thanes turned to watch and one of them said that he couldn't speak because he didn't have a tongue. Dresden and I burst with laughter at her mistake. 'Why doesn't he have a tongue?' I asked. Hrothgar answered: 'Because I couldn't stand that fucking foreign accent of his, he butchers our language, so I cut out his fucking tongue and if he ever even makes a mumble, then I'm going to cut off his fucking balls too.' The Saxons were a foulmouthed bunch and they were a terrible influence on Dresden and I, but as we got to know them we found them to be hilarious.

The mead-hall was the sleeping place of the warriors and that night it was packed with eighty drunken thanes and as the night went on the benches and tables were pushed to the side as we all prepared to sleep on the hall floor. And soon we were joined by the Saxon women and the prettiest thralls. Dresden and I were under our blanket with our heads poking out laughing as we watched all sorts unfold before our very eyes. And whilst under those covers with Dresden, I seemed to forget my love for Hild and we committed what the Christians would call a 'sin'. Twice!

I awoke that morning to a scream of laughter as Dresden was pointing at my head and laughing. During the night, whilst I was passed out from too much ale, the Saxons had shaved off my long brown hair and wiped tar onto my head and then covered me in goose feathers. 'You're a real Saxon skinhead now Hengest.' Aelfred mumbled as he patted me on the head.

The sky was grey, white and yellow and my head felt cold in the morning mist as I witnessed Aelfred and Hrothgar take almost a dozen horses and half a dozen thralls and slice open their necks. And the blood flowed as a gesture to the Gods to allow *Ocean-Mare* and the three other Viking ships a safe passage across the treacherous seas.

As I walked past one of the ships, I noticed that most of the Saxon shields were hung outside of the ship as a warning to let others know that there were thanes on board. The shields and the sail were decorated with a red cross with hooks called a swastika. I had seen the image before carved on my sword and scabbard, but I didn't know what it meant, so I asked Hrothgar. 'Its Thor's symbol, it represents Thor's hammer, bringing fire and rain to men. It brings protection against violence and the evil forces of the elves and the evil spirits that wish to do us harm. It's a symbol of kin and friendship during feasting and marriages. But most importantly Hengest, it's also a symbol of death and well-being.' I liked the swastika and much later in my life it became a prominent image of death and chaos on the battlefields of Britain.

The Saxon's were great worshippers of both Woden and Thor and were full of many great tales about their deeds in *Asgard*, but they also like to tell tales of great Saxon heroes. As we made our way to Britain we passed a ship full of commoners throwing spears at a baby whale when Hrothgar came to talk to the rowers and began to tell us a tale of his ancestors. Hrothgar spoke:

"He was a Saxon warlord; he was a giant standing as tall as a tree. The Romans called him Hermann the German. And one night he and his men ambushed three Roman legionnaires in the Teutoburg forest. The Romans had come looking for children to feed to the beasts from the darkest corners of the world. There was a major battle that lasted over two nights whilst Thor's thunder and lightening crashed over head. The Romans fought bravely, but they say that Thor could be heard laughing in the sky above and was pleased with his blood offerings given to him by the Saxons. And so the whole stinking Roman army was annihilated and us Saxons have remained safe from the Romans ever since.

Our children were once again free to grow up strong, to serve only Woden and to quench his thirst for blood with the corpses of the Romans. The legionnaires were hung from trees naked or thrown into wolf pits. Their clothes, weapons and horses were destroyed in honour of Woden. And if you go walking into the forest on a stormy night you can hear the Romans screaming and begging for mercy. I've head it myself. It was beautiful."

Dresden, Aelle and I were listening intently and I thought to myself: 'I wonder if one day people would tell stories of me like that.' I could only hope. It had been two days of pulling and pushing and rowing hard. Wipped said it would build some muscle on that oversized frame of mine. My face was numb on one side as the wind was cold and unrelenting. I saw nothing, but wind and rain for days. My clothes were soaked with sprays from the ocean wind.

My back, neck and shoulders
were aching, when finally
the British shore
was in sight.

*'A German is not so easily prevailed
on to plough the land
and wait patiently for harvest as to challenge a foe
and earn wounds for his reward.
He thinks it spiritless to accumulate slowly
by the sweat of his brow what can be got quickly
by the loss of a little blood'*

*Roman Historian Tacitus
1st Century AD*

Chapter Nine:
The Saxon Shore

Britannia 427AD
(Great Britain)

Why do they call it the Saxon shore? I asked Hrothgar as I put on my war helmet. Hrothgar spoke: 'Because the white cliffs of Dover have been washed red with the blood of the Britons at the hands of the Vikings for what the Romans call 'centuries'. And they don't know the difference between a Frank, Angle, Saxon or Jute.' We lowered our sails so that we wouldn't be spotted by lookouts and we rowed hard up the eastern coast looking for the river mouth. And as we travelled, I saw several old Roman walls along the coastline, walls designed to keep our kind out. After lots of hard graft we steered our four ships towards the entrance of the river and besides the river's edge I saw abandoned burned out villages with dogs sniffing around looking for food. There had obviously been a war of some kind. We travelled further inland when Wipped signalled to the ships behind to stop next to the riverbank. We were all told to collect our armour and shields and be prepared for battle. 'Hengest, Dres, Aelle come here.' Wipped whispered to us. 'I want you three to go towards that fort in the distance and watch them for a while and count how many soldiers you can see. And Aelle you know what a Roman soldier looks like, don't you? So you can tell us if there are any guarding the fort.'

'I can't count.' Aelle confessed. 'Don't worry we can count for you.' Dresden said as she helped herself to *Wolf-Fang* from my belt. Hrothgar then ordered for us to leave our weapons behind, as we could run faster without them. 'Just take your saxes and if anyone sees you, just kill em.'

'But what if they get away?' Dresden asked. 'Then blow on this war horn and run back here as fast as can. We'll come running and we'll bring you your weapons.' Dresden and I took off our helmets and Aelfred gave us and Aelle a lift, as the three of us climbed onto the high grass banking, grabbing the long blades of grass to help pull ourselves up. We kept our heads low as we ran towards the woods facing the old Roman fortress. Aelle was lagging behind. 'Hurry up blondie.' Dresden shouted.

There was nothing between our position and the fortress except for a long grassy field. We lifted our heads up as we lay on the forest floor hidden by the surrounding bushes. We could see people coming in and out of the gates. There were ordinary people wearing ropes of some kind. I could see cows and sheep inside the fort being attended to by the common folk. On the outside were six men, each carrying large shields and spears and were wearing strange helmets with bird feathers on them and wearing long red cloaks. 'Those men in red, they're Romans, or at least they're dressed like Romans.' The ten year old said with excitement.

Siegeferth had once explained to me that the Roman Empire had been home to all the races of the world for countless generations. The Roman's had tried to turn all their conquered people into equal Roman citizens and no longer referred to them with their own unique identities and they simply called everybody 'Romans', regardless of race or origins. And so the conquered people had gained power in Rome and this had frightened the true Roman people as they saw their own race quickly become a minority in their own country. And once the foreign races had gained power, they all favoured their own kind and all the races fought each other for their culture and identity to dominate the others. And so the Roman Empire was in a constant state of civil war and had slowly deteriated over time. And this had allowed for Rome's enemies to take advantage and crush their Roman oppressors once and for all.

The Romans were supposed to have left Britain before I was ever born to help save their own lands from invading Germanic tribes, but many had stayed behind to look after their own British families. And they have since gained the support from many of the Celts that still dream of once again being apart of the Roman Kingdom.

Aelle spoke: 'I hate the fucking Romans. I wish my dad was here for this, he hates the Romans as much as I do.' But the drunken king was at home keeping the foreigners out of his kingdom and was no doubt having a drink or two. We watched for a long time as we tried to count the number of soldiers inside the fort. But they kept walking out of view, so we didn't know if we were counting the same people or not. But we did see lots of common folk and small children, so it was probably worth the risk of an attack. The three of us ran back to the ship and reported that we think we saw about thirty Romans and about forty or fifty commoners. 'Fantastic!' Wipped said out loud. Hrothgar spoke to the men in the four ships that were lined up in the river: 'Men! Get ready for war.'

Siegeferth passed Dresden and I our war gear and told Aelle to stay behind in the ship with the guards, as the rest of us climbed up the steep banking. Ten men stayed behind in the ships to make sure that they wouldn't be stolen as none of us wanted to be trapped in those strange lands forever. And the remaining seventy trained thanes, led by the ealdorman Hrothgar, ran towards the stone wall on the left hand side of the fort gates. As the thanes stood with their backs to the wall, Dresden was told to take off her tin bucket and walk towards the main gate alone and was told to hide *Wolf-Fang* under her tunic. Dresden's long black hair made her look like one of the Celts. And we were hoping that the six Romans would see her and wish to question her as she tricked them into walking towards the thanes that were hiding around the corner so we could kill them without alerting the whole village inside.

Dresden was nervous, but she did as she was told and walked round the corner to where the Romans were gossiping something in their own language. I could hear their voices from around the corner. And suddenly the Romans started shouting to the people inside the fort. The trick hadn't worked and Dresden ran back towards the thanes, as the mix of Jutes, Angles and Saxons charged forwards pushing passed me and Dresden. The six Romans didn't stand a chance as the thanes ran over their quivering bodies as they lay in the blood sprayed grass, wounded and dying at the hands of Hrothgar's and Aelfred's swords. The seventy thanes hurried inside the fort, hacking and slashing at everything in red, before the villagers had the chance to close the gates.

I was wearing my boar-crested war helmet and my white and grey wolf skin that was attached to my leather tunic with brooches, decorated with burgundy, blue and red gems.

I screamed and yelled as I ran behind the thanes and stormed towards the Romans. They were all armed with shields, small swords or spears and were all wearing body armour. I saw one of them pullout his sword from its scabbard and I ran at him charged with battle-fury. I used a small wall to propel myself into the air like a cat and I came down with enough force to cut him straight through his thick neck. Blood squirted out of the veins in his neck and sprayed me in the face. I screamed out loud as I looked for my next kill. I then noticed that Siegeferth had pinned a Roman to the floor and Wipped had removed the Roman's helmet and was jumping on the guy's unprotected head and squashing his fragile skull. 'The Skull Crusher!' I shouted as Wipped waved in appreciation for the comment.

Mail-shirts glinted in the sun, their iron on their armour rang out as I watched as Hrothgar grabbed hold of a Roman soldier and twisted his neck, he then spat on the Roman as his limp body fell to the floor. A man charged at me with his garden fork, trying to thrust it into my belly. But I made short work of him as I sliced my blade across the wooden handle and split the garden fork in two. I then yelled out loud as I rammed *Dances with Corpses* deep into his unprotected gut. I was standing on his chest with one foot as I looked into his horrified eyes and I smiled at him as I watched him suffer. I then saw Aelfred stamp hard onto the groin of a Roman that was lying on the floor covered in his own blood.

I then looked over at Dresden as she was fighting two women armed with wooden clubs. I approached the women from behind and skewered them both onto my blade. 'Thanks!' Dresden yelled as she turned and ran after the children. She then grabbed two of them by their black hair and threw them to the floor. She then kicked them both as hard as she could in the face, breaking their noses as blood flowed from their youthful faces. Suddenly more and more Romans came rushing out of the cottages, screaming and hungry for Saxon blood. 'Group together!' Hrothgar shouted above all the chaos and disorder. No one, but my self, it seemed, could hear amongst the panic stricken village. The village began to burn and smoke filled my aching lungs. Two men shouted at me in their foreign tongue as I was covered in the blood of their people.

'You two!' I shouted pointing my sword at them. 'Come and get some.' They ran at me with spears and screams and so I had no choice, but to start dancing and swinging my blade. *Dances with Corpses* were living up to its name as it sang in the wind and danced wildly, as the bodies began to pile up. I took a firm hold of the hilt and swung the blade in an arc, a mighty blow that bit into his neck bone and severed it entirely. It became a bloodbath. A massacre.

The Romans fought well, brave and honourable, but they were no match for the savagery of the Saxons. I was soon stepping over bodies of Romans, men, women and children, intestines and puddles of mangled flesh and thick warm blood. Woden's maidens, the *Valkyries*, were not in need of Saxon warriors that day, as we lost only five men and we had gained many thralls. I counted five Romans, twelve men that looked like farmers, nineteen women and fifteen children that were all bound by ropes. They were to be taken to Frisia and sold in the Friesian markets. They were dragged to the ships, as Dresden and I looked around the village, Aelle also tagged along.

My white and grey wolf skin was now soaked in both Celtic and Roman blood as the three of us looked inside the strange stone buildings that were built by the Romans. They had strange looking people inside, they were standing still as if they were made of stone, cursed and frozen between life and death. 'Christian magic!' Aelle whispered, as if he didn't want the Christian god to hear his voice. 'Their god doesn't like people to go to *Asgard*, so he has cursed them to stone.'

'We must free them!' Yelled Dresden, as she pushed over the bodies and they smashed into dust. Aelle and I began to smash up the furniture, when we suddenly heard a shriek from inside a closed wooden door. Aelle bravely opened the door and laughed. And as I walked over to see what was in side, I could see two young boys curled up inside the cupboard, both shaking. I pulled my sword out of my scabbard and told the two boys to come out of the closet. They didn't understand me, so I ordered Dresden to drag the oldest one out by his shaggy black hair as I held my blade to his throat. 'What's your name boy?' I asked, but he didn't answer me, so I yelled: 'What's your fucking name, you waelisc scum?'

'Artorius! Artorius!' the boy quickly replied. 'That's a good boy.' I said as I punched him in the face and I spat on him as he fell to the floor. Dresden pulled out the much smaller child that was still crouching inside the closet with his eyes closed. 'Stand up you little shit.' she yelled in his ear. I told Dresden to pass Aelle *Wolf-Fang*. I then looked at Aelle: 'You hate the Romans? Then prove it.' Aelle took the blade by the bone handle and rammed it into the guts of the waelisc scum. Dresden and I laughed and screamed with words of encouragement, as Aelle went crazy, stabbing and thrusting. Blood was everywhere as his guts spewed out onto the floor.

Artorius was crying and yelling. 'Shut your fucking mouth.' I screamed as I kicked him in the face. Aelle was on his knees stabbing and stabbing at the quivering corpse that lay across the beautifully decorated marble floor. 'That's enough!' I said as I dragged Aelle off. 'I think he's dead mate.' I then took *Wolf-Fang* back and began to slice and hack at the boy's neck. I cut through flesh, bone and gristle. It was hard work and I was gasping for breathe as I finally separated the boys head from his twitching corpse. I then wiped the blood onto Artorius's robe and told him to get to his feet as I passed him the boy's head, which I believed to have been his brother's, as the two of them looked so alike. I knew the boy didn't speak Englisc, so I pointed at the closet as a gesture for him to hide.

Still sweating and gasping for air, I told him my name: 'Hengest… Hengest….my name is Hengest.' I said as I was tapping him on the head and talking to him as if he was stupid. 'Go and tell your filthy kind that Hengest did this and tell them that I'll be back for their ugly babies soon.' The boy nodded his head as if we had an understanding and I then spat on him before slamming the door in his face and the three of us returned to *Ocean-Mare*.

Before setting sail to Frisia, Hrothgar ordered for one in every ten of the thralls to be slaughtered in the name of Thor to allow safe passage. 'Kill that bastard! He isn't worth a loaf of bread.' Hrothgar said pointing to an elderly man. 'They like to have a Christian burial.' Siegeferth said. 'Their god demands it.' Hrothgar spoke: 'I don't give a shite what their fucking god demands, he ain't my fucking god. I take my orders from no fucking foreign twat of a god and if I ever see their fucking sand god then I'll bend over and tell the cunt to kiss my fucking white Saxon arse.'

We all laughed as Hrothgar then told us to burn their stinking bodies: 'If it's good enough for Woden, then its good enough for anyone.' His orders were followed through and we then set sail for Frisia, hoping to make it by morning where we planned on making much gold and silver.

After a terrible night of rowing and singing, we finally arrived on the Frisian coast early in the morning. We had heaved our ships onto dry land and I reached under the benches and grabbed my wolf skin that was hidden under a blanket to keep it dry. At least forty thanes guarded the ships and Wipped then shouted for me and Dresden to catch up. The thralls were bound by ropes as we dragged them to the marketplace. There I could see bodies swinging by their necks with no arms or legs. Wipped told us: 'That's a warning to thieves, so keep your hands to yourselves.'

Whilst the Skull Crusher and Hrothgar bartered with the thralls and the Roman and Frankish weaponry, Dresden and I spent most of the morning looking around the markets. You could buy anything there, ducks, chickens, weapons, animal skins, blubber, and even whale meat and cloaks made out of seal skins. Later Wipped gave Dresden and I our share of the silver coins. 'Don't spend it all at once on the whores Hengest.' I laughed. 'Why would I when Dresden comes free?' I said with a smile as I put my arm around her. I got a slap for that remark.

We left Frisia late in the evening on the western wind. It had been a long journey and Dresden and I were glad to be back home in England. As *Ocean-Mare* was heaved onto the beach, I was greeted by my little brother Horsa and I quickly discovered that whilst I had been away Hild had been forced into marriage with Finn. Now that Onola had passed away there was no one to stop the arranged marriage. I was horrified. That's what was wrong with her, I thought, she must have known for some time that her father had planned on using her as a peace-weaver between the Angles and Scyldings. I may have been unfaithful, but I truly loved Hildeburh and I was distraught at the news. My heart was broken and it seemed like the whole world had just crashed down on my shoulders. Dresden said nothing.

I put on my helmet and covered myself with the skin of Fenrir and with my sword in its scabbard I marched towards the hall of the king. I saw Froda; he had heard the news and told me to calm down. 'Fuck off!' I shouted as I pushed passed the commoners on my way to confront the king. I walked towards Hoc's dwellings when I was stopped by the guards that were armed with spears and shields. They knew that I had special clearance at the king's quarters, but even I had to relinquish my weapons upon entry. So I reluctantly gave up my steel and a messenger ran to alert the king that I had requested an audience with him. I was allowed straight in.

'Why?' I shouted with desperation in my voice. 'Why did you allow her to marry Finn and not me?' I was shaking with anger and frustration. Hoc stood up and yelled at me to remember who I was talking too. Hoc told me that Hild was his daughter to do with as he pleased. 'The Scyldings are powerful Hengest. I had no choice, but to form a union to protect our people. We have defeated them for now. We have taken back Jutland, but the Scyldings will regroup and will keep coming back for our lands. Don't question my decision; I did what I deemed necessary to protect my kingdom and my people-our people Hengest!'

I paused for a moment to take a deep breath, as Hoc continued: 'And I never promised her to you. Remember Hengest, I owe you nothing-it is you that owes me everything. Now that you have become a Viking warrior, I believe it's time that you swore me your oath, to be my sword! my warrior! What do you say Hengest?'

'Bollocks! I will not give you my oath, my lord. I am Aesc, son of Whitgils and I was to marry your daughter and we were to one day rule Jutland together.' I was furious and I couldn't help but think about what Wipped had suggested. But I was frightened. If I had been caught killing King Hoc then I might have been stoned to death, beheaded, drown or hanged or even burned alive. But at that moment I wanted Hoc dead. I shouted at the king: 'I love Hildeburh. I love her like the sea, the trees and the wolves and the sky. I love her like I love the Gods. I wanted her to bear me children, strong and healthy, like you once told me.' Hoc took a deep breath and sighed. 'Hengest my son, there are other girls with healthy wombs and strong hearts. What about that Jutisc girl with the black hair that's always following you around and babysitting your brother? What's her name? Dresden! I think she likes you Hengest.'

I then gestured as if I was putting my fingers down my throat and pretended to chuck up the Frisian gruel that I had eaten for breakfast. 'That's my Hengest.' Hoc said with a smile. I was extremely fond of Dresden, but I was scared that the king would learn about my drunken merry making with Dresden in Saxony. I was afraid that Hoc might cut off my balls for disrespecting his only daughter, surely a *wyrd* worse than death. Hoc spoke: 'Now Hengest! you have refused to give me your oath? I do hope you would swallow your pride and reconsider. Have I not taken care of you and your pain in the arse brother? I could have let you sleep in the horse sheds with the thralls and the fleas. But instead I have given you both a home, my warmth and my love.'

I had become quiet and withdrawn, as Hoc continued: 'Onola had kept your bellies full and your skin covered with clothes, had she not? We have raised you from a weakling and made you strong. Look at you Hengest. You're just a boy, yet half my thanes have to look up at you. You're going to be a beast.' The mention of Onola made my bottom lip begin to tremble and a tear fell from my glazed over eyes as I had become humbled. I owed my life to the king and queen. I was more grateful then I had ever shown, I had just never said the words before. And with tears rolling down my face, I knelt down on one knee and humbly offered my oath to my king. He was a man that had been more of a father to me than any other and that day I promised to give my life and my death in the protection of my king and my England.

Hoc rose to his feet, and with his thralls and guards as witnesses, he accepted my oath. Hoc told me that I could now go to his storage of weapons and select one item as a gift from a grateful king. There were expensive swords, axes, spears and shields, but I didn't hesitate to accept a fine piece of iron-meshed chain-mail. I was wearing my new chain-mail, my helmet and my wolf skin. 'Now you look like an Englisc thane, Hengest. Now bugger off and go and train the youngsters how to fight like an Angle. And Hengest……make them cry.'

I smiled as I then walked over to the other children practicing with wooden swords. I saw Dresden fighting with Horsa knocking him to his arse. She was a great fighter and my brother Horsa was only seven at the time and he was shouting at Dresden. Every time she knocked him down he would call her a bitch, pig breath and whore of Loki, the troublesome god. Dresden was laughing at him, knowing she was encouraging his spirit to grow strong, stripping him of fear and turning him into one of Woden's warriors. She was teaching him to be aggressive and to hate; it was a trait that would serve him well.

Horsa spoke: 'She keeps bloody cheating; she keeps tripping me and hitting me in the stomach.' I laughed. 'Let me show you how it's done brother. Make sure you watch and learn, as we don't want you spinning wool with the women when you grow up, do we?' He threw his wooden sword at me: 'Then you show me how its done turd breath.' Dresden looked at me with fire in her eyes: 'Let's see what you've got Wolf-Tamer.' I stood there, holding my blade, as I looked deep into Dresden's dark mysterious eyes. I remembered when I first saw Dresden in battle when she was possessed by the *Valkyries*. She had that same look in her eyes.

She seemed different somehow.

Something had

changed.

*"The feathered flight of a rumour reached the ears
of everyone in south Britain.
Their old enemies from the north were on their way.
They weren't coming to raid
but to rule the country from end to end.
But before they could defend themselves
they rushed down that wide road that leads to death.
A deadly plague killed so many
and so quickly that their weren't enough
left to bury the dead...."*

*British Historian Saint Gildas
516-570 AD*

Chapter Ten:
Touched by the hand of Hel

England to Britannia 437AD
(Southern Denmark to Great Britain)

Ten summers had passed and Dresden and I were now married with two kids. We had a son named Aesc who was eight years old and a beautiful three year old daughter with long flowing chestnut-brown hair named Rowena. There had been peace for many years in England and I had spent much of my time hunting and fishing and viking on the coasts of Britain. I had made myself very wealthy and now owned two thousand hides of land in England that I rented out to hundreds of families. And I now owned my own mead-hall that I had decorated with the spoils of war. I had built up a fierce reputation and my name was now known in all of the lands and my arms were now decorated with golden rings, many of which were gifts from Hoc.

Over the years I came to know the Saxons well and we had spent many years raiding and pillaging together. But I hadn't seen them much in the last three years, as they were now at war with the Saxon tribes in the deep-south and with the eastern Franks led by King Childeric.

King Hoc had named me as the chieftain of all the disposed Jutes living in England. And I now had a mass following of several hundred thanes and many had pledged their oaths to me, just as I had pledged my oath to King Hoc. Wipped hadn't broken his oath to my father and he too had a following of several hundred Vikings that had remained loyal to him since the death of my father. And so together, I now had a small army under my own personal command.

Much had changed in the last ten years. Finn's agreement with Hoc and his marriage to Hild had brought peace for many years between the Angles and the Scyldings. Over the years King Finn had conquered much of the lands in Frisia and Finn had become a great and powerful ruler in the south west. Frisia lay between the two great rivers, the river *Wesser* and the river *Rhine* and this was good news to us, giving us a new sense of security. But peace was not to last.

Finn's men, the Scyldings, Danes and Geates, needed Jutland, not just for the quality of the land, but also for tactical purposes. Finn had an army waiting to obey his every command in Geatland, and by possessing Jutland, Finn's thanes were one day closer to Frisia to help out with any possible rebellion by the Frisians. And of course Jutland was a vital trade route for Finn to trade with his native lands in Scandinavia. And so the Danes, Geates and the Scyldings had reignited the wars for my childhood home.

Finn had kept his oath to the Angles, but as Finn once said: 'The Angles have no right to Jutland, as the royal dynasty had been destroyed.' But as King Hoc and Hnaef knew, the rightful king of Jutland still lived. Aesc still breathed, but I was now living under the name of Hengest. And so Hoc had continued to fight the Scyldings for the kingdom of Jutland, just like he had promised. Finn's wife, and Hoc's daughter, Hildeburh, had sent many ambassadors to England asking for peace between the Scyldings and the Angles. They told us that Finn had no intensions of ever invading the Angles, but would stop at nothing for Jutland. King Hoc had fought fiercely against the invaders of Jutland, but the *Valkyries* had been watching and had selected him to join Woden in the halls of *Valhalla*.

My best friend Hnaef was now king of both England and Jutland and he had named me as his ealdorman. So I had basically become the second most powerful man in all of England and Jutland. Truly the highest honour a king can bestow on any mortal man. Hunlafing had been by the king's side since they were babies and had always been loyal to the royal family, as had his now deceased father Hunlaf. Hunlafing had always assumed that he would one day be named as Hnaef's ealdorman. Hunlafing was not happy.

The combined forces of the Scyldings, the Geates and the Danes had been battering our coastal defences for years, forcing their way into eastern Jutland. We had lost much of Jutisc territory in the north. Finn's army had become too strong for us to hold back much longer and it would only be a matter of time before Finn managed to claim Jutland as part of his growing empire. We were now forced to seek new lands for ourselves or one day accept King Finn as our overlord and master. But that was not an option for many of us Jutes. We were proud people and we refused to be bullied by anyone. It was a hopeless situation.

Wipped spoke: 'We should go to Britain. The Romans have long since abandoned it. The island is divided and civil wars have erupted and the Celts have become weak. And they are too busy fighting over their own petty differences to care about a small settlement of Jutes and Angles. The land is excellent, it never floods and it's just sitting there waiting for us to take it.' King Hnaef and I had discussed a potential invasion of Britain with Wipped and his Vikings. We had the ships, the men and the logistics for only a small attack, but we really didn't have a choice as the Scyldings were becoming stronger as each year passed. And so it was decided that we would actually try and conquer the former Roman lands in the following year. The Skull Crusher made it sound so easy, as if we could just go and take good land for ourselves, but the *Fates* had never planned for anything to be so easy.

Our scouts had reported that the entire island had fallen into chaos and disorder since the Romans had left. We heard tales of civil unrest and war. We knew that the Romans had been defeated by the Franks and had since left Gaul that lays to the south of Britain across the British sea. There had been a great Roman leader there, they say he was a Saxon, born and raised as a Roman, his name was *Germanus of Auxerre*. He and his band of Christians, mostly former Roman legionnaires, had gone to Britain in the name of their god to save their cult from the northern and western tribes that had overrun the island.

I am told that the Romans had once built a mighty wall to keep out the Pictish dwarves from the north of the island. But the wall was old and weak and they came in their hundreds. Irish invaders from the western isle that sits at the edge of the world had also come for land and plunder and the stench of death filled the air in the lands of Britannia. The world had become a dangerous place to live, and fear and panic had spread over all the lands, but there was more to fear then death and steel in Britain, much more, and none of us saw it coming.

For the last year, King Hnaef, Hunlafing, Wipped and I, had prepared for the invasion of Britain. We built up our army, we built ships and our smithies produced fine works of art as they melted, beat and twisted their steel into swords, shields, armour and spears, all beautifully decorated with runes, birds and animals. King Hnaef came up with a simple plan that would take three years to complete. We were to take two ships, each carrying fifty thanes, across the eastern coast of Britain to survey the land and look for its strengths and weaknesses. After years of raiding I had come to know the river systems well, but there had been much change in Britain in recent years and the levels of strength varied from time to time. But this time we weren't looking for slaves, we were looking for land that was within our ability to conquer and we would be taking no prisoners.

We needed the land for ourselves, for the survival of our own people and we were under no illusion that the Britons were the sharing type. The plan was that after we had chosen our target we would send for reinforcements from England. We were going there to kill everyone and everything with a pulse. We planned on taking over old Roman forts and building our own coastal defences that could be easily defended by several hundred thanes. And once we had secured our new territory we would send for the women and children and the remaining thanes that were left to defend our ancient homelands.

My brother Horsa was now eighteen and had grown up to be a fine soldier. Years of beating his arse had turned him into a mean spirited warrior with great skills and a hunger for blood. He had spent the last three or four years battling the Scyldings in Jutland and was exited about his first journey overseas. My old friends Froda and the Skull Crusher were to stay in England to help protect the Englisc border from the Scyldings. And Dresden had left the kids in the care of Saxburga, as she couldn't refuse a trip to Britain.

Thor was pleased with our blood sacrifice and was kind to us as our dragon-headed prows preened over the ocean waves. Hnaef was master and commander of his own ship that once belonged to his father. It had a big red sail with a beautiful white dragon emblem in the centre, it was called '*Wyrmhorde*', which literally means 'dragon hoard', the guardian of treasures. And I was now the master and commander of *Ocean-Mare* that I had learned to handle as though I was touched by the Gods themselves.

Horsa was wearing my old war gear as I had a new shiny helmet with a prominent boar-crest, brand new Frankish chain-mail made of iron that I wore over my black leather tunic. And I had a beautifully decorated wooden shield with a snarling black wolf in the centre. And of course my favourite accessory was hiding under a blanket beneath the benches, my wolf skin, Fenrir.

My real name was Aesc, but I had gone by the name of Hengest since I was seven years old. Hengest simply meant stallion, which was an appropriate nickname as I was now twenty five years old and I had now grown into a giant of a man, standing six feet ten inches above the ground. Many years of rowing and fighting had built muscle onto my bones and I was covered in battle scars. My hair had grown long since the Saxons had chopped it off and I now had a long brown beard. I was dressed in steel and armed with *Wolf-Fang* and *Dances with Corpses* that I now handled with grace.

'Row you slags... row.' Horsa shouted in his deep voice, as we crashed against wave after wave. I slapped him on the back of his head: 'Go and join them brother, you'll get no special treatment from me. You need to earn their respect, just like I did. Now pick up an oar and put your bleeding back into it.' It had been a long journey from the west coast of England to the eastern coast of Britain. It had taken us five days to cross the windy seas and we were sprayed constantly by the harsh winds that soaked us to the bone and rusted the gear that wasn't hidden under blankets. I hated travelling by sea and I still occasionally spent the afternoon throwing up overboard. And the youngsters, who were throwing buckets of sea water over the sides, were giving me dirty looks as they occasionally got sprayed in the face with something other than seawater.

Then finally on the horizon, I could see the coastline, looking like a cloud sitting calmly on the ocean waves. We had travelled to the north and far in the distance I could see lots of thick black smoke spread across the land. When we arrived at the coast, I waved to King Hnaef that was standing proudly in his own Viking ship, the *Wyrmhorde*. I waved to the second ship to indicate that we were to travel up the river and towards the smoke. We lowered our sterns and sails and slowly rowed up river, surveying the land. And what we saw shocked us. There were people everywhere. Some were lying in the grass with arrows in their backs. Some were burned to charcoal. And some were nailed to wooden crosses like the god of my thrall Derfel. There were wild dogs scavenging for food, they made great target practice for the archers on board.

We made our way further north until we came to the smoking villages that we had seen earlier in the day. We could see men, women and children wondering round, I assumed they were looking for their loved ones. 'What do you think has happened?' asked Horsa. 'They had a picnic that got out of hand' I said with sarcasm. 'Obviously there has been a war of some kind.' I didn't realise it at that moment, but the battle was still taking place about a mile or so up river. We continued our journey north and I began to hear screams and shouting and as we turned a corner in the river, I suddenly saw a huge stone fortress appear above the trees. There was a siege happening before our very eyes.

'What the fuck are them?' Horsa asked pointing to a pack of strange beasts that were roaming the battlefield. 'Pictish hunting dogs.' One of the thanes mentioned. 'The Picts are from the north, from beyond the great wall.' He said pointing at a band of about a hundred warriors. Most of them had long ginger or black hair. They were short in stature and dressed in what looked like carpets wrapped around their pale bodies. They were armed with spears and wooden shields. They had swords, but they were not much bigger than *Wolf-Fang* and they didn't appear to have any armour. Some of the men were naked and many of them were wearing nothing but shorts. And as Dresden had pointed out; their bodies were decorated with blue circular patterns. 'Pictish magic?' Horsa asked. 'It's not magic dickhead.' I said. 'They just think that it makes them look hard. I've seen it before in Frisia. Some Longbeards were covered in the stuff. It's nothing to fear, although it does smell a little fishy.'

I watched from a distance as I saw the Pictish battering-rams left by the gates that secured the fort. The Romans that were protecting the fort were throwing rocks at them from over the wall, forcing them to stay back. I saw the Roman archers send hundreds of arrows at the Picts, forcing them to duck and cover under their wooden shields. When the arrows stopped they all stood back up and were shouting and laughing at the Romans. We had yet to be spotted and my men had stopped rowing as we waited for the king's dragon ship to catch up. I put out my hand and reached for the hand of Hnaef, as I pulled him onto *Ocean-Mare*. 'What's that?' I asked the king, pointing up at the fortress to a flag that was flapping in the wind. 'It's the Roman eagle.' Hnaef replied. 'Exactly, then inside the fortress must be Germanus, right? What will happen if we helped the Romans defeat the Picts? If we promise to keep the Picts out of the old Roman lands then maybe they would offer us land to settle.'

Hnaef spoke: 'I don't know, it sounds too easy to me, let's go further up river and do what we came to do and survey the land.' And so we did as the king ordered and rowed further north. And as we slowly rowed passed the fortress, we were spotted by all the Picts and they all stared at us from the edge of the trees. 'Maybe they've never seen an Englisc war band before.' Hnaef said. They just stared and did nothing. We travelled for most of the afternoon, when I could suddenly smell what seemed like burnt crops. Then ahead of us we saw a small unguarded village with no walls or barriers. 'We'll stop here and stretch our legs.' the king ordered. 'Maybe we'll find real food for the men.'

We then pulled our ships onto dry land and tied them together with ropes. We could see people in the village, men, women and children. But no one seemed to mind our presence. Some of the people were just lying there motionless and some were sitting and just watched us as we walked passed. I saw two small children fighting each other for what looked like bread. I could see bread on the floor next to what looked like a bakery, it was old and mouldy. 'Is this all there is to eat? I'm fucking starving.'

'Be quiet Horsa! There's something wrong here.'

'Look at these people. They're like the living dead.' Dresden grabbed my arm. 'It's some kind of evil. Look at that guy, his face and arms are rotting.' She shrieked.

As we walked deeper into the village, I kicked open a door and was shocked to discover a full family hiding inside. They were all crouched on the floor and had a small fire in the centre to warn off evil spirits. They had dirty faces and were wearing tattered rags. They looked terrified as they stared at this big scary foreigner that was standing over them covered in the skin of Fenrir. But somehow I didn't think it was me that they feared. A man rose to his feet and made the sign of the cross. I had seen that done before by the thralls, it was some kind of Christian magic. The man didn't even look me in the eye, as he shut the door leaving me outside, as he didn't want to invite evil spirits into his home.

Dresden screamed. I ran to her, only to discover a women sitting in her home holding a baby in her arms. The baby was dead and was covered in blood. There were bodies of children lying in a heap inside that one room. All were dead. 'She's eaten them!' Dresden cried. The woman remained sitting down cuddling the rotting baby in her arms, as if it still lived. She was saying something to us, she repeated herself over and over, 'I heard the word *Hel*, *Armageddon* and *Christ*', but Dresden and I didn't understand, perhaps it was some kind of Christian disease. The madwomen then bit into the rotting flesh of the baby and snarled at us, showing us her rotten bloody teeth. Dresden screamed at her, calling her a witch, and stuck her sword into the throat of the hag, killing her instantly. Dresden was covered in the woman's blood as we left to join the others.

Some of the thanes later reported to me that they had seen people eating dogs, uncooked and bloody. They had seen people covered in black creatures that were stuck to their skin, making them go mad. And they had witnessed children coughing up blood and vomiting as they eat the flesh of their dead loved ones. Hnaef came running to me: 'It's the black death bitch! She has been. *Hel* has come to Britain. We must leave before she comes after us.'

My father had always taught me to never show any fear or intimidation, but as the men began to panic, I have no problem admitting that I too was frightened. Then over the brow of the hill, I saw the walking dead. It walked slowly as it dragged its rotting, diseased carcass towards me. It had long black hair that had been falling out as its head was rotting away. 'She's here!' One man screamed, causing the men to run back to the ships. But I stood still.

'Come on, let's go.' Horsa shouted pulling at my arm. 'No, I'm staying. I want to see it.' My heart was beating fast and I was frightened, but I was overcome with curiosity. The men called out to me from the ships wanting me to run. I had drawn my sword and I stood and waited. As *Hel* came closer, I looked into her eyes. There was nothing there, but emptiness. And with her withered, rotten arms she reached out to me. 'Fuck that!' I shouted, suddenly coming to my senses as I turned and ran to the ship.

I was pulled inside by Horsa and we turned the ships round the best we could in the narrow river. We raised our sails to catch the wind and travelled back south as fast as possible. And as we all felt the wind on our faces the men began to laugh. I don't know why they were laughing, but it was infectious and soon the whole ship burst into laughter. Our spirits were high as we arrived back at the old Roman fort. It began to turn dark and the sun was low in the late evening sky, hiding behind the grey waterlogged clouds. The Picts were still outside trying to break through the gates and get to the Romans.

'Fucking wankers!'

'Tossers!'

The Englisc shouted with laughter. Dresden and Horsa were sticking two fingers up at the Picts as we passed them in our ships. They began to shout things at us and one of them held up his sword as a challenge. 'Halt!' Hnaef yelled. We no longer cared for an alliance with the Romans, as the land was cursed; it was now a matter of stubborn Englisc pride. We were evenly matched against the Picts, as we both had about one hundred soldiers and even the Romans were watching from over the fortress wall. 'Let's show them how its done men, lets show them how the Jutes and the Englisc handle business.'

We then all grouped together, but no one discussed any tactics. 'Lets just fucking kill the foreign bastards.' ordered King Hnaef. 'You heard your orders. Kill them all.' I yelled. As we were talking the Picts had sent their dogs after us. They were ferocious little beasts, jumping up and biting down hard on our arms and legs. They were trained well and as soon as they got someone to the floor they immediately went for the throat and went for the kill. But the dogs were small and skinny and simply didn't have the size to pull down a full grown *Teutonic* man covered in heavy chain-mail and solid breastplates.

We used our shields to hit them in the face, to stun them, before swinging our axes and swords and chop them into little pieces. They only managed to seriously wound a hand full of thanes before they met their end. Dresden was one of the people that were dragged to the floor by one of the hunting dogs. And as it had its jaws around her throat, Horsa came to her rescue and spiked it on the end of a javelin.

The dogs were now dead, as the Picts looked on in anger. We all picked up the mongrels and tossed them aside, as if they were dirt. We screamed and shouted as we could feel the battle-fury and we could feel the presence of Woden on the battlefield. The world above began to pour and the rain clanged and bounced off our boar-crested helmets and shields. We then rushed forwards with more haste than caution, throwing ourselves against the Picts with a horrible grinding of teeth and our usual fury. They charged at us with their hair streamed behind them and a kind of madness flashed from their eyes. We had the advantage of strength and height, but the Picts seemed fearless as we all crashed together on the wet muddy slopes, as the Romans watched from above the wall.

'Woden has you!' Dresden screamed as she gored a spear all the way through the unprotected gut of a Pictish warrior. The battlefield soon filled with blood and I witnessed Horsa skewer a dwarf with his sword, as the rain poured down his smiling face. Dresden and I laughed as Horsa held down the twitching corpse with his foot and struggled to yank out the bloodied blade.

One man dispatched a spear and I saw it just in time as it smashed against my shield. We were besieged with throwing axes and spears and javelins. We knelt down and protected ourselves with our shields. Horsa looked at me with a grin as he knelt in the soaking mud, holding his shield high like Dresden and I had taught him. An axe bounced off a shield and skimmed past my face, as I then turned to look at Dresden and I noticed that she had her eyes closed and she struggled to hold up her shield. The spears and axes had stopped and we were again charged by the Picts.

The blacksmiths art shone and sparkled as men fought for the glory of the Gods on the battlefield. One man ran at me and with all his might as he jumped into the air and gave me a thrust with his shield. But I was twice his size and I didn't budge. I simply stood up and towered above the little man and laughed as I struck down hard with *Dances with Corpses*, splitting the man from his neck to his breast. Another dwarf soon replaced him and screamed like a wild man as he charged at me with his sword high above his head. And I felt the grip of

Woden on my sword hand, forcing my blade deep into the belly of the Pictish warrior, and the blood dripped down his pale white flesh.

I saw Horsa and Hnaef dancing in the middle of the chaos, their swords singing a beautiful song. The rain poured down hard as I frantically searched for Dresden, calling her name above the screams. Then I saw her on her knees. 'Where are you hurt?' I yelled. 'I don't know. There's something wrong, I feel like shit.' She said as she dropped her sword. I then picked her up and carried her to *Ocean-Mare*. I put her down on the deck at the back of the ship on a couple of old blankets. 'Stay there!' I shouted, as I returned to the fight. I was now pissed and the dwarfish Picts were going to pay.

I screamed as I carelessly ran back into the mix, my armour clanging and banging as I ran. The rain came down hard and I could hear Thor charging overhead as the sky thundered and crackled. The Picts had begun to group together as their numbers were dwindling. They were now surrounded and I could see it in their eyes that they were ready for death. We then satisfied the thirst of the Gods and the thirst of our swords. They died honourably.

I heard Horsa shouting at the Romans that were watching from above the wall. The field was full of puddles of blood and twitching dismembered corpses and stank of shit that had spilled from open stomachs. 'That's how you fucking do it, you Roman cowards.' I then returned to Dresden in the ship, as the men screamed and shouted insults at the Romans. The journey had been a failure; the Romans under Germanus seemed strong and impenetrable. The land was cursed and diseased and so we made the long journey back home.

As we crossed over the ocean waves, I could hear the thanes in the other ship singing and bragging over their kills. I wasn't aware of how many men we had lost that day. I didn't care. Dresden was seriously ill and coughing up blood. She was lying at the back of *Ocean-Mare* sweating and puking. One of the thanes was brave enough to speak to me, as the rain washed away the blood stained armour: 'I think she's dying, my lord. She is not wounded and she was covered in the blood of the madwoman.'

'Dying?'

'It's the blood, my lord. Once it's cursed, it spreads like fire across a summer meadow.'

'Is there not a cure? What about the witches?'

'I'm afraid not. No one, not even the shamans and the priestesses have ever been able to break a curse like this. She will die and she will infect more, unless_____'

'Unless what?' I demanded. Horsa put his head into the palm of his hands crying tears that only the Gods could see. He had known Dresden his entire life; she was like an older sister to him. My heart sank, my loving heart lost in the dark, not knowing what to do.

'I can hear you. I'm not sleeping. I know what he says is the truth.' I saw the sadness in her eyes, as Dresden spoke with a solemn face trying to smile and failing miserably. Her skin turned white, her face looked tired. I prayed to the Gods, 'let her stay', but not even they could help now. The thunder crashed overhead, the rain poured down from above, it was dark and dangerous on those seas, as Dresden laid there begging: 'Don't let me die like this Hengest. Don't let *Hel* have me. Send me to the *Lord of Hosts*; I can hear him calling me. Woden whispers in the wind, asking me to come. Send me to him, my love.'

'Damn it woman! Don't talk crazy, you'll be okay. You just need a good nights sleep.'

'Stop it Hengest!' Dresden cried out in a bout of coughing. 'I'm cursed!' she shrieked. 'And I'm only going to suffer more and spread this evil to England and to our children.' Dresden had hoped to become a *Valkyrie* one day and she now wished for them to come and claim her. She was crying hopelessly and coughing up blood. Dresden spoke: 'Now be a man Hengest and do what I would do. Do what needs to be done.'

'I can't!' I cried. 'I'm weak.'

'We're all weak Hengest. But we'll see each other again. I'll be waiting for you in *Asgard*. I'll be watching you Hengest. Make me proud. Promise me that you won't give up on our kid's futures. Promise me you'll find land for our children and our children's children.' I stood tall as I looked up at the white horse sail that was flapping ferociously in the strong winds: 'I promise my love, I'll slaughter the entire world if I have to. But I will find land for our kin, our blood and for our people.'

I then picked up a throwing axe and stepped closer to Dresden. The entire ship was silent; the only noise was coming from the creaking wood, the storm above and the splash of the waves. Dresden looked me in the eyes and whispered: 'If you be the one to cut me, then I'll bleed forever.' I froze. Then Horsa stood up and grabbed my shaking hand: 'Sit down brother.' He said with glum, as he took the axe from my hand. I then looked at Dresden and with silent tears rolling down my cheek, I said: 'There's so much to say, but I just can't find the words.'

'The last eighteen years has said everything I ever needed to know. I love you my Wolf-Tamer.'

'Me too my lady.'

Horsa then mumbled something under his breath, whispering to the Gods, as he then stepped closer to Dresden. Before covering his mouth with a cloth to protect himself from the cursed blood, Horsa spoke the final words that any of us ever said to the one that we had loved so much and was now to be taken from us: 'Now rest your head and go to sleep. Because my sister,

this is not our

farewell.'

*'When not engaged in warfare
they spend a certain
amount of time hunting,
but much more in idleness,
thinking nothing else
but sleeping and eating'*

*Roman Historian Tacitus
1st Century AD*

Chapter Eleven:
The Battle of Finnesburh-Part One

England to Frisia 448 AD
(Southern Denmark to Belgium)

Ten years had passed since I had lost my Dresden and she was fed into the jaws of *Aegir*, the God of the sea. The Scyldings and their allies now ruled over all of Jutland and even after all these years Finn had kept his word and had never attacked England. Finn had been married to Hnaef's sister Hild, my former lover, for twenty one years and they now had three children together. Their first child was a girl named Freawynn; she was now twenty years old. She had a younger brother named Frithuwulf and he was eighteen years old. And they both had a younger brother named Frealaf, who was about ten years old.

Hild's brother, King Hnaef of England, had not yet fathered a son, and so Hnaef had adopted his nephew Frithuwulf from the age of eight. Frithuwulf had lived with his uncle in England for the last ten years. It was purely for tactful reasons. It was common for a king with no heir to adopt a nephew from one of his brothers or sisters, providing they had at least two sons. This way, if and when Hnaef is struck down in battle, his heir would be of blood kin and would be made king and he would be accepted by the people of England as one of their own. This would save many lives from a potential civil war amongst the Englisc and would provide unity between the Scyldings and the Englisc tribes long after Hnaef's death.

King Finn would never attack England, oath or not, if his own son lived there and was heir to the kingdom and so we had known peace in England for many years, but the wars for Jutland had continued to the present day. But the day had come when I turned to my best friend and king and told him that the battle for Jutland was over. We had lost and no more men need die for a hopeless cause. I had accepted that I could never be King of Jutland; the Gods simply wouldn't allow it. They had other plans for me. I just didn't know what.

King Hnaef and his foster son Frithuwulf had been invited by King Finn and Queen Hildeburh to celebrate Yule in Frisia. And Hnaef was going to use this occasion to tell Finn that he would end the wars with the Scyldings over Jutland and discuss peace negotiations. We had simply become too weak to continue the fight and Finn had become the most powerful king in all the lands. He had a mighty empire, he was rich and powerful, both feared and respected. I hated Finn with a passion, but I had always admired his courage in battle and I had admired his quest for power.

Hnaef and I were aware that we had both caused much trouble for Finn over the years by continually fighting for Jutland and we had killed many of Finn's men. And we knew that it was in Finn's best interest to have Hnaef murdered to allow Frithuwulf, who had come of age, to become king and essentially give Finn power and influence over our homelands in England. And so Hnaef took no chances and invited me and sixty of our best thanes, both Angles and Jutes, to Finn's stronghold to spend the winter. The *Fates* were weaving their tangled webs.

After four days on the rough winter sea, Hnaef, Hunlafing, I, Siegeferth, Horsa and Hnaef's foster son, Frithuwulf, arrived in Frisia. The weather had been wet and cold and it had been snowing for days, but Thor was kind and allowed us to cross the sea safely, having lost only one man at sea as he was taking a shit at the back of the ship. I saw a line of small islands and sand dunes where the earth seemed to melt into the water. As we passed the two islands that lay at the mouth of the river *Ems*, we were greeted by a small army of Finn's men. They were ready with their weapons and shields and hounds. We were asked to relinquish our weapons as a sign of goodwill.

'Bollocks!' I shouted. We would not surrender our weapons. I told Finn's dogs that we were the personal bodyguards of our king and we will remain armed at all times. We were then taken to Finnesburh further down river. The entire area looked like it had been built on a swamp, as Frisia was constantly flooded. England had its fair share of floods, but they say it is so bad in Frisia that the Frisians are born with webbed-feet and lived on their boats.

Finnesburh was a huge stone fortress with the Scylding banners riding high over the stone walls, showing the world who was king in those lands. And the main gates were as tall as mountains and it was heavily guarded by many Scyldings and Frisians. And inside the fort were several mead-halls and stone buildings and it had an impressive stone tower where the king resided. Hnaef had told me that Finn was a very rich and powerful king, but I was still shocked at how big Finn's kingdom was. It simply dwarfed my fathers and even Hnaef's fortress seemed insignificant in comparison.

I was nervous as I entered the kingdom of the man, who along with his dead father was responsible for the destruction of my village and the death of my loved ones. It had been twenty eight years since I came home from the Black Forest with Horsa wrapped in my arms to discover that the Scyldings had wiped out my entire village in Jutland. And it had been twenty one years since Dresden and I had fought with King Folcwald and killed him on the battlefield with *Wolf-Fang*. And Finn had no idea that the son of King Whitgils still lived or that I had been responsible for Folcwald's death. He simply invited me and the king into his fortress with *Wolf-Fang* tucked into my belt, perhaps still with traces of Folcwald's blood on the blade.

Finn did know me as 'Hengest the Wolf-Tamer' the young brash kid that he had met all those years ago in Jutland. And he knew of me as the Englisc ealdorman that had been slaughtering his men for a generation and he obviously didn't like me or trust me, but I do hope that he respected me. And as Hnaef had reminded me all the way to Frisia, we weren't there for trouble, or for blood-feuds, we were there only for peace and union and for Frithuwulf to spend Yule with his mother and father.

We were all shown to the mead-hall where Finn had a feast prepared for us and after days and nights at sea we were all starved. Finn's hall was huge and was beautifully decorated with golden shields that hung on every wall, nobody on earth knew of another hall like it, it was spectacular. It was the most lavish of mead-hall's that was radiant with the gold of many conquests. And I confess to being jealous of Finn, he had achieved success that I could only dream of and he was married to the first woman that I had ever loved. I had not seen Hildeburh for many years and I still remembered the nights when I would sneak into her room and she would teach me how to be a man. But that was a lifetime ago and I was a little nervous about seeing her after all these years.

Frithuwulf was sitting at the table sucking on a peace of chicken like he hadn't eaten for days. He was Finn's kid, but I do confess to liking him. He had a great sense of humour and he was a great fighter, just like his father, who I had grown up watching in battle when I was just a kid. Frithuwulf was now eighteen years old and had practically grown up in King Hnaef's mead-hall in England getting shit-faced with his uncle and I. Horsa, Hunlafing and Siegeferth were at the table too, stuffing their faces full of meat and ale and that's when King Finn entered the hall. And we could immediately feel the intense atmosphere.

Finn was wearing his trademark black bear skin over his chain-mail. His hair was long and as grey as the winter night sky, his chin was shaved and his arms were covered in golden rings, showing off his wealth and status. The king entered with a large band of thanes; amongst them was a Frisian lord by the name of Guthere and another man whose face I recognised instantly. My heart was beating fast as the king walked towards us. I turned to Hnaef and told him that standing next to the king was Garulf. Hnaef and I didn't believe it.

Garulf was a western Jute and the son of the murdered Gefwulf. Hnaef's father, King Hoc, had ordered Gefwulf's death to prevent a rebellion in Jutland. And it now looked like the exiled Jutes and Garulf had sided with their former enemy. And I would later learn from Hnaef that Garulf was now the King of Jutland. Hnaef and I had known Garulf since he was a kid and we had gone to war together against the Scyldings, but that was a long time ago and Hnaef and I now had a blood-feud on our hands.

Hnaef stood up as the king made his way to our table, but I just sat there ignoring the king and avoided eye contact as I carried on eating, even though I felt a little sick. 'Good to see you my friend.' Finn said to Hnaef as he embraced his brother in-law. Then Finn turned and addressed me: 'Welcome Hengest, it's an honour to have such a decorated champion such as yourself here at Finnesburh. They tell me you are big and strong, but they didn't tell me that you had grown into a giant. You were such a small child when I first laid my eyes on you. And you were a cheeky little bastard too, if I remember correctly.' Finn laughed. 'I do hope we can put our grievances aside and maybe one day become friends. I would like that; there is nothing that I would want more than for Geatland, Jutland, England and Frisia to one day unite under one roof. Think about it Hengest, our people would rule the world and no one could ever beat us.'

Finn was irritating me as he told me about his fantasy and told of a future where we would be great friends. And so I stood up and replied: 'In this lifetime, I don't care to be your friend, but I also don't wish to be at war with you any longer. You have proven to be a great king, you are a brave warrior and you are kind and generous to your people. But I know that you have been brutalising the Frisians that are under your rule. And I could never trust you to be kind to my people like the way you are with your own. And so I don't care for us to become butt buddies because I think you're an arsehole. However, I do respect you and your accomplishments, but I can never forgive you for what you did to my people. But I do come in peace and I wish you and your family no harm. I am here on the request of my king, to serve and protect him with my honour and nothing more.'

Finn looked up at me and replied: 'Very well, I can accept that and I thank you for your honesty. Now please continue your meal before it gets cold. And if there is anything that I can arrange for you and your men to make your stay more pleasurable, then please ask.'

I then sat back down and continued eating as Horsa gave me a funny look. Frithuwulf was sitting next to me and just belched loudly as he gulped down his father's mead. Frithuwulf didn't know his father very well as he had only seen him a few times in the last ten years and he greeted Finn almost like he was a stranger. 'Alright mate!' he said to the king, not even bothering to get up. Horsa and I gave a sly smile to each other as we thought that it was hilarious that the king's son didn't care for his father. 'Get up son and give your old man a proper embrace.' Finn demanded. Frithuwulf then stood up and shook his father's hand as Horsa spat out his mead with a laugh that he tried so hard to keep inside.

'Where's my mother?' Frithuwulf demanded to know. 'She's just fetching your brother and sister; she'll be here in a minute.' My heart began to skip beats. I don't know why, but I suddenly became terrified at the thought of seeing Hild, even more so then with Finn standing next to me and with Garulf staring a hole right through me. And then I saw her walking with her maidens and her two kids. Adorned in her gold, she graciously saluted the men in the hall, queenly and dignified, decked out in jewellery that sparkled from the light emitting from the flame torches that surrounded the extravagant mead-head. She looked beautiful and elegant. Her hair still wild and curly, her face just as beautiful as I last saw her. She wore a long violet satin gown and had on a magnificent headband that sparkled with gems and emeralds.

Frealaf and Freawynn ran to their brother and the three of them embraced. Queen Hildeburh approached the table and greeted her brother in a formal manner. I had wiped my mouth on my sleeve before standing to greet the queen: 'Nice to see you my lady, you look very beautiful this evening.' My hands were shaking and my voice was trembling and I felt like such a faggot talking to her that way. Her arms were decorated with sparkling bracelets that were worthy of only a true goddess.

I then kissed her hand and looked into her blue eyes, but she didn't look back. She turned her head and smiled at her son that she had not seen for some time and avoided eye contact with me. Her face looked the same, calm, familiar and friendly, but her eyes were different. It was as if she was a different person that didn't know me. It felt strange and bizarre. It was as if someone had cast an evil spell and she had forgotten who I was and had forgotten the many years we shared together.

I noticed that her arms had markings on them, that she was hiding under her sleeves; she then quickly pulled her hand away and greeted her son. I then sat back down, deflated. She didn't even greet Horsa whom she had known since he was a baby and her mother had practically raised him. Hnaef then joined his sister and his brother in-law in their private quarters, as the rest of us finished our meal and got plastered on the mead.

Later that night, Hnaef and Frithuwulf returned to the hall with news of the peace agreement. Hnaef told me that we would spend the winter at Finnesburh as planned, and when winter turned to summer, he and his men would return to England without me. Hnaef had negotiated for me to stay in Finnesburh with a small band of men for the entire summer, the traditional war season, as a token of peace and unity. I was second to the king and the most important man in Hnaef's band of warriors and so I would become Finn's hostage. And in exchange, Hnaef would be accompanied by Finn's most valuable advisor, Guthere. And so if Hnaef was to trick Finn into lowering his defences in Jutland and then attacked him during the summer months, I would be killed by Finn's men at Finnesburh. I wasn't happy with the arrangement, in fact I was livid, but I accepted my duty to my king and I knew of no plan to attack the Scyldings in Jutland and so there was no reason for me to fear treachery. Everything had been planned well and we had secured peace in Jutland. Or so we thought, as that night a blood-feud would arise and swords would be drawn.

My old instructor Siegeferth and Horsa joined me that night by getting rat-arsed on the mead and ale and the Jutes and Englisc thanes joined us in a sing song. But Hnaef and Hunlafing didn't join in. Hunlafing told me that he didn't trust the Frisians or the Jutes that had aligned themselves with Finn and feared an attack. In the early hours of the morning, as I began to sober up, I heard a knock on the door. Hnaef told us to be quiet and not to respond. Frithuwulf, Horsa, Siegeferth and the sixty thanes that filled the hall were all armed and ready for any surprises. Then the door began to slowly turn on its hinge and the huge thick wooden iron-braced doors slowly creaked open and in poured dozens of warriors bearing torches and spears that rushed into the hall and they were led by a very determined Garulf. Hunlafing was right and all *Niflheim* broke loose at Finnesburh.

Hnaef and I ordered the men, including a very enthusiastic Frithuwulf, to charge at the enemy. And as we did so, our shields clashed against theirs, sending shock-waves down my arms and through my upper body and the clash of steel and bronze echoed throughout the mighty hall. My feet slid backwards on the stone floor as the Jutes pushed forwards, forcing there way into the hall. Hnaef and I were at the front, pushing and pushing, with the support of sixty battle hardened thanes behind us using our shields to force the enemy back and out into the courtyard. I then ordered the men to barricade the doors and secure the hall using the tables and chairs that we had prepared earlier.

We now knew that we were at war and that Garulf hadn't come for his blood-money, he had come for our blood.

Frithuwulf slapped my hand and screamed with joy as he was exited about fighting the exiled Jutes. From what we could see there were no obvious Scyldings amongst the attackers. And Hnaef suggested, after his long talk with Finn earlier in the night, that Finn was not involved in the attack and Garulf and the Jutes had independently sought there revenge against the people that they blamed for the murder of their chieftain and their forced exile. And Hnaef made an interesting point that Finn had no reason to attack us and he wouldn't have put his eldest son at risk. I believed that Finn wouldn't have sent Garulf into battle with us as he was the King of Jutland and far too important to Finn to risk his life. And so I am convinced that Garulf was the one that orchestrated the attack at Finnesburh.

We decided to hold out the night and wait for Finn's help in the morning, hoping to come to an agreement with the exiled Jutes. We could hear Garulf's men outside the hall planning their next attack and as we settled back down in the hall, I heard Hnaef bragging to the lads that the edges of his sword were famous amongst the Jutes and Scyldings and was greatly feared. I then pulled *Dances with Corpses* out of its scabbard and interrupted the king: 'If I had a notch on this sword for every man I have killed, then I wouldn't have a sword, as it would have turned to splinters.'

'Hail Hengest!' Horsa yelled. 'Hail Hengest!' the men shouted as they raised their drinking horns in a toast. Hunlafing didn't raise his ale; instead he just scowled at me, obviously still brooding over the fact that I was made Hnaef's ealdorman.

We had no idea what time of day it was as there were no windows in the great hall and we became bored as we sat and waited. We tried to keep ourselves entertained with sagas of old heroes. I had fallen asleep numerous times and lost all sense of day and night and I had no idea how long we had been hauled up in that big dark hall. There had been lots of food and water and of course more importantly there was lots of ale and mead to help keep the boredom away. We had eaten all the good meat that Finn had his thralls prepare for us on our arrival and we were now living off the leftovers. We eat old gruel, stale porridge, days old fruit and veg, and stale bread, once we had cut off the furry green bits. We were starving and bored and very drunk. The hall stank of gone-off food, sweat, piss, farts, puke and shite. Then after what seemed like days, we heard a loud bang as something heavy crashed against the doors that secured the hall.

'They're using a battering ram.' someone yelled. 'Get ready!' I told the men as we waited patiently seeing if the doors would hold. They didn't. And after many attempts at breaking the doors open they finally managed it and the exiled Jutes came charging against our shields and spears. I then saw Garulf charging into the mix of flesh, bone and steel with his yellow hair flowing behind him from underneath his helmet, his eyes crazed and wild. He was shouting 'Murderers! Traitors!' and all sorts of obscenities as he charged forward feeling the battle-fury.

'He's mine!' I yelled to the men on the front ranks as I broke away and swung *Dances with Corpses* above my head with Garulf in my sights. There were thanes everywhere, swinging swords and axes and goring with their boar-headed spears. I charged through the men whilst avoiding spears and javelins as I lunged forward towards Garulf. We were friends once, when we were young, but that didn't stop me running through him with my blade.

As my sword crashed against him, I suddenly fell backwards and we both fell to the ground. My sword had hit his steel breastplate and it had broken the tip of my blade. I was on the dusty floor fearing being trampled on as got to my knees and tried to get back to my feet. But there was too much weight crashing against me and men began to trample over my legs. I screamed and yelled for them to get off, but no one cared as the exiled Jutes poured into the hall. Their screams and shouts echoed off the stone surroundings as I managed to crawl to the wall and pull myself to my feet. I could see Finn's son smashing against the intruders with his shield that had been a gift from his uncle and foster father Hnaef. I saw my old instructor Siegeferth hacking and slashing into the ranks of the enemy.

I then looked over and saw that Garulf had gotten to his feet and so I joined the carnage once again and pushed and shoved my way back to the front. 'Move you fucking arseholes!' I shouted at my own men as I squeezed my way past and headed for Garulf. I then put my sword back into its scabbard and used all of my weight as I then rammed my wooden shield against Garulf. And as he stumbled backwards and fell into his own men, I then reached over and pulled off his protective war helmet and violently slit across his bearded throat with *Wolf-Fang* and blood squirted out, painting my face crimson red. I felt like I was in *Valhalla* as I gave out a primal war cry, loud enough to be heard by the Gods themselves. Garulf was the first to die in the battle of Finnesburh, but he wouldn't be the last.

I could hear the winter gales blowing outside the hall gates as the doors were slamming against the wall in the fierce winds. I could hear yelling and death screams all around me as I joined the front ranks of the shieldwall. But we were undisciplined in the Roman style of fighting and the exiled Jutes quickly broke our ranks, as our shields were not locked together properly. And the whole hall flowed red with blood, as it descended into chaos and anarchy and I loved every second of it.

I immediately targeted a thane and introduced him to *Dances with Corpses* as I hacked and hacked. I'm not sure how many parts he was left in, maybe three or four. A man in armour then got in my way and so I swung my decorated sword that came down ringing and singing on his head, splitting him in two. I was stepping over bodies and dismembered limbs as I chose my next target.

I saw that Frithuwulf had been cornered against the wall by two Jutes; obviously they didn't know that it was King Finn's eldest son hiding under that helmet. And so I rushed to his defence and with *Dances with Corpses* in both hands, I cut one of his attackers right through his crotch, nearly cutting his leg off as I lifted him in the air, tearing his balls in half. I had just pulled my left shoulder, but I didn't care as the battle-fury owned me now and I was its humble servant. I then turned towards the other guy and kicked him in the balls as Frithuwulf stabbed him in his unprotected kidneys. 'Well done kid!' I yelled over the noise, as Frithuwulf adjusted his helmet.

The sparks were flying and people were dying and I was having the time of my life fighting by the side of my brother Horsa and my king. I then looked into the mix of flesh and steel to see how Hnaef was doing when I saw that he was outnumbered by the pissed off Jutes. He was surrounded and I desperately tried to push through the carnage to get to his aid, but I couldn't do it as I was been squashed between the warring thanes. I witnessed Hnaef's sword flickering in the light coming from the flamed torches that were hung around the walls. His sword *Battle-*

Flame was singing and dancing as it took the lives of the Jutes. Hnaef was in a blaze of fury, his sword and his movements became a blur as he fought to the death against his attackers.

King Hnaef died honourably that morning. He died like a man, like a king, like a warrior and like a son of Woden. He died with his sword in his hands and had earned himself a place in the warrior-hall of the slain by the side of his father in *Valhalla*. I was devastated at Hnaef's death, but I was in the middle of a warzone and the battle continued.

It was a tight squeeze inside the hall and I had to resort to only using my long knife *Wolf-Fang* to try and gut my opponents and spill their innards on the stone floor in Finn's hall. I could smell the leather and the sweat as I crashed against shield and bone, stabbing and thrusting wildly at everyone and everything that moved. The fighting was intense and as the night went on things were going to get worse, much worse. As the fighting progressed, the body's piled up and the stench of death violated the air. After what seemed like an eternity fighting, I became exhausted and disorientated. And as I was thrashing and kicking, I thrust my blade deep into the guts of the man in front of me. His eyes bulged widely, blood poured out of his mouth as he stared into my crazed eyes. It was Frithuwulf.

I had just stabbed my best friend's nephew and foster son. I didn't know who it was until I heard his death scream. I was horrified. Even though I had detested his father, Finn, I had grown fond of Frithuwulf and was sick and disgusted at the events that unfolded that night. As the night dragged on and bodies continued to fall, the Angles and the Jutes managed to force the intruders out of the hall. We used our shields and our last ounce of energy to drive the exhausted enemy out and barricaded the doors once more.

We were all resting inside the hall surrounded by the dead and of course our king and his heir were amongst them. The men were checking the fallen for armour and better weapons as Hunlafing and I discussed our next move. England had just lost its king and I had been the second in command and so many of the Jutes that had grown up in England decided to accept me as their new leader. Hunlafing opposed this idea, as his family had been close to the Hocings for countless generations and many of the Englisc saw him as their rightful leader. Hunlafing's father had been the ealdorman of King Hoc, a man that many had once pledged their oaths too and had since given their oath to his son, Hnaef. And so the group was divided into two camps, on one side was the Jutes led by me and the Angles on the other, led by Hunlafing.

I explained to the men that King Hoc had tried his best to avoid this happening by uniting the Jutes and Angles under one kingdom and that's what got us into this mess with the exiled Jutes in the first place. But most men didn't understand the concept of 'irony'.

Later, King Finn arrived at the hall and banged on the doors demanding to know what had happened. He explained that he didn't order the attack and was horrified to learn that his two guests, his son and brother in-law, had been killed at his home. Finn seemed sickened that he now had to tell his wife that her brother and eldest son lay dead in their famous mead-hall. And he seemed disgusted with the fact that he also had to tell his two children that their uncle and brother were now dead.

I listened as I heard Finn talking at the other side of the wooden doors to Hunlafing. Finn explained to Hunlafing that he didn't have a problem with the Angles and now wished to accept Hunlafing as the rightful King of England, as long as he rejected his alliance with my self and my fellow Jutes.

I then whispered to Hunlafing and explained that Finn had lost so many men that he couldn't force his way back in and wouldn't burn down his own hall. We knew that Finn wouldn't be able to raise an army for months, as it was a harsh winter and travel was almost impossible. And so I convinced Hunlafing not to betray the Jutes and leave us to the mercy of Finn's men. I explained that Finn was not to be trusted and that if Hunlafing betrayed the Jutes, then he would cause a civil war in England with the hundreds of Jutes that were loyal to me. And Finn would simply take advantage and order an attack to kill all the highest ranking Angles and Jutes and name himself King of England. Hunlafing agreed that I was right and tried to negotiate with Finn, asking the king to swear an oath of peace with the Englisc and the Jutes, giving Finn no choice, but to accept.

I then asked Finn personally to acknowledge that he knows that neither I nor him self had started the fight and so neither of us were responsible for the deaths of our loved ones. Finn agreed. And whilst talking to him through the doors, I asked the king for separate quarters from the exiled Jutes for the remaining winter. Finn agreed. I then asked the king for the finest fur rugs for the men to sleep on. 'Ask for whores.' Siegeferth whispered. 'And Siegeferth would like the prettiest whores in Frisia to keep us warm throughout the remaining cold winter nights. And my brother Horsa requests a couple of young boys for himself.'

'Piss off! Its Hengest that wants the boys.' Horsa shouted. I had personally asked Finn to bring his wife Hildeburh to the doors and swear an oath of peace with his name and honour on the line. And in front of his nobles and his wife, Finn swore his oath and gave us all status whilst staying at Finnesburh for the long winter months and promised death to any of his men that broke that oath. And so we laid down our arms and opened the doors.

It was impossible to survive a journey at sea, as the ocean raged with wind and storms and no horse was able to travel through the deep freezing snow that now covered the world. And so the plan now was to stay at Finn's throughout the winter, officially under Finn's protection.

Hnaef had no children of his own and often spoke of Frithuwulf as his own son and later that night Hnaef and Frithuwulf were laid together on the funeral pyre. The pyre was heaped with boar-crested helmets forged in gold; there were shields, silver drinking vessels and other treasures. And Finn and I had each placed a sword in Hnaef's and Frithuwulf's hands and we watched with sorrow as the pyre was set alight by the archer's flaming arrows. And the fire lit up the night sky; as we watched their heads crumbling, their flesh bursting open,

>spurting and sizzling as the
>Gods consumed
>them.

*'Both prestige and power
depend on being continually
attended by a large
train of picked warriors,
which is a distinction
in peace
and a protection
in war'*

*Roman Historian 'Tacitus'
1ˢᵗ Century AD*

Chapter Twelve:
The Battle of Finnesburh-Part Two

Frisia 449 AD
(Belgium)

    Finn had agreed that his men and my men were to be kept apart during the winter and we were to have our own hall and our own thralls. Hunlafing had kept Hnaef's famous sword *Battle-Flame* and as we sat in the mead-hall brooding over the king's death and waiting for the good summer weather, Hunlafing placed Hnaef's sword across my lap. He wanted me to kill Finn for the king's inability to keep the Angles and Jutes safe upon our arrival at Finnesburh. But I was confused. Should I avenge Hnaef's death or honour my peace agreement with Finn? Hunlafing spoke: 'Remember Hengest, you didn't swear an oath to Finn, it was Finn that swore an oath to you.' And the men sitting around the table agreed to the murder of King Finn. 'All is fair in love and war.' Finn's father once told me and so I agreed to avenge the death of Hnaef.

    Summer came round and the snow had melted and Hunlafing and the Angles went back home to England, as agreed with Finn. And the rest of us stayed at Finnesburh to honour the peace agreement with the Frisian lord. But what Finn didn't know was that Hunlafing was to tell of Hnaef's death and blame everything on the unsuspecting king. And then raise an army of thousands for the sacking of Finnesburh. Horsa, Siegeferth and I, along with a small band of men, stayed at Finnesburh and we kept out of Finn's way whilst anticipating a surprise attack.

Finn was king of a mighty empire, but his men were stretched across the lands and Hunlafing was going to make sure he brought a massive army that dwarfed the number of Scyldings, Jutes and Frisians that occupied Finnesburh. England had been safe from the Scyldings for over ten years and was safe from other attackers and so I told Hunlafing to bring every available thane and leave no able man behind.

When the night came I was nervous and exited as I knew that the *wyrd* of England and the *wyrd* of my children all rested on that one night. And Horsa and I couldn't afford to make one mistake, otherwise our plan would fall apart, and Horsa and I would have been murdered. And I dread to think what would have happened to my kids.

I had been waiting for this moment since I was seven years old, for a chance of revenge against the last remaining people that were responsible for the murder of my family. Finn and his father had made a surprise attack on my village and they say: 'revenge is a dish best served cold'. And now the time had come and the swords were drawn.

It was warm and sticky as Horsa and I sneaked out of our hall in the dead of night. We were careful not to disturb the lookouts in their watchtowers as we sneaked around the courtyard looking for the guards that we were going to put to our blades. We had ventured round many times in the night, talking to the guards, and planning our route to the watchtowers. There were eight watchtowers in total, each with a guard at the bottom of the staircase. Months earlier, I had planned the attack with Hunlafing and we had decided it would be best to kill the two guards watching over the main gates from their watchtowers and then allow Hunlafing to bring the army to the front of the fort, unnoticed.

Horsa walked up to one of the guards that we had become familiar with: 'Alright pal?' he said just before he pulled out his sword. The guard immediately held out his spear and put up his shield. But before he could call for help, I had grabbed him from behind and twisted his neck, snapping his spine. I slowly allowed his body to drop to the floor and dragged him around the corner. 'One down, three to go.' I whispered to Horsa.

We then both took off our armour to stop it clanging as we sneaked up the stone stairs to the guard watching over the fort walls. We began to crawl as we reached the top and we held our breath as we prepared to murder him. The guard seemed to be sleeping in his chair and it was too easy as Horsa gently slit his throat and blood gushed out silently, as the man shook and quivered on the floor.

We then went back down stairs and put on our armour and ran to the second watchtower. I was wearing my war helmet as I approached the weary guard that was standing at the bottom of the tower. He was only a kid, no older than my own son, Aesc. And the boy was only half my size as I smashed my protected head onto his forehead, knocking him silly. And I felt a little guilty as I had no choice, but to rip apart his throat with *Wolf-Fang*.

We then did the same routine as we sneaked up the spiral stairs and confronted the final guard. He was standing up as he watched over the fort walls. He was standing on his chair, taking a piss over the wall, when I turned to Horsa and made sure that he was watching. I then sneaked over to the guard and simply pushed him over the stone wall. He screamed with fear moments before his body splattered all over the marshy floor on the outside of the fort.

I then heard voices as the scream had alerted the Frisians, Jutes and the Scyldings. Horsa began to laugh and shout with excitement as we both ran as fast as possible to the main gates that secured the fortress. I knocked gently on the gates three times. I then waited for a response, hoping that the guards on the other side were already dead. I then heard two knocks, it was Hunlafing, as two knocks meant that everyone outside of the fort was dead and I had an army outside waiting to raise Finnesburh to the ground.

I then opened the gates and they made a huge creek as I was greeted by a big grinning ginger man and behind Hunlafing was a mass of flesh, bone and steel. The combined Englisc and Jutisc thanes had lost land and loved ones at the hands of Finn and his men and we all hungered for revenge.

The men of Finnesburh began to stir and thanes began to walk the courtyard, wondering what all the noise was, as hundreds of warriors poured through the gates. The Scyldings and Frisians shouted for help before they were cut down by my soldiers and soon the entire fort was awake and chaos ensued. I drew *Dances with Corpses* from its swastika engraved scabbard and led my men into battle. 'No prisoners!' I shouted, as we began the slaughter.

My heart was racing as I charged at Finn's men; my eyes were wide and crazed as I clashed against their shields and sliced across their unprotected chests with my long repaired sword. I had broken my sword in Finn's hall during the fight with Garulf and I found it amusing that I had had it repaired at Finn's expense and I now used it against his own men.

Finn's thanes began to pour out of the mead-halls that were scattered around the fortress. Hundreds of men had been awakened from their dreams, not knowing that their nightmares had just begun. My men simply overwhelmed the Scyldings and their allies and the fight resembled more of a massacre than a war.

As I desperately looked for the king, I was challenged by a brave thane who had singled me out for combat. I nodded to the soldier as I had accepted his challenge. I began to walk towards the enemy when I was attacked by two other men. But I made short work of them as I kicked one in the balls and cut his throat, and I then hit the other one in the face with my spiked shield boss and shattered his eye socket. I left him alive on the floor as he screamed in agony, holding his right eye. I merely walked past him and stepped over bodies that were starting to fill up the courtyard.

I then came face to face with the Frisian. It was Guthere, Finn's top advisor and ealdorman. He was protected by a boar-crested war helmet and an impressive round shield, decorated with black swastikas. He wore chain-mail and a breastplate and was armed with a spear and sax. He then suddenly threw the spear at me as though it was a javelin and it crashed like thunder against my shield. And my heart sank as he then pulled from his belt a spiked-ball on a chain. He then gave me a wicked smile, as I'm sure he thought he was going to defeat the mighty Hengest in battle, a tale that the poets would be able to sing about until *Ragnarok*.

I held up my shield, cautiously, as I began to encircle him, breathing heavily. He swung his spiked-ball at me and I nearly shat myself as I desperately tried to avoid the killer blow. My body was big and heavy and I moved much slower than I had wished. Guthere was fearless as he charged at me, feeling the battle-fury. I knew that I was at a great disadvantage against Guthere and it was hard to get anywhere near him without being smacked in the teeth with the spiked-ball. I knew that

I wasn't going to win this battle with brawn alone and I needed to use brains and outsmart him.

I was feeling the battle-fury myself, but I couldn't go charging at such a dangerous opponent and so I took deep breaths and tried to relax and think. And as the battle continued all around us, I then suddenly had a brainwave. It was simple really, I was so big and strong that I simply grabbed a thane that was half my size and launched him at Guthere. I didn't know if it was my own man or not, as I threw him into the air like he was a small child. Guthere put up his shield and tried to dodge out of the way as the thane crashed against him, knocking Guthere to the ground. I then rushed over to the Frisian lord and with one foot on his chest; I stabbed him in the neck with *Dances with Corpses* and blood squirted everywhere as I yanked out my blade. I then picked up his spiked-ball by the chain and swung it with all my might and I smashed him in the face. And I took great joy as his facial-features crumbled and his head made an imprint into the soft ground beneath him.

As the war continued, I could clearly see that the Scyldings and Frisians were the better soldiers and were far more disciplined and better trained. One side was wild and turbulent, the other deliberate and cautious. But I wasn't concerned as my men outnumbered Finn's men by several thousand. I then backed away from the fighting and desperately looked for King Finn as I was worried that he might have been able to escape. I never saw Hild or her two children during my time under Finn's protection, but I was worried that she might still be at Finnesburh. I was responsible for Frithuwulf's death and so I felt a sense of responsibility for the protection of Hild and her two remaining children, whilst at the same time desperately looking for their blood kin for a final showdown.

I then ran towards the tower where Finn had resided and easily killed the two guards at the bottom of the stairs. I killed one of them with the spiked-ball and the other with the flamed torch that was on the wall. I held the flame to his face and screamed with joy as his skin melted away. I then charged up the spiralling stone stairs like a crazed man, I was breathing heavily as my armour clanged and echoed off the walls. I then kicked open the wooden doors at the top of the stairs and burst into the room with my spiked-ball and chain. I entered the room to a loud scream from Hild's only daughter, Freawynn.

'Get out Hengest!' Hild shouted as she was grabbing her personal things, obviously she was planning a hasty retreat. 'Where is he!?' I demanded. 'He's not here; he grabbed his sword and ran down stairs. Now go away Hengest, you've caused enough damage to our lives.' I then did as the queen asked and rushed back downstairs and entered the courtyard.

The yard was full of thanes, each battling to the death. Finn's men were falling at the feet of the Jutes and Angles as we were winning the war and everything was going to plan. There had been archers standing on the rooftops of the halls that were picking off my thanes one at a time. But now I noticed that several of the halls had been boarded shut and set alight and Finn's men were trapped inside and were simply burned alive. The archers sitting on the roofs were now forced to jump down and join the slaughter.

Smoke and burnt flesh now filled the air as I looked around the fort, calling Finn's name. My voice couldn't be heard over the warring thanes, but I was easily recognisable as I was the tallest of all the men and soon Finn spotted me from across the courtyard. The king had just slaughtered a couple of my men as our eyes locked for the first time that night. We both screamed a war cry and with fire and death behind him, Finn began to run towards me with his sword drawn.

He must have known that I was responsible for the attack and he came at me with determination as he pushed past the thanes with furious anger. I remembered when I first laid eyes on Finn when I was only seven years old. I looked up at him as he sat like a champion on his black and white horse and I admired him and wished to emulate him. But that was a long time ago and now I looked down at the grey haired king, as I was no longer a boy, but a full grown Jutisc and Englisc warlord. Finn was wearing his beautifully decorated dragon masked war helmet and my smile widened as Finn pulled out a huge sword, it was a thing of beauty. And I swung my new spiked-ball, drawing a circle in the air, as we stood off against each other.

The sky was lit up as fire burned around us and all we could hear were screams and the smash and bang as swords met shields and spears met flesh. Finn was furiously shouting something at me, but I didn't understand a word. I was sucking in oxygen as I tried to anticipate Finn's first move and we didn't take our eyes off each other. We were standing in the centre of the courtyard surrounded by warring thanes, when I furiously swung my spiked-ball at Finn. Finn quickly jumped out of the way and allowed his shield to take the blow. He then tried to counterattack by thrusting his sword towards my beer gut.

We were both protected by chain-mail, helmets and breastplates and Finn's blade had winded me as it hit me in the steel. But I wasn't hurt as I then suddenly swung and threw the spiked-ball at him using all of my strength. I had aimed at his face, but as he turned to protect himself, it hit him in the shoulder and shattered the bone. Finn then dropped his shield as his left arm was now useless. I laughed at him as I drew *Dances with Corpses* from its scabbard and asked: 'Is this all the mighty Finn has to offer? You're pathetic! You make me sick.'

Finn was standing favouring his shoulder whilst still holding his sword with his one good arm. He then jumped at me with his sword and I just stepped aside and easily avoided him. I was hopelessly disappointed. I had waited a lifetime for this opportunity and I somehow seemed robbed of glory. Finn was old, weak and pathetic and I felt no honour in killing an old worthless king. I was deflated and angry as I shouted at Finn, calling him a worthless piece of shite. I had lowered my guard as Finn then saw an opportunity and with both hands he gripped his sword and slashed me across my right thigh. My leg buckled as it bled out and I fell to the floor. Finn had tricked me.

There was nothing wrong with his shoulder as his iron chain-mail was strong. I knew that Finn was a smart man and I was furious that he had managed to make a fool out of me. I now lay on the floor, holding my gash together, as blood began to form a puddle around me. Finn then locked eyes with me from behind his dragon-mask as he held up his sword preparing to deliver the killer blow. 'Wait!' I yelled. 'I have something you need to know.'

Finn now had the advantage over me, however it was clear that my men were going to win the war as Finn was down to his last hundred men and I still had at least a thousand. Finn looked shocked as he suddenly paused and listened to whatever I had to say, perhaps hoping for a truce to save the necks of his men. I then scrambled to my feet, my thigh felt as if it was on fire as blood dripped down my legs. I then shouted out as loud as possible to the warring thanes, asking them to stop the fight. Finn then ordered one of his men to blow into the war horn and slowly the intense fighting finally came to an end. And Finn and I exchanged our final words in front of our armies.

Finn removed the mask part of his helmet and yelled with authority: 'Before I kill this treacherous piece of crap, he has something to say. And apparently he wants you all to hear it.' My leg was weak and trembling with pain as I wrapped a leather strap around my thigh. I then turned to Finn and laughed at him. 'Do you remember the battle at Garulfsburh when your father laid dead face first in the mud? I then held up *Wolf-Fang*. 'I killed your father with this very blade.' I shouted as loud as possible so the men could hear my voice. 'Well actually, that's not quite true, because it wasn't me that gave him the killer blow; it was Dresden, the mother of my two kids.' I was laughing out loud as I was trying to ignore the pain in my leg. 'She was only thirteen. Your father, the king, was killed by a little girl.' I was laughing hysterically and coughing, as I wiped the spittle from my mouth. 'She was possessed by the *Valkyries*, as she then licked Folcwald's blood off this very blade.' Finn was furious. But I continued: 'You know me as Hengest, don't you, my lord?' I asked with arrogance. 'But that's not who I really am. My name isn't Hengest and I'm not an Angle. I'm a Jute and my name is Aesc, son of Whitgils.' Finn looked horrified. I began to take off my armour and placed my weapons on the ground, as I continued telling Finn the truth about my hidden identity: 'Aesc still lives!' I yelled as I took off my war helmet, allowing my long brown hair to flow freely.

There were murmurs in the crowd. But I continued: 'And I am the rightful King of Jutland, a kingdom that you've stolen from me, Finn. And now I challenge you to a fight, one on one, to end this blood-feud, once and for all.'

The crowd was silent as they waited for Finn's response. But Finn didn't say a word, as he then took off his helmet and threw his weapons and armour to the floor and accepted my challenge. And so in front of the two armies, Finn and I agreed to fight to the death and no weapons would be involved.

With fires burning and crackling behind him, Finn's long grey hair was blowing in the breeze as he stood before me. I tried to ignore the pain in my leg as I stretched my neck to the side and cracked my fingers as I prepared to pound Finn's head into oblivion. I then stepped forward, limping slightly, and charged at Finn, taking him to the ground with a strong tackle. The men cheered. I was punching Finn hard in the face with a thunderous force. He put up his arms to protect himself, but I had managed to break his nose and blood was everywhere. Finn then poked me in the eye and hit me in the jaw, knocking me over. He got to his feet and began kicking me in the ribs and head.

I was gasping for air as I tried to block his attack and get to my feet. I then grabbed Finn and head-butted him square on his already broken nose. Finn screamed in agony as blood flowed from his face. Finn looked tired and disoriented as I smashed him in the face with my fists, knocking him to the ground. I saw Horsa smiling as he watched me batter and pound at Finn's face.

'Come on Hengest, kill the bastard!' the men screamed. Siegeferth spoke: 'Remember what I taught you Hengest, no mercy!' As Finn lay on the floor, I raised my good leg into the air and stamped down hard on Finn's head several times, using all of my weight. The women were screaming, as I then picked up Finn's tired and limp body that was dripping in blood, and dragged him across the courtyard towards the fires. Horsa yelled words of encouragement as Finn's men looked on with horror. I had a smile on my face and evil intensions on my mind as I took Finn and threw him onto the open fire.

The men gasped with horror and Finn's screams could be heard in the halls of *Valhalla*. Finn ran around the courtyard, falling and tripping over the dead bodies, as he desperately tried to put out the fire that had engulfed his flesh. I was then shocked as Horsa used Hnaef's old sword, *Battle-Flame*, and rammed it into Finn's belly and up behind his ribs, piercing his heart and putting him out of his misery.

I had burned my arm on the fire that had consumed Finn's body, but I hadn't noticed it at the time as I was enraged with the battle-fury. And I gave out a primal victory scream with the support of my thanes and much to the horror of Finn's men. I then used *Battle-Flame* to cut off Finn's head and I grabbed his long greasy hair as I held his decapitated head for all to see and my men all cheered and applauded, as Finn's blood dripped down my right arm. I then threw Finn's lifeless and head-less corpse onto the fire and allowed the flames to claim him. And to show my respect to the warring thanes and to honour the courage of Finn, I then placed his sword into his charcoal hands, as even Finn deserved his rightful place amongst the Gods.

I noticed that Hild had walked away and watched from a distance as her kids hid their faces in their mother's bosom. I then walked over to my armour and weapons that lay on the floor. And as I decked myself out in my war gear, I noticed Finn's war helmet lying on the courtyard. The helmet was a thing of beauty; it was a magnificent piece of *Nordic* art and craftsmanship. It was made from solid gold and iron and had pictures of warriors in combat, beautifully decorating the entire helmet. On the sides were panels made from tin-covered bronze-foil, also with decorative pictures of warriors in combat.

The helmet had a thick leather lining for a comfortable fit and on the back was a large neck guard made from the strongest iron. The helmet also had big long eyebrows and each brow ended with a boar's head and was lined with red garnets. Hanging from the front of the helmet was a mask to protect the face and flaps to protect the wearer's ears and jaw whilst in battle. The mask also has a gold-covered-bronze nose and moustache. And there was a dragon on the front made of gold-covered-bronze and the dragon had eyes made of red jewels and had a tail and wings. I then gave Horsa my old helmet and placed Finn's magnificent glittering dragon masked helmet over my long bloodied locks.

As Finn's corpse vanished before our very eyes on the fire, I called out to his thanes that were still standing staring into the flames. The sun had risen slowly over the distant clouds, fires crackled around me, the smell of burning flesh violated the air and my adrenaline was pumping, as I addressed the Frisians: 'Your king is dead and I now ask you to surrender your weapons and go home to your families. You fought well tonight, you fought with honour and I salute you. You have been loyal to your king, but you are no longer bound by oaths to a dead man, you are now free. The Angles and Jutes have no quarrel with Frisia.'

I knew that Finn had several forts scattered around Frisia and he still had thousands of men that were loyal to him. But as I explained to the Frisians, now Finn was dead, the oppressed Frisians would rebel and fight for their freedom and civil war would break out. Many of the Frisians were Vikings and mercenaries and they were now in need of a new king or ealdorman. And so after killing the Scyldings amongst the men at Finnesburh, many of the Frisians knelt down on one knee and offered me their oaths. I then pulled out *Dances with Corpses* and held it out to the men on their knees and accepted their oaths. And I told the men that I would one day be calling on them for help.

As I held out my blade to the Frisians, one man at the front reached for my sword and held the blade delicately, as if he feared cutting himself. His name was Hereswith and I would come to know him as a mighty warrior and a great friend and in front of hundreds of thanes, he then kissed my blade as if it was a lady. 'Don't be so gay.' I said, as the men laughed.

The Frisians then went home and the Jutes and Angles then took all things of value from Finnesburh. There were astonishing treasures to be found and it took us several days to load the ships with all the golden wall hangings, glittering gold buried beneath the floorboards. Finnesburh was packed with jewel-studded goblets, silver headbands, jewel-studded pattern-welded swords and a magnificent emblem of Thor's hammer made of pure gold and inlaid with emeralds that I put around my neck.

There were also Brooches, gems, a golden war horn, splendid furs, jewelled-brooches and glinting golden harps, golden ornaments and jewelled shields and more swords of excellent Germanic craftsmanship. I also found a belt buckle made of pure gold and inlaid with garnets and jewels that I pinned to my black leather belt. And there was also a worm-looped-patterned shield with red, orange and purple jewels that I kept for myself.

We then left Finnesburh and burned the fort to the ground, leaving nothing, but an empty shell behind. Hild and her children accompanied us as we made our way back to England and there she was announced as the rightful Queen of the Angles. Many of the Frisians went back home and I had hoped to see them again one day along with their families.

It was like old times in the echoing hall, with proud talk and the people were happy, loud and exited. Once I had settled in back home and filled my hall with the treasures of my conquest, I then received a visit by the most unlikely of ambassadors. Their names were strange and foreign and it would take me a long time to be able to pronounce them correctly. Mauricius and Valeninian were ambassadors from the High King of the Celts in Britain, his title was Vortigern, and I now forget his real name. Vortigern wished for me and my brother to help them fight against the northern Pictish tribes that had invaded their lands in the south of the island.

The Jutes and Angles still needed better lands, as our coastal villages had been constantly flooded over the years and we were now forced to live further inland. And now with Finn dead, we knew that the alliance with the Scyldings was over and nothing was stopping them from attacking England. And so we accepted their offer to work with the Celts as hired mercenaries, hoping this would lead to a permanent settlement in Britain. And the Gods were watching with baited breath and the *Fates* were weaving their tangled webs as the *wyrd* of my people began to unfold before my very eyes.

'Gaeth a wyrd swa hio scel!'
'Fate goes ever as fate must!'

> "A council was held to decide the best way
> of dealing with the brutal invasions and bloody raids.
> All the members of the council and the Great King (Vortigern)
> were struck blind. To hold back the northern enemies
> they brought to this island the vile, unspeakable
> Saxons led by brothers Hengest and Horsa.
> These Saxons are hated by God and humans alike.
> Nothing more frightful has happened
> to this island,
> nothing more bitter."
>
> British Historian Saint Gildas
> 516-570 AD

Chapter Thirteen: Tides of Destiny

England to Britannia 449 AD
(Southern Denmark to Great Britain)

    The three ships, *Wyrmhorde*, *Ocean-Mare* and *Dancing Wolves*, bearing the emblems of the white dragon, the white horse and the two dancing wolves, were loaded with a cargo of weapons and armour. The three ships that sailed to Britain were each carrying sixty thanes, amongst them was my thrall Derfel and he would be most valuable as he spoke much better Englisc than Vortigern's two dogs. I spoke to Derfel: 'Try and run away and I'll cut your fucking balls off. Do you understand?'

    'Yes, my lord.' Derfel whimpered. 'Good man.' I said as I tapped Derfel's cheek with *Wolf-Fang*.

    The curved dragon prow preened on the waves and the wind was behind her and froth formed at her neck as she flew like a bird over the British seas. I sailed in *Wyrmhorde*, along with my old trainer Siegeferth, and Horsa was the commander of *Ocean-Mare*, embroidered with the white horse emblem that Horsa has since become famous for. And in the third ship was the Skull Crusher, whom had grown a long beard down to his waist that had long since turned grey and was platted down each side.

    After a lifetime of raiding the British coast, I knew our route well and I knew of its winds, tides and treacheries. We rode those waves as if our keels were being carried by Woden's eight legged horse *Sleipnir*.

We were embarking on a new adventure for riches and glory; we came in peace and friendship with the Celts, only looking for land for our own prosperity. But the *Fates* laughed at that and the Gods had a more interesting *wyrd* for the Jutisc and Englisc races.

My name was known well in Britain and I was shocked that Vortigern would hire me and my men as mercenaries to help protect Britain from its attackers. But I later understood that Vortigern had little choice, as the Romans had long since abandoned the island and Britain was told to defend itself against the invaders that came from the north, the west, the south and the east. And civil war had broken out amongst the Romano-British led by *Germanus of Auxerre* and the native Celts led by Vortigern. And Vortigern needed all the help he could get. It was a decision that would change the course of British history forever and change the *wyrd* of my people for all time.

Upon our arrival on the British shore, we had removed the dragon headed prows, as was custom, as to not frighten the friendly land spirits away and we were greeted by several dozen of Vortigern's men, each carrying round shields and swords. The men were wearing chain-mail and Roman standard helmets, each with red feathers down the middle of the helm. And several of the men were holding long staffs showing off the Celtic emblem of a red dragon on a green background. The leader told us that Vortigern salutes our arrival from across the seas and welcomes our help. He told me that it was his God's wish that we came to the island and help the Celt's in their hour of need. Their God had a sense of humour.

Valeninian and Mauricius led us to Vortigern's stronghold whilst riding their brown and white horses, as my thanes rowed up the river behind them. I could see the fort's watchtower in the distance, poking out over the brow of a hill. I could see the flag of the Celts flapping in the wind as it hung proudly overlooking the lush green lands of Britain. We then got out of our ships and made our way across the fields to the fort. The fortress looked old and battered and was probably Roman. As I scouted the fort from a distance, looking for its weaknesses, I turned to Horsa and whispered: 'Keep your eyes peeled, as one day we might be at war with these sheep shaggers.'

'I know I'm not an idiot.'

'Keep your bloody voice down, I don't want Derfel to hear us, because I know he'll go running to his own filthy kind and start spreading rumours.'

'Then let me cut out his tongue and rip off his fingers.'

'Don't be bloody stupid, I need Derfel to talk to these sub-humans.'

'But I can still rip his fingers off?'

'No! I might need Derfel to write messages to the Celts as he can write in Latin and he would be most valuable. And besides, I'm thinking about making Derfel write my sagas one day so we'll be remembered.'

'But he would have to write it in the Roman letters, who's ever going to read that?'

'Our Christian thralls, of course. They can read them out loud in our mead-halls and entertain our guests.'

'But you'll probably just exaggerate everything anyway so people think your some kind of hero.' I laughed at Horsa's comment. 'No, I don't give a fucking shite what people think about me. I'm sick of people telling others what they can and cannot think. People should be told the truth, the facts, and then be allowed to come to their own conclusions about what was right and what was wrong, even if it's not the popular opinion.'

I then took a deep breath. 'And besides, the Christians are always reading boring children's stories about strange elf-like people with big noses from the desert. And if I get Derfel to write my sagas then they can read about interesting stuff that actually happened. My life is far more exiting then old Christian sagas about a bunch of weirdo's that don't drink, don't fight and don't have sex with women.' Horsa laughed out loud as we crossed the field next to the fort and we got a few stares from the British.

Horsa continued: 'If they don't have sex with women, then what do they do for fun?'

'They have sex on their own, when they think nobody is looking.' Horsa couldn't control his laughter. 'And then they go to their sacred temples and tell their god what they did. He then tells them to beat themselves until they bleed and then he forgives them.' We were both laughing hysterically. 'Their god sounds like a bundle of joy, what a faggot!'

'Be quiet!' Wipped whispered. 'But how do they make babies?' Horsa asked. 'Their men have sex with young boys and then the monks perform miracles and virgins give birth to their ugly babies.'

'Stop your bullshit!' demanded Wipped. 'You're acting like children.'

'Sorry grandpa!'

I then stretched my shoulders back as we finally entered the gates to Vortigern's palace. I saw chickens, goats, cows and shit all over the place and it stunk like Horsa's breath in a morning. The British foreigners, or 'waelisc', as we call them, were watching us and giving us dirty looks. They called us all 'Saxons' which they thought meant 'sons of the sax', or 'sons of the sword' or they simply called us all 'pagans', whatever that meant. They never used the words Englisc or Jutisc.

The waelisc looked horrified as we entered their stronghold, decorated head to toe in iron, steel and bronze. I was holding my dragon helmet in my hand and was wearing the bloodstained skin of Fenrir. I had *Dances with Corpses* in its scabbard and *Wolf-Fang* tucked into my belt and in my other hand was my worm-looped-patterned shield and my arms were decorated with golden rings.

The faces of the Celts looked strange and foreign to me, most of them looked like the fire was lit, but no one was home. It seemed as though they were all greasy and spotty and they were all bred from the same litter. They all had vague and empty expressions on their miserable dark faces and their jaws were slack, a little like a dead fish and I couldn't tell one from the other. They all looked like hairy animals that were trying to impersonate a human being, poorly, and their women looked like men. The women had huge faces with massive jaws, wide, flat noses and evil looking dark eyes with dark eyebrows that joined in the middle. Most of them were dressed in long robes, completely covered up to the neck, even though it was a scorching hot day.

I saw a bunch of them kneeling on the floor with their hands together, crying and begging. 'They're begging for their god to feed them.' Siegeferth whispered. 'Lazy bastards.' Horsa mumbled. 'Why don't they feed themselves, as it's bleeding obvious that even their own god doesn't like them?' I saw one of the waelisc kissing a dead man's toe that was nailed to a cross. 'What a bunch of faggots.' Horsa said to himself. 'This strange, foreign cult will never catch on.' The Christians were strange people.

I then saw the High King of the waelisc, Vortigern, enter the courtyard. Vortigern was a small and puny man, he looked like he was about forty and was well dressed. He had a long weather beaten face and looked like he had been in many battles and was well distinguished. He had long reddish hair and a short well groomed beard. He wore some sort of crown upon his funny shaped head, but it didn't impress me, as I thought it made him look a twat. He had a large round shield made of bronze and was decorated with the same sort of blue spirals that I had seen before with the Picts from the north. He was covered in chain-mail and had a long shiny sword that only a man of great status would own.

Upon my first meeting with the High King, Vortigern explained to me, through my interpreter Derfel, that he wished for me to cleanse the south eastern corner of the island from the Germans that had settled there since the previous summer. Vortigern called that stretch of land *Cantii*, but I hated all those foreign words and so I simply called it Cent. Vortigern offered us half a chest full of silver and other riches for our troubles.

We were given food and shelter for the night and we kept a few men on constant watch and guard in the hall that had been given to us by the king. There was a constant feeling of unease amongst the thanes, as we all knew that the Celts didn't want us there. The rest of us tried to get some sleep, because in the morning we were going to go to Cent and solve the little problem of a few Germans that had settled in Vortigern's lands.

I woke up the next morning after Horsa belched out loudly waking everyone up in the hall. The waelisc fed us that morning, but were mortified when Wipped asked for some animals for a ritual sacrifice before we went to war. The waelisc refused to allow such a blasphemy on their lands. I have no idea what the word blasphemy meant, nor did I care, as I demanded to be allowed to honour the Gods with fresh blood. Finally, Vortigern came from his quarters and granted us our request and we took great pleasure in spilling blood in front of the snivelling Christians. It was time for war.

We then travelled to Cent on horses provided by Vortigern and was guided by a couple of his most trusted men. Vortigern had given me a mighty stallion called *Chestnut*; it was a well trained war horse that was used to all the noise and chaos seen on a battlefield. And he even gave me a beautiful golden horse bridle as a gift to show his appreciation. 'I bet there's lot's more gold where that came from.' Siegeferth told me.

The British countryside was beautiful with hills and small rivers and my arse was killing me as we finally arrived in the county of Cent. The British noble that owned the land was called 'Lord Gwyrangon' and he had arranged for his men to meet us on top of a sacred site. It was a large grassy hill with a giant white horse. They say that it was made with chalk by an ancient race of giants that once roamed the island before the races of man were created. The entire southern landscape was marked with strange stone pillars; Britain was a place of magic and mystery.

It was a hot and sticky summer afternoon and I was dying of thirst by the time we reached the ancient meeting site. From on top of the hill, I could see Lord Gwyrangon's Roman style villas in the distance. I could also see a huge round hill with a flattened top called 'Dragon's Hill'. Our guide told me that it was the site of the very last battle between the Celt's and the last dragon seen in Britain. I could see the German settlement at the bottom of the hill. I saw small huts and several Viking ships along the narrow river that stretched across the landscape. From the number of ships and the number of houses, I estimated the number of Germans to be about two hundred.

I took off my dragon masked helmet and had a good look at the patterns on the sails to see if I recognised any of them. I saw animals and birds and runic symbols. I then turned to Wipped and asked: 'Do you see what I see?' Wipped nodded. I then told Lord Gwyrangon's men and our guides to wait there, as the rest of us slowly made our way down the steep hill on our horses and made our way towards the settlement. We were clearly visible to the Germans and their scouts rushed ahead to warn them of our presence.

Wipped was holding the staff with the Jutisc emblem high in the sky to alert the Germans that they were being visited by the Jutes. And I myself was holding the emblem of the Englisc, a huge red flag with a beautiful white dragon in the centre. The Germans began to rush around gathering their armour and weapons as we slowly trotted along the fields towards a small wooden bridge. And as our horses crossed the river, we were greeted by a band of thanes, armed and ready to fight.

I then told my men to wait where they were, as I slowly made my way towards the centre of the field, holding my flag with pride. The leader of the Germans did the same, as he brought with him his own banner of a red swastika emblem. They were Saxons.

And as the German took off his helmet, I could see an old friendly face with a smile as wide as the ocean. His hair was long, silver and platted. It was Hrothgar. I first met Hrothgar over twenty years ago and we had been on many slave raids together, but we hadn't seen each other for many years. And he recognised my emblem as he jumped off his war horse and put his sword back into its scabbard.

I then did the same and Hrothgar shouted as he walked towards me: 'Hengest! You big bastard, long time no see. How have you been?' I had jumped off my horse *Chestnut* and began to walk towards Hrothgar, still with a slight limp from my battle with Finn. 'Alright mate, you grey headed twat.' I said with humour. He then embraced me as he wrapped his arms around me and tried to lift me off the ground. 'Get off you big puff.' I said as he put me back down. 'Fucking *Hel* Hengest, who ate all the pies?'

'Fuck off.' I said as I looked down at my old friend. I then waved over the rest of my men and we joined the Saxons at the bottom of Dragon's Hill, as Vortigern's guides and their allies looked on from the hilltops. Amongst the Saxons were my old friend Aelfred, he was young when I first met him over twenty years ago, and he just looked the same to me, still with a shaved head and chin. Aelfred spoke: 'Look at the fucking size of him. You look like a fucking bear Hengest. And where the fuck did you swipe that dragon helmet from, its beautiful.'

'I took it off the Frisian King's head after I had decapitated him.' I said as I ran my fingers through my long brown beard, picking out my breakfast. The Saxons were a feared tribe and were well known in Britain since their days in the legionnaires. And I wasn't surprised that Vortigern had sent my men to fight them, rather than his own. But Vortigern hadn't counted on us knowing each other and our plan for a better future seemed more likely now. We had just doubled our army and we both had thousands of followers waiting across the seas and it seemed as if the Gods were smiling down on us.

Amongst the Saxons was my old friend Wynn, she was Hrothgar's sister in-law and she had recently lost her husband to the waelisc attacks on their settlement in Cent. Hrothgar forced the locals to pay the Saxons monthly tributes and so they had finally retaliated and Wynn had lost her husband and two of her kids during the struggles against the Celtic mercenaries. I had known Wynn since my days raiding the British coasts with the Saxons when I was younger and she was a good friend of Dresden's. The two of them had always wished to become *Valkyries* and loved going into battle and slaughtering the men. And I would look forward to going into battle with Wynn again, just like the good ole days.

Wynn was incredibly beautiful and after seeing nothing, but foreign looking, hairy women for days, Wynn's *Teutonic* features were a sight for sore eyes. Her neck was decorated with a golden chain covered in beads and little red gems and at her breast was a beautiful golden hammer of Thor. She had rubies and gems gleaming from her wrists and she had breasts as white as untrodden snow. She had the largest breasts that I had ever seen on such a slim figure. And I definitely would.

Wynn, or Wynnie, as I liked to call her, was the sweetest, nicest woman that I had ever met, her name literally meaning 'joy' and 'happiness'. All the kids loved her and she had a smile that could brighten up even the gloomiest British sky. But when she puts on that war helmet, she becomes something different, something frightening, and even her own kids wouldn't recognise her. She becomes possessed, wicked, evil and blood thirsty. She becomes a *Valkyrie*.

As we entered the huts at the Saxon settlement at the bottom of Dragon's Hill, that were made out of woven branches and dried mud, Hrothgar spoke. He told me how the Saxon King, Eadward, had drunk himself to death and that his son, Aelle, had now become a greatly feared warlord on the continent and they had since parted ways. Hrothgar and Aelfred had hired themselves out as mercenaries for a living, but they both now had families and were looking for land of their own and they too had turned to Britain as their promised land. Aelfred told me that the waelisc were worthless and the land was excellent.

That evening the Saxons made a pact with us Jutes and Angles and we all swore oaths to each other and promised to band together and do whatever it took to take good land for ourselves. And they had all agreed to accept me as their lord, king and ruler and I accepted on one condition. Hrothgar was a former Roman soldier and was well trained in Roman warfare and I asked him to teach my men how to fight in the Roman style and to teach us how to fight in a shieldwall. And so it was agreed that Hrothgar would become my ealdorman and I would become the king of all the Germanic peoples living in Britain.

Our plan was simple. We were going to preach friendship and unity with the British whilst fighting the enemies of Vortigern. And then invite more and more of our kind and settle them into Britain to boost our numbers and make us stronger together. And when the time was right we were going to cleanse the land of the waelisc and make room for our own people to take over. And the British were too stupid to see the calm before the storm. And anyone that distrusted us and dared to speak out in defiance against our settlement were ostracised and called 'ignorant' and 'intolerant' and were accused of hatred against our race. It was like watching a nation build its own funeral pyre. It was hilarious.

I later returned to Vortigern and explained to him that I had saved many lives by not fighting the Saxons. I explained that I had recruited the Saxons and they were now going to help Vortigern fight the Picts and the Irish tribes. Vortigern accepted my proposal, but refused me the half chest of silver. I slammed my fists onto the table and told Derfel to explain that I needed that money to help pay the men as they don't work for free. And we needed more money to help build and repair the coastal defences to help prevent more Germans from trying to settle the lands.

Vortigern's advisors were warning him about something, but Vortigern had little choice and agreed to pay me a full chest of silver. Horsa and I tried not to smile as his men brought us the heavy chest. Vortigern was actually paying us to settle his lands and to build forts that we planned on using as a defence against his own men one day. The *Fates* must have been pissing themselves with laughter.

That night Horsa and I returned to the Dragon's Hill with the good news. We were to fight the Picts in two days time and so Hrothgar began to teach us the shieldwall. Hrothgar spoke: 'When you fight in a shieldwall forget all those big killer blows and aim for their feet. Put your main swords away, as they're fucking useless in a shieldwall and use your saxes. Aim for their ankles and try and cut off their feet. Stab them up and under their shields, right into their balls.'

We had practised for two days and Hrothgar believed that we were now ready for battle against even the greatest of the Roman legionnaires. The Picts were making there way south and so we headed north, looking for a fight. But this time Hrothgar and I weren't looking for slaves,

we were looking for blood,

honour and

glory.

*'Take pity on them.
For they themselves
are saying
"we are of one blood
and one bone
with you"*

*St Boniface
Telling how the continental Saxons
(Germans) regard themselves
as one and the same
as the English*

Chapter Fourteen: Puddles of Crimson

Britannia 449 AD

(Great Britain)

    Vortigern and his Celts made their way east to continue their fight with the old Roman General *Ambrosius Aurelianus* for the leadership of the whole western side of the island. Vortigern was a very ambitious man. He already ruled over a vast kingdom in the south and east of the island and his reason for hiring my men was for us to help defend his lands whilst he was away in battle and to help expel the Picts from his lands, once and for all.

    Our original plan was to simply hold back the Picts and prevent them from coming into Vortigern's territories. But the night before we set off up north, a visitor arrived at Dragon's Hill. It was Mauricius and he had come with a message from the king. Mauricius told me that Vortigern's eldest son, Vortimer, was under-siege from the Picts and he and his nobles were trapped inside, surrounded by the dwarfish Celts from the north. And so our main objective was to free his son and restore Vortigern's rule across the northern border of his kingdom.

    I had noticed earlier that Aelfred had lots of human skulls tied together through their empty eye sockets using a thick twisted rope and they were wrapped around his horse for decoration. Over breakfast he explained to me that he now enjoyed collecting one head for every battle that he'd been in for the past two years and it was some sort of hobby of his. Hrothgar had also picked up a strange habit since I last saw him all those years ago. He used the blood of his victims as decoration, as he liked to paint the Saxon swastika emblem onto the fur of his white horse. And I really liked it; I thought that it looked amazing.

After the ritual sacrifice of a dozen hares, I, Hrothgar, Wynn and the troops jumped on our horses, provided by Vortigern, and made our way north. We journeyed for days, over hills, across woodland and through small villages, often getting dirty looks by the locals. Hrothgar, and his sister in-law Wynn, wanted to slay the waelisc for the death of their blood kin, but I forbid any trouble with the locals. I had sworn an oath to King Vortigern promising to protect his people on my honour. And I planned on keeping that oath until the day I got a sign from the Gods telling me to rip the head of Vortigern and to give his lands to my own people.

Once we had arrived at the old Roman fort, I could see the Celtic dragon flapping in the wind, high above the walls, as the Picts camped outside. The Picts could clearly see us from over the river, but we couldn't engage in warfare until we found a crossing and so we had to travel the long way round. It took us ages to travel round the old Roman road on our horses. The Picts had about five hundred men that were wild, crazed and fearless. And I only had three hundred thanes under my command, as many had to stay at Dragon's Hill to protect the island from other Vikings. We knew that the Picts would be more than prepared for us by the time we finally arrived, but I didn't care as our plan was foolproof.

Horsa was by my side as we slowly trotted along the Roman road on our horses and we could see the Picts in the distance, just standing there waiting for us. 'This should be easy.' Horsa said with a deflated voice. 'Yeah, I know, but we could do with some practice using the shieldwall.'

'Yeah, I suppose.'

Wynn spoke: 'What's wrong with you two? Aren't you excited? We're going into battle. I can't wait to bathe my blade into the warm flesh of these sheep shaggers.' I then heard a massive scream coming from the woods on Horsa's side of the track and I saw my brother being dragged off his horse by a naked Pict. Wynn too, was dragged off her horse. We had been ambushed. And I barely had chance to reach for my steel when I too was dragged off my horse *Chestnut* by a wild, flame-haired dwarf. And I think I banged my head on the floor as my body hit the ground hard. And I felt a little dizzy as the ginger, naked dwarf covered in blue plant extract, thrust his blade into my breastplate. I then put up my shield that was still attached to my left arm by leather straps and jumped to my feet. There were yelling all around me, as the Picts at the end of the track came running at us to join the fray.

I then pulled out my spiked-ball on a chain, that I now called *Gertrude*, and began swinging it in a circle. The dwarf looked like he just shat himself as I towered above him and swung Gertrude straight into his teeth. And as he lay on the floor with blood pouring from his mouth, I swung with all my might, as I smashed his face into oblivion. I could hear Wynn screaming wildly as she swung her sword violently at the carrot-tops that had attacked us. I was then surrounded by Picts and so I reached for *Dances with Corpses* and challenged the flame-haired bastards to come and get some. They looked at me with their dark evil looking eyes and eyed up my weaponry, as I quickly glanced over at Horsa to see if he still lived.

'I'm alright!' he shouted as he held his bleeding arm. I then turned to the Picts with my back to my horse and spat blood on the floor. One of them charged at me with a spear and so I held up my shield and deflected his energy away from me. And as he had his back to me, I then slashed my sword all the way down his unprotected back and the dwarf fell to the floor in agony. Wynn then came into view and I looked into her eyes as she raised her sword and rammed its tip into the throat of the fallen Pict. Blood was everywhere, spraying all over the field and all over Wynn and I. Her eyes were wide and round, her hair was flowing behind her and she was smiling in such a way that it reminded me of when my son was placed into the arms of Dresden for the very first time. And just then I saw the gates open at the Roman fort and Vortigern's son, Vortimer, came running along the road with a large band of men.

'Saxons!' Hrothgar shouted. 'Shieldwall-now!!!' and just like in practice, we all banded together and locked our shields with the man to our left. We had to protect the man to our left with the shield and attack using only our right arm. We were either to use a sax or a spear for the fight and nothing else, as *Gertrude* and *Dances with Corpses* were ineffective in such close combat. Vortimer's men did the same and locked their shields together, trapping the Picts in the middle of the two bands of warriors, leaving them to our mercy. And as Hrothgar once told me: 'Mercy? I know nothing of this word.' It was now a massacre.

I was on the front ranks along with my ealdorman Hrothgar and his sister in-law Wynn and with us were Horsa, Wipped, Siegeferth and Aelfred. I couldn't see anything as I was being squashed by all the weight of the men and we were all pushed forward by the thanes behind us. 'Stab their ankles.' Aelfred shouted. 'Stab their fucking balls.' Wynn shouted even louder.

The Picts were not trained in the Roman style of warfare and so didn't know how to form a shieldwall of their own and they just jumped on our shields, stabbing and thrashing, trying to break through and find a weakness. But we were strong and the Picts kept jumping onto our spears and saxes. It was hilarious, as all I could see was their hairy legs and swinging sacks, as the Picts often fought naked. Maybe they thought it was more masculine or something. But it didn't matter to me as I took great pleasure in aiming for their balls, knowing that they weren't going to be making any more of their foreign, ugly babies ever again.

I remember holding *Wolf-Fang* tightly by its bone handle, as I watched a Pict trying to force my shield down. I could see his balls swinging forwards and backwards, as he pushed his way onto my shield. I then took *Wolf-Fang* and sliced open the pair of big, saggy, hairy, ginger bollocks. I sliced open his scrotum and his balls just fell out and dangled towards the ground, hanging on by bloody and mangled flesh. It was disgusting, but effective.

The Picts were attacked on both sides by the Saxons and by Vortimer's men and they were simply erased from this world and butchered into dog meat. After the battle was over, I walked over to a Pict that was quivering on the floor holding his crotch. He was slowly bleeding to death as he said something to me in his awful foreign tongue, probably asking for a hero's death. And so I swung *Gertrude* and sent him to his god and left his corpse to the birds and the beasts.

As I wondered the battleground, Horsa called to me and showed me the blood-spitting, bloodied face of a fatefully wounded Siegeferth. Siegeferth had been the one to train me and toughen me up in my youth and we had been on many Viking adventures together and we had become like brethren. And as I knelt over to him in his final moments, I thanked him for been such a good friend and I thanked him for been such an arsehole of a trainer. Siegeferth spoke: 'Just remember what I taught you Hengest. Show no mercy to your enemies, as they will have no mercy for you.'

'Burn him!' I ordered, after Siegeferth was taken by the *Valkyries*.

'I'm not dead yet!' Siegeferth yelled, as he spat blood all over himself. 'One more thing Hengest, kill that ginger tosser, Vortigern, before he kills you. Take his lands and share them with our people, just like we had talked about.' His spirit was then taken away by the *Valkyries*, but I kicked him several times, just to make sure.

Along with the British aristocracy, Vortimer was now free and Vortigern's rule was safe in the northern lands once again. The British king now owed my men a chest full of gold as promised; it was an easy day's work. Before leaving for Cent, I had witnessed Aelfred cutting the head off one of the Picts and attach it to his collection. He got many dirty looks from the Christian nobles that looked on in horror and spat on the floor with disgust. Vortimer was to come back south with me, as he was officially under my own personal protection and I escorted him back to his father's Roman palace.

Three years later my small band of mercenaries were still living at Dragon's Hill and Wynnie and I had since gotten married. We had lived a life of adventure and danger, never knowing if we were going to live until tomorrow and so we had grown close and fallen in love. I remember our exact conversation when we discussed getting married for the first time, it went as follows: 'I'd sooner my brother in-law, Hrothgar, think of me as your wife, rather than your whore.'

'But you are my whore.' We married the next day. Black eye and all.

I had kept my oath to the British king and my men had since defeated the Picts and the Irish and had successfully kept them out of Vortigern's empire. One year ago, I had received word from across the northern sea that Queen Hildeburh had since lost power with the southern tribes of England and new leaders had emerged and civil war had broken out. My childhood lands had descended into darkness and a new dark age had begun. I had a choice whether to stay and fight for new and better lands in Britain, or leave and break my oath to the king and go back and fight for my homeland, England. It was a dark choice and my honour was now at stake and all the paths before me were waiting to be lined with bloodied corpses.

Living in England seemed to me the least practicable as the lands were constantly being flooded and the harvests were poor and it was under constant threat from the Scyldings, Geates and Danes. It seemed to me that the Gods were making the decision for me and so I decided to stick to the original plan of settling Britain. I simply had to leave England to its *wyrd* that had been given to it by the *Fates*. And later in life, I would learn that England's destiny was to be ruled by the Scyldings, Geates and the Danes that it had since been named after. Both England and Jutland would now be forever known as Dane Mark, after its Scandinavian invaders. And as I had once said to Horsa: 'If I can no longer live in my beloved England, then I would simply bring England to me here, in Britain.' And so I sent word for the first wave of migration to take place.

It was deep into a dying day on the Centish coast, as I stood next to Horsa watching over the horizon. I stood there on the hills, overlooking the sea, with the white dragon, the swastika and the white horse emblems, flapping in the wind, as I watched sixteen Viking ships sail the calm summer sea. They had come from England and they had come to stay in the new lands that we believed were fated to us and had been given to us by the Gods.

As the ships came closer, I could see a young woman standing proudly at the front of the dragon headed prow. She had long dark brown hair blowing in the sea breeze. Her name was Rowena; she was seventeen years old and was the daughter of Dresden and I. She was the apple of my eye and the reason that I get up every morning and put on my armour, preparing for war. 'If we don't fight for our babies, then we fight for nothing!' I told Horsa.

A huge black figure then appeared from behind Rowena. He looked like a giant, standing tall as he gripped the ropes to the sail. He was a menacing presence as he was decorated in iron, steel and bronze and was clearly a mighty warrior. His name was Aesc; he was twenty two years old

and he was Rowena's brother,
he was my
son.

*In one of the ships was Hengest's daughter,
a very beautiful girl.
Hengest arranged a feast for Vortigern and his soldiers.
They got very drunk and the Devil entered into Vortigern's heart,
making him fall in love with the girl.
He asked Hengest for her hand in marriage and said,
'I will give anything you want in return,
even half my kingdom!'*

*British Historian Saint Gildas
516-570 AD*

Chapter Fifteen: A New Dawn

Britannia 454 AD
(Great Britain)

Rowena was a very beautiful girl and was well skilled in charm and herb-lore. Her eyes were dark and mysterious like her mother's, Dresden, but when the sun caught her face, her eyes sparkled like emeralds. Her hair was long and braided under a red jewelled-headband and she had on a long satin gown and looked like the princess that she was. Her arms were decorated with sparkling bracelets and her gown shone with the most dazzling of golden brooches.

Vortigern had fallen in love with my daughter since the moment he first laid his eyes on her. I had only agreed to the union of my only daughter to the British king, as it was for the entire county of Cent. Rowena had secured the future of the Englisc, Saxon and Jutisc races with her marriage to Vortigern. And I was now the official ruler of the south east corner of Britain. I had become a '*Bretwalda*', a 'Britain ruler'. I was born a Jute and raised as an Angle, but the British knew me as simply the 'Saxon Warrior King'.

Also in the ships was my son Aesc, whom was now tall and handsome, just like his father. He dressed like me, like a warrior king, he wore a boar-crested war helmet, iron chain-mail, but did not yet own a sword of his own. He was still young and had lots of time to earn one for himself. Amongst the wave of immigrants were hundreds of families, men, women and children. I remember seeing young children with beautiful faces and warm smiles; I saw them helping their mothers and fathers building new huts and makeshift tents. The children also helped farm the land and everyone was helping the community, helping everyone to settle into the British countryside. A new age had dawned.

Vortigern was already married to his first wife Sevira; she had been a Christian and was loved by the nobles, until her forced exile by Vortigern. The Christians hated us 'none believers' and hated Vortigern for marrying one. But it seemed that Vortigern was under Rowena's spell, as he was besotted with her and seemed oblivious to the concerns of his own people.

Vortigern showed more warmth towards the foreigners that had settled his lands, than he did to his own people and he had simply thrown his nobles and dukes off their lands and gave them to me and my men. And I used that land; along with all the gold and silver that Vortigern often supplied me with, as payment for my army of thanes that now numbered a thousand. The British aristocracy were furious with Vortigern's actions and I often feared a rebellion by the waelisc, it was an uneasy alliance. I had men riding every road and ruling every fort and we had built fantastic defences, but we were still outnumbered by the waelisc as their numbers were in the millions.

Rowena had made the ultimate sacrifice for our people by marrying into the British royal family and she has since become known as the *Modor of Angelcynn* the 'Mother of the English nation'. She never wanted to marry an old man, but I had little choice if I was to secure land for our people to permanently settle.

Before her marriage to Vortigern, I had told Rowena that if she ever got pregnant by the waelisc king, that I would take her baby and throw the humanoid into the nearest fire. I had warned her not to breed with those sub-humans, as I didn't want an unnatural half-human half-vermin monster-child carrying my *Teutonic* blood. 'Don't worry father!' Rowena assured me. 'If I was to spawn Vortigern's child, then I will throw the vermin into the flames myself.'

'That's my girl.' I said as we embraced. I hadn't seen much of Rowena since she was a child and she had grown up to be a beautiful and intelligent young woman, just like her mother Dresden.

Three years had passed since Rowena's marriage to Vortigern and my brother and I had been living in Britain now for six years and had an interesting relationship with the Celts, a tolerant relationship. Vortigern had now been married to my daughter, Queen Rowena, for three years and for the third year running I was invited to Vortigern's palace to celebrate Yule, or as the Christians call it *"Christmas"*.

Yule was an ancient tradition in my culture where we worship the holy night of '*Modraniht*', 'Mothers' Night, where we honour the Goddesses and this would be done every Winter Solstice. Yule was a time for feasting and gift-giving and for animal sacrifice such as the *sonargoltr*, the Yule pig. It was a time when Woden, also known as *Wish-Giver*, would ride the night sky on one of His wild hunts looking for the souls of the unwary. Yule is also a time when the veil between the realms of the living and the dead is thin and communication with the ancestors is made possible. Yule is a magical time when wishes are granted and oaths are made and *wyrd* is decided amongst mortals. And before entering Vortigern's stronghold, the Saxons, Angles and Jutes had made our own new years' *wyrd*.

I brought along my family and a few hundred armed bodyguards that had to wait outside. I was sitting at the king's table, inside a huge stone hall, and I could feel the tension in the air. There was a Yule tree decorated with colourful sparkly things. There were decorations hanging from the ceiling and on our tables were sparkling crosses and other bits of rubbish scattered around.

By my side was my wife, Wynn, and my brother Horsa and also my son, Aesc, and opposite us was Vortigern's son, Vortimer, and I could tell that he didn't like nor trust us. The room was full of British nobles and they were all giving us dirty looks as if we didn't belong, as though they were better than us. And they all rose to their feet as the king and queen entered the room. Vortigern and his son had learned many Englisc words and could now speak to me in my native tongue.

'Stand up!' Vortimer said with authority. Horsa looked at me, as though he didn't understand the awful British accent. And we simply ignored his demand and began to eat before the king and queen had seated. We had eaten before prayers and many of the men and women at our table were horrified, as though we had done something to offend them.

My wife, Aesc, Horsa and I were stuffing our greedy faces with the king's chicken, as the king and queen were greeted by the nobles as they slowly made their way to the top table and joined us. I then stood up and kissed the hand of my beautiful daughter, the Queen of Britannia. I then greeted the king: 'Alright mate!'

'Good evening Hengest.' Vortigern replied, as his son was still giving me the evils. The two queens then gave each other a formal and queenly greeting. Wynn spoke:

'Alright darling? How's these bleeding foreigners been treating you?'

'Alright I suppose, at least they give me lots of ale so that I can get rat-arsed and numb the pain of their company.' Wynn laughed as the Celts looked at each other to see if either of them understood our foreign words. Aesc burped out loudly as he greeted his sister: 'Alright shit-breath!'

'Alright dick-face!' The other guests were muttering under their breath and Horsa was smiling at his niece and nephew as they exchanged insults at each other. The Christian women had been trained to be quiet and obedient to their husbands and they were horrified by my wife, Wynnie, and my daughter, Rowena. 'Behave yourself woman!' Vortimer demanded. 'A queen must learn to be a lady.'

'Fuck off dickhead! I'm no lady!' Rowena yelled. Vortimer then slammed his fists onto the table, causing my drink to spill over. 'What makes a woman think she can talk to me that way?' Vortimer demanded. 'This does!' I said as I placed *Gertrude* on the table. Only the king and his guards were allowed to be armed, but I too was a king, and so I was allowed to be armed as well. Vortimer sank back into his chair and Vortigern simply laughed it off, as I put *Gertrude* away.

As my son gulped down the Roman wine, he began talking to Vortimer: 'You're a bit of a faggot you, aren't you mate?' Vortimer looked confused, as he pretended not to understand the insult. 'Picking on a fucking girl? Do you think that makes you a man? Do you think that makes you look tough in front of your sissy mates? How about me and you go outside and see if you're a real man or not?' Vortimer's face turned bright red and refused to answer and I didn't blame him. Vortimer was as small and puny as his father and Aesc was as tall and as strong as I was. He had long brown hair and a broad chest and round shoulders and was a frightening man. 'Calm down lad! You're going to make him piss himself in front of his guests' I said as I patted my son on the back. Vortigern was a placid man and enjoyed talking to his wife for much of the dinner, but Vortimer was suspicious and war was brewing.

Late that evening, we had returned to Dragon's Hill, leaving Rowena behind at Vortigern's Palace, and I was convinced of a rebellion by Vortimer and his men. I was asking for the Skull Crusher's advice as we were walking alongside the horse stables. And we knew it was a good omen, as we witnessed a raven pecking at the rotten flesh on one of Aelfred's skulls. And we decided that the time was now right to bring in reinforcements and take Britain for ourselves. I ordered my ambassadors to go to the continent and tell our Saxon, Englisc, Jutisc and Frisian allies to bring everyone that wished to escape the chaos that now flowed throughout the continent and wished for better lands.

I told the ambassadors: 'Bring every man, woman and child and tell them to bring their possessions, their wealth and their livestock. Tell the men that I demand their loyalty and their oaths to me and they had to accept me as their king and overlord.'

I told the ambassadors to let the men on the continent know that I expected all men to be trained in combat, including the farmers, and they would be called the *Fyrd*. And whenever I needed extra men to join the thanes in war, I would be calling up the *Fyrd* without their complaint. 'What about the lame, the old and the sick, my lord?'

'Leave them behind.' I ordered. 'For we will not harbour the weak and the parasites, bleeding us dry.' We were to build a new nation, a strong nation and for that we needed only the best *Teutonic* blood.

Several days had passed, and I had scouts everywhere waiting to alert me to any possible invasion by the waelisc, led by the king's son, Vortimer. And whilst I was sleeping in my bed next to my wife, Wynnie, I was awoken by one of my guards, warning me that the waelisc had attacked in the north. I immediately got up and with my heart beating like crazy; I got dressed in my war gear and gathered the army. As I went outside, I could see fires in the distance, as the Saxon villages had been attacked by the Celts. I had built defences around my new kingdom, but most of them were along the coastline. And the wall that protected the villages was incomplete and utterly useless at that time.

The Saxon thanes, that I had been originally told to cleanse, were defending themselves against their attackers, as Wynn, Wipped, Horsa and I rushed to help Hrothgar and the Saxons that we had sworn to defend. My armour was heavy, as I rushed to the flames, screaming for the blood of the waelisc. 'No prisoners!' I yelled as I drew *Dances with Corpses* from its scabbard. There were women and children in those homes that were on fire, they were our future and the waelisc would pay a great price for their crimes.

I smashed my shield into a Briton, knocking him to the ground with ease. I then stuck my blade into his throat, momentarily blinding myself, as blood sprayed me in the face. I wiped the blood from my eyes, as I looked through the smoke to try and find Vortimer. I was then jumped on by two Brits and I welcomed their challenge as I swung at one with my sword. He raised his shield to protect himself as he stumbled backwards. The other guy then ran at me with a spear and I quickly moved out of the way as I grabbed the shaft under my arm and snapped it using my own body weight. I then rammed my sword under his chin, as I witnessed my son Aesc take the other guy out and spike him onto his sword from behind. 'Cheers son!' I shouted over the chaos. 'No worries old man.'

Wynn then came by my side and she was covered in blood, the three of us were then surrounded by about five or six Brits that had encircled us. 'Dance!' I shouted as we began to swing our swords and they sung a beautiful song of death, whilst Aesc gored them with his spear. The waelisc began to fall on Saxon swords, as blood soaked the lush green lands of Britain. I swung my sword wildly at the Celtic intruders, whilst I still looked for Vortimer, whom I believed was responsible for the attack. But it was hard to recognise anyone, as all the waelisc were dressed the same, in chain-mail and Roman style helmets.

The villages were burning down and the common folk were panicking as they were running in all directions. The battle continued, as I rushed to the side of a small child that were running to his mother. I tried to run to the boy's aid, but I was too late, as I watched a waelisc soldier grab hold of him and punched him in the face. And as he was on the floor, the soldier raised his spear and rammed it into the young boy's belly.

The Celt then grabbed the boy's mother by her hair and tried to drag her into one of the remaining unburned huts. I then grabbed the soldier from behind and twisted his neck, using his helmet as extra weight, as I drove his head forwards and then twisted it to the side and pulled it backwards.

I was screaming for Vortimer, but I couldn't see him anywhere as the smoke began to blur my vision and fill my aching lungs. As I tried to look through the black smoke, I could just make out a small shieldwall that had formed at the front of the village by Hrothgar. Wynn then cut the head clean off the waelisc soldier that was standing in front of me, when I suddenly heard a horn blow and the waelisc began to retreat. 'Vortimer! You fucking coward!' Aesc was shouting as he had wanted to challenge the prince to a duel.

The sun began to rise, as the waelisc jumped on their horses and fled the battle-scene, and I began to survey the damage. I saw Wipped opening the gates to the horse stables that had been set on fire and the horses ran wildly across the blood-soaked field. I saw women and children scouring the field, turning over dead bodies, as they looked for their loved ones. There were women and children lying in the grass with gaping wounds as they lay dead from waelisc spears. The women were clutching to their dead husbands and lifeless children. The screams and cries of my own people scorned my ears and pained my heart. 'Payback is a bitch!' Aesc muttered to himself. Wynn spoke: 'This is what happened many years ago when we first came here looking for land. I lost my husband and kids in an attack like this. The British don't want us here, they never did, our kind and their kind don't mix, and sooner or later one of us will be wiped out forever.'

The following week we had buried the dead and had begun rebuilding the villages and the front wall that was to protect us against further attacks by the waelisc. One hot morning whilst repairing the defensive wall, we were surprised with a visit from Vortimer himself. He was being escorted by about twenty soldiers, each carrying the Celtic dragon, and they had clearly not come to fight as the Celts were outnumbered by a thousand thanes. Aesc, Horsa, and Hrothgar joined me as we grabbed our swords and walked up to the fence on top of the sloping hill where Vortimer was waiting on his horse.

As we got closer, I was shocked to discover that Rowena was riding on the back of Vortimer's horse. I was happy to see that she was well, as I had been worried about her safety after the earlier attack by the British. 'What-in the name of Woden's hairy arse-are you doing here?' I asked my daughter. Rowena popped her head shyly from around Vortimer's shoulder as she gave me a friendly smile, just like her mother used to. Vortimer spoke: 'I bring her to you' he said with his strange British accent, as he struggled to remember the right words. 'We can no longer feed your people, as your numbers have grown too much. We don't need you anymore, now go away to your own country, you are no longer welcome.'

Vortimer had told me how trade with Rome had collapsed and his father could no longer support the Saxons. He said that we had bled them dry, as our demand for clothes, food and riches were too great and that we were no longer needed and we had to leave the island and go back home. 'And are these the wishes of the king?' I asked, as Aesc helped Rowena down from the horse. Vortimer spoke: 'Those that God wishes to destroy, he will first make mad. My father is a fool and you Saxons have been taking advantage of him. And so I bring to you his wife and end your agreement on his behalf. Now you can go home and leave us in peace.'

'You fucking what?' Aesc yelled, as he gritted his teeth in anger. 'You fucking come here and kill our women and children and then run from us like cowards and expect us to just leave…….. Bollocks to that.'

I then spoke to Vortimer: 'I'm the rightful king in these lands. We have earned them by fighting your enemies for you. And on my honour and with the will of the Gods, we will not leave. And we will have our vengeance for your cowardly attack.'

I was now angry as I held up *Dances with Corpses* and raised my voice to the British prince: 'And you can tell that father of yours that I don't care what his orders are as I now consider him to have broken his oath to me and my men. And so I'm no longer bound by my oath to protect you fucking Celts. And your Christian *Armageddon* is now upon you.' Vortimer laughed, as he turned and rode away with his men, leaving Hrothgar and I to decide our next move.

Two weeks had passed when Horsa came to me with a message: 'They're here!' he said with enthusiasm, as we rushed to the coastline on our decorated horses. And it was a beautiful sight as I stood on the cliffs overlooking the sea with my two kids, my wife and my brother. The red sun was rising, lighting up the sky with an array of beautiful colours. A grey bearded Wipped, Hrothgar and Aelfred were there too as we witnessed an ocean of ships with sails blowing in the glorious winds given by Thor himself. 'The ground will shake beneath him and the seas will disappear at his command.' Horsa said, as I was getting shivers down my spine.

The sails were black, red, white and many other colours and were all decorated in runes, swastikas and pictures of animals and birds, bears and wolves. There were hundreds of ships, each carrying a massive army from England, Saxony and Frisia. They were carrying the future of our young country and the future of our race and they would be the ones to tell our tales in the mead-halls, long after our bones had turned to ashes or we were placed under burial mounds.

The wind and rain beat against my face as I rushed towards the fleet on my horse. The men helped heave the ships onto the Centish beach, as I welcomed our new guests, many of which I had never laid eyes on before, but they had come to grant me their oaths in return for my protection and land. And aboard one of the ships were my old friends Saxburga and her husband and a great Jutisc thane by the name of Froda. I had known Froda since I was a small child and he was the one that took me to the Angles after my village had been sacked. He had known me as a spoilt child, born into power, but I had since earned his respect. I now had a fierce reputation as a warlord and I was now Hengest the Wolf-Tamer, *Bretwalda*, and the King of Cent.

Froda and I had been on many battles together against the Scyldings, but he never liked to travel much and I hadn't seen him in many years, as he had remained in England for most of his life. Saxburga looked old as she was helped off the ship and walked towards me gracefully. She had helped look after me when I was young and I often thought of her as an older sister. Froda then popped his head over the ship: 'You look well, my lord!' he said with respect.

'Don't be soft Froda; you're one of my oldest friends, you don't have to call me lord. You can just call me master.' Froda laughed. 'I've known you since you were a little piece of shit that had fallen out of Loki's arse.' He said with humour. 'And out of respect for your rank,

I'll call you lord, when in front of the thanes. But when in private, well that's another matter.'

'Very well.' I said as I held out my arm and helped him onto the beach. Froda then grabbed me and hugged me like a brother. 'Get off you big puff! I'm not that way inclined.' I said as I held the old man back. And just then I saw a face that I hadn't seen since the battle at Finnesburh, it was the Frisian lord, Hereswith. When I last saw Hereswith he had given me his oath along with many other Frisians that had been freed from King Finn's tyranny. He had since taken hundreds of his people to northern England and had been living in Queen Hildeburh's court ever since. As he came towards me he took off his boar-crested helmet and allowed his long blonde hair to flow freely in the gentle shore breeze. 'My lord!' he said as he knelt to one knee. 'It's an honour for my people to offer our services to you.'

Hereswith and his men were great archers and a welcomed addition to my growing army. The army in Britain had begun with less than two hundred men, but over six years it had swelled to tens of thousands and nothing was going to stop us from taking anything we wanted. The Gods had been kind.

Wipped and I had not anticipated that amount of men when we sent for reinforcements and we struggled to accommodate them. Our defences against the waelisc were still very poor and I feared loosing many of the men in a surprise attack. The Celt's under Vortigern still outnumbered us by hundreds of thousands and so I had decided to attack them first. During an emergency meeting with my most trusted men, I gave the orders to cleanse the lands directly outside of my territory with fire. 'But what about the waelisc, my lord? Froda asked. 'I'm talking about the fucking waelisc!' I yelled. 'I see dark shadows gathering round my kingdom, wanting our people gone and they will stop at nothing to erase us from these lands. We must burn their villages and crops and kill every last one of them without exception. This is our world and our reality.' Aesc interrupted: 'It's us or them and they're probably discussing the same thing as we speak. And we would be fools if we didn't act accordingly.'

'There is no right or wrong here, only survival.' Wynn added.

Froda voiced his opinion: 'But what about the women and children? They are innocent in all of this. Why can't we spare the children and raise them as Englisc and Saxons?'

I sighed as I took a deep breath and shouted: 'Because they are not us! They are not the sons and daughters of Woden and Frigg. They don't share our *Teutonic* blood and they are not the same. And we will not lower ourselves to their level in order to become their equals. We can give them our language and they can talk like us and act like us, and begin to look like us, but they will never be us. They are vermin no matter how you dress it up. They will become dependant on us and we'll feel sorry for them and gave them everything that we have. And then they'll want more and more from us and from our children and soon they'll start believing that it is their right to walk into our lands and take food from our children's mouths.

They are parasites that will feed on us like a leech from a swamp. They will breed with us and piss into our *Teutonic blood* and soon we'll forget who we are and become like them and we'll be erased. Our children will become half human and simple minded. They'll call us 'British' and make us believe that we are the same as them, like worthless vermin. And our children will be forced to become Christian slaves and forget where they came from.

We cannot allow this to happen, otherwise our race will die and our gods will abandon us. It's the will of the gods that we make martyrs out of them; they even wish it upon themselves. They say martyrs go to heaven and are rewarded with seventy two grapes, just for dying. So I say lets drown them all in a great lake of fire, lets holocaust them into oblivion. It's the will of Woden.'

'Yes that's true, the Gods told me last night.' Aesc said as Hrothgar laughed at his mockery.

But I continued: 'We must burn their churches and drive away their evil spirits before we become infected by them. We must purify the land against their priests and bishops. We must accept that they are evil and infectious and we must protect our children from them, for all time. We must view the foreign races for what they are and not for what we wish them to be.'

Wynn spoke: 'We will be forever outsiders and we will be pushed back into the sea or face extermination if we don't fight for our kind

today. Its not the Gods wishes for us to waste our courage in bad lands, it is Woden's wish for us to fight for the British lands. May the Devine Lord of War, Woden, grant victory to which ever race he sees worthy.' I then looked around the room and stared into each of their eyes. 'Are we all agreed to what must be done for our
children's futures?'
They agreed.

*"All the great towns fell to the Saxon's battering rams.
Bishops, priests and people were all chopped down together
while swords flashed and flames crackled.
It was horrible to see the stones of towers thrown down
to mix with pieces of human bodies.
Broken alters were covered with a purple crust of clotted blood.
There was no burial except under ruins
and bodies were eaten by the birds and the beasts."*

*British Historian Saint Gildas
516-570 AD*

Chapter Sixteen: The Great Lake of Fire

Britannia 455 AD
(Great Britain)

    The following morning, I ordered for the men to polish their blood-plastered coats of mail, weapons and armour and to paint fresh symbols on their shields, especially the swastika and other religious symbols. I wanted all the power of the Gods on our side, as we rampaged across the lands of Britain in the name of Thor and Woden. The darkness had surrounded us as the sun disappeared behind the water-logged clouds and my son passed me my dragon-masked war helmet as we prepared for a holy extermination.

    Rowena spoke as she blessed our lands:

Hal wes thu, folde, fira modor.
Beo thu growende on Godes faethme,
fodre gefylled firum to nytte

'Hail to thee Earthan Modor, mother of men.
Be thou fruitful in God's embrace,
filled with food for the use of men.'

    Rowena had begun her training as a Wicca many years ago, she was still just an amateur, but she insisted on been the one to evoke the

Gods at our next battle. 'With this blood, we will spill the blood of our enemies.' Rowena said as she slit the throat of the most beautiful of horses. It was penned in as Rowena used a sax on the sacred animal and gathered its sacred blood in tin buckets. She then showered herself in its warm essence, covering herself in a mass of crimson. The blood dripped from her hair and she blessed many of the weapons being carried by the men by smearing them with the fresh sacrifice.

As the men prepared themselves for battle, I rode forwards on *Chestnut* and addressed the army: 'Saxons! Angles! Jutes! Frisians! A new age has dawned, a new era has begun and our actions today will echo throughout the ages as we cleanse the land of the filth that inhabits it. Today we extinguish the flame of the foreign God that wishes to enslave our children and enslave our souls.'

The men were cheering in their thousands as I called to them and rode my horse amongst the ranks that faded into the distance. My beard and hair blew into the wind and I was wearing my dragon war helmet, with the mask removed, that glinted in the sun.

I had on my chain-mail, my breastplate and I was protected with my swastika shield that had been a gift from my ealdorman, Hrothgar. I had *Wolf-Fang* and *Gertrude* tucked into my belt and I was draped in my blood-stained wolf skin, Fenrir. And I was holding up *Dances with Corpses*, as I continued addressing the army:

'Today, we write our names onto the lands of this island with the blood of our enemies. We do this, not for ourselves, not for power, but for glory and for our children and our children's children. Do you want your kids to be murdered in their beds by the foreign scum that walks this land?'

The men screamed No!!!

'Do you want your daughters to be raped by the foreign filth?'

No!!!

'Do you want your beautiful daughters giving birth to the dark haired races?

No!!!! They screamed in their thousands.

'Do you wish to witness your *Teutonic* blood wiped out by inferior dwarves and hairy woman?

No!!! they roared waving their weapons in the air.

'The people have spoken. Now come with me and we'll drown our enemies in the great lake of fire.'

I then rushed across the field riding *Chestnut* and headed towards the lands of the waelisc, whilst an army of Saxons, Angles, Jutes and Frisians followed. The young men behind me, dressed in glinting mail-shirts, marched in good spirits as we all had bad intensions on our minds. Before the journey, I had surprised my son, Aesc, with a gift for his bravery against the Celts. It was a beautiful pattern-welded sword, encrusted with emeralds and decorated with runes, it once belonged to Finn.

After a long time travelling by horse, I had jumped off, and I allowed one of the infantry to ride the beast, as I chose to walk the rest of the way. I was followed by Wynn, Horsa, Rowena, Aesc, Wipped, Hrothgar and Aelfred as we travelled over the beautiful lands of Britain. But beauty always came with dark thoughts and those were to be the darkest of times.

Rowena was in front skipping with a childlike innocence, as the rest of us marched across the damp grassy fields in heavy war gear. And then in the distance, between the hills, I could see smoke from a little waelisc village. And as we marched towards the village, Aesc began to scream and howl like a wolf, as he was overcome with excitement and the rest of the gang began to copy.

It was called 'becoming a *Berserker*' and whenever a person became a *Berserker*, Woden would eliminate them from fear and pain. And they became as strong as bears and neither iron nor fire could harm them. We howled like creatures of the night as we ran towards the village with our swords drawn and lusting for the kill.

Perhaps it was easier that way, to see ourselves as monsters, rather than men, as we were prepared to do horrible things, terrible things, things that should only be whispered about. But it's not my wish to be known as a liar and so I'll tell you the truth, I'll tell you everything, I'll tell you the story just like it really happened.

The men on horses had reached the village before us and I could see the smoke as I marched forwards. I remember seeing a flock of birds fly overhead in the shape of an arrow and I imagined they were dragons breathing fire onto the village. 'Kill them all!' Wynn screamed like a *Valkyrie* as she ran towards the village, still lusting after vengeance for the death of her blood kin. As I entered the village, I saw my men slaughter the helpless waelisc, as they tried to run to safety, but it was hopeless for them, as my men were everywhere. There were several hundred guards around the village, but they were no match for thousands of Saxons.

A man armed with only a garden fork, came running towards me, screaming for my blood. I simply stepped aside and slashed his wooden pole in two and sliced the man's head clean off and blood gushed into the air like a fountain of water. I ran through the centre of the burning village and carnage was all around me. I then noticed a small hut that was unaffected by the fires and I thought that I saw movement from inside. I walked over to the entrance and pulled out *Dances with Corpses*, as I carefully walked inside. And there I saw a young boy, maybe nine or ten years old.

He was alone and armed with only a wooden cross that he held out to me, as if he was warning me against the power of his god. He looked at me, stone faced, as he held out the religious cross that he believed protected him against the demons from the Christian underworld. And standing nearly seven feet tall and wearing my wolf skin and my face covered with the mask of the dragon helmet and wielding *Dances with Corpses*, I must have looked like the red eyed lord that the Christians feared so much. He was muttering something to himself as he held out the cross, perhaps calling for protection from his saviour, but there was no Christ to save him on that day.

I looked into the eyes of the boy and slowly placed my sword back into its seal-skin-lined scabbard. I then rotated my right arm and shoulder and slowly reached to my belt and released *Gertrude*. I dropped the spiked-ball as I held onto the chain and then slowly wrapped the chain around my fist. I didn't say a word as I stood over the boy, my shadow blackening his youthful face. I then swung *Gertrude* and smashed into the boy's skull, killing him instantly. I then lifted *Gertrude* as her spikes gripped to the boy's face, forcing me to hold down the tiny quivering carcass. I then yanked her from what was once the boy's face and blood smeared the room, as I casually walked back outside.

I laughed as I witnessed Aesc drag some kind of Christian priestess across the centre of the village. She was wearing black and white ropes and only her face was visible as Aesc threw her onto the fire and held her down face first with his boot, as he gave me a little wave. There were people running in all directions desperately tying to escape the revenge of the Saxons. And as a woman with long ginger hair brushed against me, screaming, I suddenly grabbed her by the hair. I then stabbed her in the back and through her stomach with *Dances with Corpses*, before realising she was heavy with child. 'One less breeder of vermin.' I quietly said to myself as I spat on her.

That day I bathed *Dances with Corpses* in the warm blood of the waelisc whilst their hearts still beat. And after the waelisc guards were defeated, I remember burning the Celtic dragon emblem on the fires by the side of the women and children. They were nailed to the wooden crosses that Rowena and her uncle Horsa had put together. And whilst they screamed in agony, as their flesh melted away, I witnessed Hereswith using the Celts for target practice. And he was pretty good, managing to hit a boy right in his eye socket.

I remember seeing Froda crouching down, he was alone and appeared to be crying as her stared at the blood that dripped off his hands and ran down the blade of his axe. I felt bad for him, he had been burdened with a conscience and he generally cared for folk, even foreigners. But I was more fortunate, as I had grown up with hate and anger and so I didn't feel anything except joy and laughter at the misfortune of others.

I saw Horsa and Aesc betting on who could throw the children the highest into the air and then catch them on spears. I witnessed Hrothgar and Aelfred giving the children 'a leg and a wing' and tossing them down the hill, breaking their legs, arms and necks, as they crashed to the floor.

I remember seeing Wynn grab hold of several children and slash at their throats with furious anger and an unrivalled passion. She hated the waelisc more than I did and she seemed possessed by the *Valkyries* as she dragged two small children and drown them in the pig troth that was full of water. She screamed and howled as I witnessed her forcing her thumbs, long nails and all, into the eyes of the children. Even Rowena looked on, horrified. Wynn screamed: 'Vermin, they're everywhere, they're all around us and they're going to kill us all. We have to get rid of them in the only language that they understand.' she shrieked as she thrust her sax into the guts of the little girls.

Blood and intestines of small children filled the air with death, as their remains were thrown onto the fires. The Celts were praying to their god for a miracle, but he wasn't listening, and the torture and mayhem continued all night long. Sceneries painted beautifully in British blood.

We stayed in the village that night and eat all the food we could find, before venturing out the following morning looking for more plunder. As we came to the next village, I could see that it had a huge wooden church that stood tall overlooking the whole village. We had expected that the waelisc might barricade themselves inside some of the buildings and so we had brought several battering rams. We rode into the village, unopposed, as clearly the British hadn't expected us to have travelled so far into the waelisc lands. And the village was unprotected against the assault of the Saxon mercenaries.

I kicked at my horse, *Chestnut*, as I rampaged into the village, swinging *Gertrude* wildly. I smashed over their market stalls as the peasants ran for their miserable lives. Many had run into the church and many were slain by Saxon steel, as the whole village descended into anarchy. I saw a family running with their small children being dragged by their parents. One of the women was holding a young baby in her arms and as I rode my horse towards them, I swung *Gertrude* at the back of her head. Wynn screamed with delight, as I then dragged her corpse along the dirt path, as my spikes had stuck into her skull and her baby was trampled on by the horses.

I had to jump off my horse and pick *Gertrude* out of the woman's skull and it had blood and torn flesh sticking to the spikes. My men were slaying the waelisc from on top of their horses and as they lay on the floor quivering, I would finish them off with a quick swing from *Gertrude*. I was blood-drunk, as I screamed out loud, beating my chest in the centre of the horror stricken village.

After much slaughter, I ordered the battering rams to be brought into the village, as many of the waelisc had barricaded themselves inside of their sacred church, just like we had anticipated. We could have set fire to the wooden building, but the men needed to have their fun with the women and so we began to smash our way inside. 'Is it wise to destroy the sacred site, my lord?' Froda asked. 'What if their angels exact revenge on us?'

'Don't be a fool Froda. Their god is weak and a coward and has no testicles. He doesn't like fighting and he would be no match for Thor or Woden, as they would burn their angel wings to dust.' I said, as I ordered for the doors to be smashed open. It didn't take long as the old wooden doors had never been reinforced and soon we were inside.

There were all sorts of religious weirdo's inside on their knees at the front of the church. The Christian monks had hoods covering their mysterious faces: 'Don't let them go to their knees; they're calling on their god!' I yelled, as the men rushed past and began the slaughter.

Many of the men and women were hiding themselves in-between the benches, hoping that we would ignore them. But some of them were incredibly brave, as they chose to fight, rather than sit and wait to die. And whilst I was giving orders to the thanes, I was suddenly attacked, when I least expected it. I had been stabbed in my side by a crazed flame-haired woman. I felt sick and dizzy as I suddenly let go of my weapons and grabbed her by the throat. I was angry and confused, as I suddenly sunk my teeth into the side of her neck and ripped at her flesh like a wild beast.

Blood poured down my mouth, as Rowena rushed to my aid and thrust a blade into the woman's, already bleeding, throat. She then told me to sit on the benches, as the rest of the waelisc were beaten down. Rowena then began patching me up, as I gritted my teeth in agony. 'Stop being a big puff.' She said as she sewed up the hole in my side. 'Be gentle woman!' I said as she closed up my gash. 'Stop your whinging, you're meant to be a king.' I then laughed. 'You remind me of your mother, Dresden. She used to patch me up when we were kids and she was as annoying as you.' Rowena smiled, as she liked it when I talked about her mother, which wasn't very often.

That night we stayed in the church and there were no god to end the wild fires and screams, the drunken rapes, the wild dancing and the burning of corpses. My body was wracked with pain, as I laughed and laughed, as I witnessed the waelisc being tied to two different horses by their arms and legs. And then the horses were forced to walk away in opposite directions, splitting the British in half. The men had competitions to see who could invent the worst punishment for the Celts. And it was hilarious to see eyes being gauged out, balls being cut off and then rammed down the victims' throat, forcing him to choke on his own scrotum.

We forced some of the men to fight to the death, promising that we would let the winner run away. And after one man killed his friend, by hitting him in the head with a rock, Hereswith then allowed the man to run away, before shooting him with a dozen arrows, making him look like a hedgehog. Aesc, Horsa, Hrothgar and Aelfred had a strongman competition to see who could behead a full grown man with one clean swing of an axe. Aesc won.

As the sun rose, the screaming had finally stopped, and after burning the church to the ground with everyone left inside, we then made our way to the next village, leaving only ruins behind. My armour had begun to rust from the dried blood of the waelisc and I was ordered to stay on my horse, *Chestnut*, by Rowena and wasn't allowed to take part in the slaughter.

We had been away from Dragon's Hill for almost two weeks, slaughtering and burning everything across the British countryside. We had used up all our supplies and the waelisc hadn't much food of their own,

as a famine had swept the lands,
and so we finally
went back home
to Cent.

*'For the boldest and most warlike men
have no regular employment, the care of house,
home and fields being left to the women,
old men and weaklings
of the family'*

*Roman Historian Tacitus
1st Century AD*

Chapter Seventeen: The War of the Dragons

Britannia 455 AD
(Great Britain)

Several weeks had passed and my wound had almost healed, when I received word of an army of hundreds marching across the countryside, led by King Vortigern. And in the dark heart of the night, the men of Cent marched southwards to head off Vortigern in the little town of Aylesford. It was a cold, wet night and the grass was slippery and I could smell the burning of crops in the distance, as the waelisc were trying to starve us out of the British lands.

Horsa was riding by my side, when I looked at him and got a cold chill down my side. I remembered when he was only a baby and I took him outside of my father's fort and into the woods, chasing the ancient spirit. And how on our return, the village had been burned down and everyone was dead. My real brother had died during birth, along with my mother, and so I told people that Horsa was my brother. And even after all those years, I still felt guilty, as I had never told Horsa the truth. He believed that he was my blood kin, but as we rode south, I suddenly felt a sense of responsibility. I felt that I owed Horsa the truth and so I told him everything.

I told Horsa that he was really the son of a thrall and was destined to be a slave. I told him, how at the age of seven, I had saved him from certain death and raised him as my own brother: 'I held you in my arms and kept you warm that night. I was only a child myself and I was frightened and scared and when Froda asked me who you were I said: "He is my brother, his name is Horsa!"' Horsa kept his head low as I told him his true identity, but he then raised his head and looked me in the eye: 'You saved me and together we became kings and you gave me one fantastic *wyrd* and for that I thank you. And Hengest don't look so glum, for we have always been brothers, we are the sons of Woden and our meeting was the will of the Gods.' I smiled as we trotted along on our horses. Horsa then laughed: 'Just don't try and hug me, you ugly bastard.'

It was dark and gloomy and the visibility was poor, as we rode over the hills and through the forests, as we made our way to Aylesford. And then finally, I saw the fires from across the fields and I could see Vortigern's men positioned outside the old Roman fort. Hrothgar ordered the men to form a shieldwall, but his orders fell on deaf ears, as the men charged at the waelisc like wild boars. It was dark and dangerous on those cobbled streets, as my men rushed forwards with their spears and javelins. The waelisc also rushed forwards and the two armies crashed in a haze of steel, flesh and bone.

The only light was coming from the moon and the wild fires from down the alleyway and I watched as I tried to see what was happening. But it was so dark that I couldn't tell who was waelisc and who was Saxon. I ordered my men back, but they didn't hear me as they were in a fight with the Celts and they were all dragging each other off the horses and fighting on the ground. I heard Hrothgar calling my name and so I left my men to their own devices and joined my ealdorman on the frontline with the bulk of the army behind us.

Nobody discussed tactics, as Froda was at the front, charging into battle, and so the rest of us followed. We rushed across the Roman streets and out into the open field, as our swords smashed against waelisc shields. I charged at one guy on my horse and raised my sword in the air and as he lifted his shield for protection, I slashed against the throat of his horse. And both the horse and the warrior came crashing down to the wet muddy grass with a thump. I then dismounted and smashed the back of his head with *Gertrude*. He wasn't wearing a helmet and I made a bloody mess, as his brains hung onto the spikes of *Gertrude* and blood poured from his smashed-in skull.

I saw Aesc and Horsa fighting side by side, as Wynn and I began searching for Vortigern and Vortimer. We had both wished to be the one's to slay them both in battle and have our names be remembered for all time on this tiny, yet bloody, isle. I saw men carrying the waelisc banner, but I didn't recognise any of them as royalty. The Saxons, Angles and Jutes preferred to fight as infantry and dismount from our horses and the Celts preferred to stay on the horses during battle. And so I had to keep a look out for horses coming up from behind and I was always trying to thrust *Dances with Corpses* up and into the throat of an oncoming, rampaging, horse.

I saw Hrothgar and Aelfred stabbing their blades into the guts of a fallen warrior. I saw Froda swinging his great big axe, taking the legs off the horses. And then Wipped, the Skull Crusher, would live up to his name, as he jumped on the faces of the fallen men using all of his weight and believe me that was a lot of weight. I swung my sword round my head, slashing at the horses, as my blade began singing its beautiful song of death, as I danced round and round.

The white and grey fur of my wolf skin was now blood-red and I looked for my next kill in the abyss of steel and swords. I saw that my son and brother were outnumbered, as they were surrounded by the Celts. I saw one of their faces, as he attacked Aesc and Horsa; it was the waelisc prince, Vortimer. It began raining, as I rushed to help my family, but I was too slow as I witnessed my brother and best friend Horsa; fall to the blade of Vortimer.

Vortimer had just mortally wounded my brother, and my son, Aesc, then rammed his sword into the throat of Vortimer and his quivering body began shaking on the muddy, wet grass next to Horsa. I rushed to Horsa's side, as his guts and intestines hung out all over the place. The rain began washing the blood off my sword, as Wynn tried pushing Horsa's guts back inside his open stomach. But Horsa begged her to stop, as he screamed out in agony. Aesc stood over us and looked on as rain poured down from the stars and soaked our faces. And I promised Horsa that I would make all the waelisc fall and bleed down at my feet.

Horsa then spoke: 'Just smile and laugh, even when death stares you in the face. Because you know what, we all die, but only a handful of us change the *wyrd* of an entire people……like we did.'

Horsa then leaned over and screamed in pain as he took off his golden rings from around his arms and then gave them to his nephew, Aesc, and told him that he had earned them. Wynn then took *Battle-Flame*, Hnaef's former sword, and placed it in Horsa's hands to make sure that he would be taken by the *Valkyries* and took to the hall of *Valhalla*. 'Dresden's coming to claim me.' Horsa whispered. And just before he closed his eyes for the very last time, I managed to say my final words to my baby brother: 'We will meet again soon, my friend, make sure you keep my seat warm in *Valhalla* and let them know that your brother will be coming to join the never ending battle in the sky.' Horsa gave a weak smile, just before slipping away from this world and on to the next.

I then turned to Aesc and as he stood tall, covered in blood as it flowed down his body being carried by the rain, I told him: 'One day, son, you'll be king. And if you want respect from the men, then you honour the brave and the fallen. And my son, it's always better to avenge blood kin, than mourn their loss.' Aesc then nodded his head and we both gripped our swords and along with Wynn, we began yelling a war cry as we charged into the mix of flesh and steel. We were infected with rage and furious anger, as we began dragging the vermin off their horses and began a killing frenzy.

I used *Dances with Corpses* to slice open the throat of a great war horse and as the horse fell to the ground, shaking and kicking its legs, I swung my sword so hard that I cut the man right through the top of his war helmet and into his neck. His head was split into two and his brain flopped out, as I then fixed my eyes on my next kill.

He was a tall man that had dismounted from his horse, he then ran at me with his black hair streamed behind him, as he raised his heavy axe over his head. He was covered in chain-mail and seemed fearless as he swung a great axe at my head. I then stepped aside and swung *Dances with Corpses* at his waist and slashed open his chain-mail, as if it was made of human flesh. I then used the blade as a spear, as I charged at him and thrust my sword deep into his stomach, opening him up with ease. His guts then spilled out as he fell to the floor screaming like a girl. I then left him there to suffer a slow and agonising death. Puddles of blood and entrails were everywhere.

I then looked for Aesc to make sure he was still alive and I witnessed him slash at another man's stomach and his victim then tripped over his own intestines as he crashed face first into the mud. And as the man still breathed, Aesc then cut off his head and held it up by the long black hair and screamed a war cry, as he was drenched in blood and rain. I never told him, but he made me proud that day.

As the battle raged on, I took a little rest with the wounded and there I saw Wipped sitting in the mud and his long beard was dripping in blood. 'That's not your blood, I hope?' I asked, as I took off my heavy dented dragon war helmet. 'No, no, don't worry, it's not my blood, it's the blood of scum. I'm fine. I'm just having a breather. I'm not as young as I used to be.'

'Me neither, my bones ach and too much mead has had its effects.' I said as I wobbled my beer gut. Wipped laughed and looked in the direction of my son that was still in battle. 'What I'd give to be young and handsome again.'

'Handsome? I've known you since you were in your early twenties and I don't remember you ever being handsome.'

'Piss off! you cheeky fucker.' Wipped laughed. 'It will be left to them soon.' Wipped said with a serious tone, as he was referring to the younger generation. 'And it's up to us old ones to tell our tales and sagas so the younger ones never forget. They should never forget what has happened in these lands. The sacrifice, the blood and the brave souls that have fought for this country should never be forgotten and lost to time.'

'I agree.' I said, as I told Wipped that Horsa had given his life for our new country and I would be horrified if his name was lost to history.

'What would you do if we could go back and live our lives again?' I asked the old man, as we watched the battle continue. The Skull Crusher laughed, as he told me: 'I would kill more vermin, drink more ale and make more babies.' I then laughed as I put on my dragon masked war helmet and joined the battle once more.

It looked like it had been raining blood, as the men were covered in crimson that flowed down their shiny armour and dripped off their weapons. Bodies were everywhere, horses and men lay in the grass, some twitching, and some still breathing, but most had been taken by the *Valkyries*.

Ryan West

As the sun began to rise from behind the morning clouds, I saw that we were winning the fight, as the waelisc began to retreat to the west like cowards. And the Saxons, Jutes, Frisians and Englisc had left a feast for Woden on the battlefield and he came for his gifts in the form of a dozen ravens.

*"in so dawling away their time
they show a strange inconsistency –
at the same time loving indolence and yet hating peace"*

*Roman Historian Tacitus
1ˢᵗ Century AD*

Chapter Eighteen: Night of the Long Knives

Britannia 456 AD
(Great Britain)

One year had passed since my brother was buried in his famous Viking ship *Ocean-Mare* along with his sword *Battle-Flame*. And in the ship with him was his favourite stallion, a gift for the afterlife. Our villages in Cent, or as many of us older ones called it 'England' after our home across the sea, had been rebuilt by men, women, children and thralls that worked night and day as the whole community rallied together. Our defences had been finished securing the common folk from more waelisc attacks and we were now using the ancient hill forts that scattered the countryside as strategic defences for our most noble thanes and ealdorman.

We were invited to Britain as mercenaries, as friends, and we arrived looking only for land and security. But a clash of culture brought distrust and paranoia, and war had broken out, and now we fight for our survival in this hostile world that we have inherited through no fault of our own. And we were prepared to fight to the very last man for England and for our children's futures. But the wars and endless death, the burning of crops and the starvation of our people, had to come to an end.

I had lived a long time and I was covered in battlescars and I had become old and wise and I did what I knew was the only thing that could bring harmony to my young country. And so I sent my thrall Derfel to the Celtic King, Vortigern, to arrange for a truce between our people and to end the daily struggle for survival once and for all.

The High King of the Celts had agreed to meet me at an ancient meeting place on the other side of the island. It was an ancient custom in Britain to meet bearing no arms when leaders met to discuss peace negotiations at one of the strange stone sites that covered the ancient landscape. I rode for several days along the British countryside as I made my way to meet Vortigern and his council of nobles and dukes, on what was fated to become an historic night that would change the history of Britain forever.

I was accompanied by Wynn, Aelfred, Wipped, Froda, Hereswith and my two kids Aesc and Rowena, as we were battered by wind and rain. We were guided by Vortigern's two ambassadors, Mauricius and Valeninian, and they were both dressed in Roman style robes that made them look like important figures, but I wasn't impressed, as I knew they were just Vortigern's filthy dogs.

Rowena told me how she looked forward to seeing her husband for the first time since she ran away when Vortimer brought her to me at Dragon's Hill. Aesc was also keen to see the Celtic king, as he had been the one to kill his son, Vortimer, at Aylesford, a year earlier. But I told them both to keep their big mouths shut and leave all the talking to me and Wipped and I demanded their obedience, as I didn't want them to ruin this very important meeting. And so they both promised to behave themselves on this fateful night.

It had begun raining as we finally arrived at the chosen meeting place of Vortigern's council. The unarmed Celtic warriors nodded their heads in a show of respect as we passed them whilst riding our horses. None of us were carrying weapons, but we were all wearing armour and carrying our dragon and horse emblems with pride. The glow of the flames on the ancient stones was the first thing I noticed as we jumped off our horses and gave them to Vortigern's thralls to tie up. The ground was wet and muddy, as we all stared in amazement at the ancient circle that looked like it had been built by a race of giants. The Celts had a strange and foreign word for the site, but I couldn't get my *Teutonic* tongue around their harsh words. It was a henge, it was made of stone, and so I called it 'Stonehenge'.

The flamed torches were flickering in the wind and rain as we cautiously walked towards Vortigern and his council that waited patiently in the centre of the strange stone structure. I was given a torch myself by a thrall as I was greeted by Vortigern himself. 'Welcome my brothers.' He said with open arms and a smile on his face. He then shook my hand and the hands of my men and his council followed as we were all greeted as though we were family by the men we had been at war with. Vortigern even shook the hand of his wife Rowena and she smiled at Vortigern, even though she despised the old fool.

I noticed a look of great unease on the faces of Vortigern's nobles, even though they had fixed smiles on their faces. And I'm sure I must have looked menacing under my dragon masked war helmet, so I took it off and allowed the rain to soak my long locks that flowed down my back.

We were all given soaking wet, wooden chairs to sit on, as Vortigern stood up and gave us a well-rehearsed speech on brotherly love. He kept quoting people from a book written by sand elves on the request of their god, much to the delight of his nobles. But me and my men were looking at each other with smirks on our faces, as we were bored to tears. We didn't understand much of what Vortigern was saying as his accent and his knowledge of our language was awful and cringe-worthy. Rowena turned to me and whispered: 'I had to listen to this crap for three years.' I laughed as I felt her pain. 'And we are all grateful *Modor of Angelcynn*.' I whispered. 'You bloody better be.' She said with scorn.

We were all dripping wet, as Vortigern continued his speech. 'Were we not all created equally?' Vortigern asked, as his men cheered and hung on every word. 'That ugly bastard isn't my equal.' Aesc whispered, before I told him to keep quiet. Vortigern continued. 'It is the will of God that our two races come together and live in peace side by side.'

'It's not the will of my god.' Aelfred added under his breath. 'Shut the fuck up!' I told the men, as I listened to King Vortigern continue. 'We have both lost loved ones because of our petty differences and I believe in a society that is equal and fair. Where there are no more wars, only peace and unity with each other. I believe in a world where all races and cultures can live together as one and share a love of God and embrace his love with each passing day.'

'This god sounds like a faggot to me.' Whispered Aesc. Vortigern continued: 'I believe in a Britain that welcomes our friends from across the seas with open arms. And I believe in a Britain that refuses to see race and differences. We can become a nation that only sees fellow human beings, friends, brothers and sisters. We will be better and stronger together. A new age has dawned, has it not? An age of fairness and equality, an age of brotherly love has begun.' Vortigern's council stood up and applauded, as my men were staring at me, eagerly waiting for my signal for the slaughter to begin.

I then stood up and asked Vortigern a series of questions: 'If what you say is your true intensions, then what would you do if the people that you have welcomed into this country with open arms become more powerful than you? What if they decide that they don't want you in what has now become their lands? And what if they don't like your culture and wished to destroy it and force their ways on your children? By refusing to see race, then is not possible to invite a foreign enemy under your own roof and be too blind to see the horrors to come? Have you already forgotten what happened to the mighty Roman empire? Do you wish to share the same *wyrd*?

Vortigern looked horrified by my questions, but I continued: 'What if your god doesn't wish for the races of man to live together in peace and harmony? What will happen to your children if your God has created the world with a –dog eat dog-mentality and his wish is too see the world at war and allow for only the strongest race to survive? What if you're wrong, Vortigern, and you've just invited the destruction of your own people and your liberal views have struck you too blind to see it coming?'

I then knelt down on one knee and pulled out *Wolf-Fang* that had been concealed inside of my boot, I then held it up to the night sky as the rain poured from the heavens and asked in a stern and cold voice: 'What have you done Vortigern? What have you done?' I said, as I laughed at his stupidity. And just then my men knelt down and pulled out their own saxes, or long knives, that were concealed in their boots, as I continued to address Vortigern: 'Your god has deceived you and now your race and your children will pay the price for your treason against your own kind. Your fields will be filled with corpses and your rivers will flow with the blood of British children.' I then gave the signal for the slaughter to begin.

It was a British custom to come to Stonehenge unarmed, but it wasn't my custom, as I wasn't British. I was a Jute, I was Englisc and I was a Saxon Warrior King that did the only thing that I knew would secure the future of my people, and that was to eliminate the competition. I understood the desires of man and I understood the true nature of man. I knew that Vortigern was trying to create a fantasy world where he believed he would be king and have power over all of Britain.

I knew he wished to create his own Roman empire and convert my beautiful race to the oppressive horrors of his sand cult and erase our sense of identity. His wish was for us to allow foreign and strange beings from around the world to come to our lands for his own economic power and greed. And I knew that the only real way of protecting my race and children was to annihilate the enemy and wipe them from Britain, before they did it to us first.

The unarmed Celtic guards that surrounded Stonehenge were quickly wiped out by a sneak attack led by Hrothgar. And the rest of my men grabbed Vortigern's nobles and dukes and had their fun with them, as they punched, kicked and slit throats. I had since put on my dragon helmet and grabbed hold of Vortigern and head-butted him on his unprotected nose. The rain poured down as I ordered the king to lie in the wet grass and don't move if he still wished to live. Vortigern didn't dare move as he witnessed the horrors been done to his own brethren.

I laughed out loud with words of encouragement as Aesc began to gauge out the eyes of one of Vortigern's ambassadors. He rammed his two thumbs into the eyes of the scrawny little man and Mauricius screamed loud enough to wake the dead, as blood ran down his face. And he was one of the lucky ones as he lay dead in the wet grass and was unable to witness the dreaded *Blood-Eagle* being done to his friend, Valeninian.

Valeninian screamed and begged for mercy as Hrothgar grabbed him by his hair and forced him to lie backwards over a small stone in the centre of Stonehenge. He then used his sax to tear open Valeninian's torso and allow his ribs to be opened up. As Hrothgar cut open the chest of the waelisc man, his ribs began to split and poke out one at a time. His lungs were then pulled out past the ribs to make it look like an eagle had spread its wings. And this was done as I held Vortigern by his hair and forced him to watch.

'Take a good look Vortigern, this is what we really think of your people and you invited us here with open arms. You're a fool Vortigern. A fool.' I then threw Vortigern onto the grass, as I had a little fun of my own and smashed one of his nobles head first into the towering stone pillars, smearing them in blood that was quickly washed away by the rain. Rowena then spat on Vortigern and kicked him in the balls, as Thor was heard riding in the sky that night. I then cut off the waelisc man's head and held up the decapitated lump by the long ginger hair and screamed into the midnight sky. 'That's for you England! That's for you!'

I then told a petrified Vortigern that he was responsible for the death of his men and the utter destruction of Celtic Britain and all he could do was lay there and cry like a worm and beg his god for forgiveness. I then walked over to Valeninian that still lay across the stone with his chest wide open. I then removed his heart and held it up to the heavens as a symbolic gesture of the Jutes, Englisc, Frisians and Saxons tearing out the heart of British resistance. I then licked the blade that was stained with the blood of a defeated people.

The Englisc had
arrived.

*'We will dismiss from the kingdom
all foreign born knights, crossbowmen, serjeants,
and mercenary soldiers who have come with horses
and arms to the nuisance thereof.'*

*The English Magna Carta
1215 AD*

Chapter Nineteen: England Rising!

Britannia 457 AD
(Great Britain)

    One year had passed since the historic *Night of the Long Knives* and I had allowed Vortigern to walk away in one piece, as he had agreed to give me most of his lands in exchange for his worthless life. By allowing Vortigern to live, I was able to expand my kingdom without any resistance from the waelisc and without losing a single man. Vortigern simply threw his remaining nobles and dukes off their properties and gave their lands and properties to me. I then shared those lands with the army as payment for their services, just like I had promised. And now the Saxons, Englisc, Jutes and Frisians occupied all of the former Celtic strongholds within my growing young country.

    Food and trade now flourished across the British channel, that I had renamed the Englisc channel. The British used to say that we were uncivilised people, I had no idea what that word meant, but I do know that it was some kind of snobbish insult. And I now laugh at those who insult us, as their 'civilised' and 'superior' culture had crumbled away and my native Germanic culture was thriving.

    The English channel was filled with trading vessels carrying food and the greatest Germanic and Nordic art of the greatest craftsmanship that the world had ever seen. My people now had more food then they could eat and so we were trading with our German cousins from across the continent. The world had entered a dark-age, but here in England, we thrived, and I thank the Gods for their blessings. And I say 'bollocks' to all those that say we were no good. Aye men!

Vortigern would pay the ultimate price for his treachery against his own people, as he was found dead at one of our new Celtic forts. He was probably killed by his own people for his act of treason against the British. He had let in the foreigners against the will of the people and we had taken over their lands and destroyed their livelihoods. His body was found bloodied and beaten, he had paid dearly. And I'm told that when they found him thunder reigned across the clouds. Perhaps it was a good omen.

Vortigern was dead, but the fight against the waelisc continued as new leaders had emerged and once again we were thrust into battle. 'Get your tools lads, we're going to war.' I ordered, as I laced up my wolf skin boots and Derfel placed my dragon masked war helmet over my long fair locks that I confess to being a little grey. I had *Gertrude* and *Wolf-Fang* tucked into my leather belt and *Dances with Corpses* was placed in its seal-skin-lined scabbard. I was wearing my iron chain-mail that had rusted with the blood of the waelisc and around my neck was my lucky Thor's hammer made from the finest riches. And both my arms were decorated with golden rings to show my wealth and power.

I then looked over at my wife and helped her dress into her leather tunic and iron chain-mail and I placed her bashed up, dented, war helmet over her blonde and grey locks. 'Let's kill the ugly fuckers.' yelled Wynn, from under her war helmet.

The battle was supposed to take place in the west, but the waelisc had gone back on their word and had invaded us on the eastern coast. They had tricked us and came into our territory from the least protected northern borders and so the battle would now take place at Crecanford.

My scouts had warned me of a massive army that had invaded our northern lands. They say that it was so big that the ranks of men faded into the distance and over the hills. I was told that the waelisc had brought their best soldiers from the western lands and that they all had Celtic courage mixed with Roman discipline and skills. And so I gathered every thane, ealdorman and the entire *Fyrd* and forced them to march north.

The swastika, the white dragon and the white horse were flapping in the winds as they were being carried with pride and we were pounded by rain, as our horses trod our path to glory. We were greeted by the women and children as we passed through a small village. And I could see small boys and girls waving at us, smiling and some of them saluting us, showing us their appreciation, reminding us who we are fighting for.

The number of Saxons, Angles, Frisians and Jutes that were prepared to put their lives on the line for our new country had grown into tens of thousands. And I was at the front leading the way on my war horse *Chestnut* complete with its gilded bridle and decoration. And by my side were my band of warlords, my son Aesc, my ealdorman, Hrothgar, the Saxon, Aelfred, my champion archer the Frisian, Hereswith, and my fellow Jutes, Froda and the Skull Crusher.

We were also joined by the women, their wives, daughters, girlfriends and mothers and with them was my beautiful wife, Wynn, and my beautiful daughter, Rowena. They had come to offer inspiration and moral support and help stitch up a gash or two.

As I looked back over my shoulder, I failed to see where the rows of men ended, as they stretched for miles across my young fertile kingdom. I then turned to Wipped and said: 'It's not Jutland, but we got our kingdom in the end.'

'It's the will of Woden.' Wipped said with a wise voice. 'Our people have been blessed by the Gods. We have it all, brains, beauty, courage and wisdom. And whenever we pull ourselves together and fight as one unit, the world will fall and bleed down at our feet. And only when that happens will our children know the meaning of freedom and forget the fear of what lurks in the shadows of the night.' Aesc interrupted: 'And it's up to us to make that happen.' Aesc said, as he admired his broad sword shining in the sunlight. And with an army of thousands behind me, I was confident of success against the foreign vermin that stood in our way, wishing to push us back into the sea from which we came.

It had stopped raining as we finally arrived on the battlefield and facing us were an army of what seemed like millions. I saw their Celtic emblem of a red dragon on a green background being carried by hundreds of men on long staffs. Crecanford field was the perfect location for a fair fight as it had a long flat field in the middle and two long, steep embankments on either side.

I then turned to Hrothgar and told him to prepare the men into battle formations. I saw the Celts lined up with eighty men and women across their front ranks and their troops fell back so far into the distance that I was unable to count them all. But my best guess was there were at least twenty thousand men and women against our fifteen thousand. Many were wearing chain-mail and were armed with swords and shields. But most seemed to be unprotected and were only armed by spears and wooden shields, decorated with blue circles and patterns.

I was sitting high up on my horse, as I witnessed the British monks walking up and down the battlefield throwing what looked like water on the ground. It was as if they were calling on their god against us, the monks chose to fight us by pursuing us with hostile prayers. But I no longer feared their god, as he had proved himself weak in battle and couldn't match the power of Woden.

I then ordered my own shaman and priestesses to begin the ritual sacrifice. Rowena then led several horses round to the front ranks and she was followed by several priests and priestesses, along with a few chosen thanes. And between them they forced several worthy war horses to lie in the grass and the men then slashed their throats, as Rowena allowed the blood to flow into the buckets. And after splashing the field with the offering, she then carried the buckets of blood to the men and showered many of us in the thick warm blood of the honoured beasts. Rowena had blessed both the fields and the men, as she evoked the power of the God of War, Woden, and his warrior maidens the *Valkyries*.

My wolf skin was soaked, as blood ran down my dragon masked war helmet and dripped down my long hair and onto the floor. The runes had been cut and the charms had been spoken and it was now time for war. I saw the *Berserkers* biting on their shields, rabid and crazed, waiting for the slaughter to begin, and so I turned to address my champion archer Hereswith: 'Blow the fucking horn and lets get this thing started.'

My first order was for the archers on the front line to begin firing at the Celts that were neatly formed on the other side of the field. And once in place, the arrows were set alight, before Hereswith shouted the word '*FIRE!*' The afternoon sky was dark, as the sun was hiding behind the thick waterlogged greyish clouds. And as the horn sounded, the sky was light up with fire, as arrows blotted out the little light that shone from behind the clouds.

The men then cheered, as the waelisc were bombarded with arrows, as they hunched behind their shields for protection. Many of the Celtic shields were made of wood and as they stood back up to put out the flames, they were once again hit with a second wave of flamed arrows. I witnessed as the Britons were hit in the face with bronzed arrow tips that crashed into their eye sockets, legs, arms and chests.

The archers roared with cheers and laughter as the waelisc took a battering. The British didn't retaliate, as their bows couldn't match the range of the superior Saxon bows. Hereswith then ordered a third wave of arrows that was quickly followed by a fourth and a fifth wave of the flamed demons of the sky.

The bows and arrows were made in northern Germany, in the Saxon lands, and were over two meters long and had an impressive range. But whilst sitting on the horse watching the sky turn to fire once more, I suddenly turned to Hereswith and told him to stop the archers. I then turned to the big Saxon, Hrothgar, and told him to blow the war horn and send in the infantry. And it seemed like the gates of *Valhalla* had opened as thousands of Saxons, Englisc, Jutes and Frisians rushed towards the waelisc like crazed mad men.

I then watched from a distance, as Froda led the men into the mix of swords, steel, flesh and bone. 'Kill the fucking cunts!' Hrothgar shouted in his usual pleasant way, as I, Wynn, Hrothgar, Wipped, Aesc and Aelfred watched on from on top of our war horses. I could see Froda running across the battlefield, followed by a mass of steel, as he clashed against the charging waelisc, wielding their weapons, ruthless and determined.

Froda was armed with his famous double-edged axe and we watched with delight as he began swinging his steel and the heads of the waelisc began to fall to the floor, quickly followed by their spurting headless, twitching corpses. I was feeling the hilt of my sword as I began to feel the excitement of such an epic and historic encounter. And I knew the Gods and the *Fates* were watching with baited breath, as the slaughter continued.

Blood began to soak the battlefield, as Saxons, Celts, Jutes, Englisc and Frisians began to fall in a pile of quivering corpses and dismembered limbs. 'Fucking what?' Aesc shouted, as he pointed at a waelisc man charging at our thanes like he was possessed by a wild boar. And we watched on with amazement as he defeated three of our men single-handedly, as he swung his sword with grace and expertise.

I was now feeling restless as I began tapping the horse with both feet and I watched as the battle began to heat up. 'You fucking arseholes!'

Hrothgar shouted as he watched his fellow Saxons begin to fall by the feet of the wild-eyed, flame-haired Celts. 'This is madness.' Hrothgar said, as he became increasingly agitated by what he was witnessing on the battlefield. 'What the fuck?' He yelled, as we all saw one of our men get skewered on a British spear. Wipped then turned to me and asked me what I was waiting for? to which I replied: 'I'm seeing how the British fight and how good we really are against their very best.'

'We're fucking shite.' Aesc added. 'Relax lads.' I said with a patient voice. 'Most of them are the *Fyrd*, they are young or old. Most of them are farmers and inexperienced. The best thanes are stood behind us, watching and learning how the Celts fight.'

'Now what?' Hrothgar asked. I then called for Hereswith: 'Do what you do best and blow that fucking horn.'

'I always worried about you and Hereswith.' Aesc joked.

'You're not too old for a slap.' I told the cheeky bastard, as Wynn and Rowena laughed. Hereswith then blew the war horn and the thanes in battle quickly retreated, as the sky once again became a blaze of fire, as the waelisc were slain by thousands of arrows.

The dried horse blood was causing my skin to itch under all of my armour and the sun was in my eyes, as I watched from on top of the hill as the arrows filled the afternoon sky with fire. But then the Gods had given us a sign, as it suddenly began raining once more and as the sky poured, the rain clanged and bounced off our helmets and armour. And the thousands of thanes behind me roared and cheered, as I then sounded the horn and led the cavalry.

We then charged down the steep, slippery hill towards the British with our swords, spears and emblems held up high with pride. And the earth began to move as the stallions charged forward and my eyes were watering as the wind and rain blew into my face. My hair was flowing behind me as the blood of the sacrifice washed away.

My infantry had once again joined the battle as I witnessed the British send in their own cavalry to meet us in the middle of the chaos that had engulfed Crecanford. And I could feel the battle-fury as I raised my sword high and tried to avoid my own horses and men that were tumbling over as we rampaged down the slippery hill. Wynn, Hrothgar, Aelfred, Hereswith and Wipped stayed behind with the remaining ten thousand men that were biting their shields in anticipation of going into battle.

Once at the bottom of the hill, Aesc and I dismounted and joined the mix of steel, flesh, bone and twitching corpses. Sweat dripped down my face, as I rushed into battle and slashed against the face of a dark haired, blue faced Celt. His face and body was painted in blue dye, he was wearing no armour and was only armed with a wooden shield and spear. But he now lay dead in the wet grass, painted beautifully with the colour of his own blood.

I then looked up and saw a woman charging at me with wide blue eyes and grinding teeth. Her body was covered in blue dye, her hair was long and black and as she got closer I could see that her face was young and beautiful. Perhaps she was protecting her young as she bravely charged at the foreigners that had taken over her lands. She was wielding a long knife at me, determined to defend her lands. I then slashed her from her navel to her neck and split her wide open. And as her blood dripped off my mask, I then looked down at her bloodied corpse and I found myself feeling respect for her bravery and determination. I then knelt and picked up the chain that had been cut from her neck. It was a wooden cross, it was covered in blood, and then I felt an overwhelming desire to place her knife across her gaping wound and place her wooden cross into her tiny hands that were dripping red and allow her God to claim her soul. I then gently closed her eyes and honoured the stranger's death.

Most of my men had dismounted as we found it awkward to manoeuvre and fight whilst trying to control an animal the size of a horse. But the waelisc loved their horses and struck us down with their swords, spears and axes. I was constantly surrounded by horses and wild men and women that tried to slash across my head and neck. I was keeping my shield high as I kept moving around in circles to avoid standing still for too long, as I didn't want to fall victim to British steel and iron.

I slashed at human legs that dangled over the horse's ribs. I ducked and weaved as the British infantry flung throwing axes and javelins at my face, trying to be the ones that took down the Saxon king that in their minds had invaded their lands. But this was my land and my kingdom now. I had earned that land by helping the Celts fight off the Picts and Irish. I had earned that land with the blood and sweat of my people. And the Gods wouldn't allow a worthless Celt be the one to take down Hengest the Wolf-Tamer.

I was then challenged by a man whose face I recognised from Vortigern's court. He was dressed in chain-mail and was obviously a man of great power and importance and I welcomed his challenge with a smile. He was armed with a sword and shield and wore some kind of bronze helmet. I then swung *Dances with Corpses* at his chest and arms, but he was fast and moved swiftly out of the way. He retaliated by smashing me with his shield to try and throw me off guard. But the Celt was simply too small and weak and I didn't budge an inch.

I then swung my blade ferociously at his neck using all of my weight, but I had missed and made almost a fateful error, as I suddenly lost balance and fell to the floor. I had dropped my sword and I saw the expression of delight on the Celt's face as he charged at me, wielding his sword in the air and came down at me with a killer blow. I then raised my swastika decorated shield over my face and held out my sax as the Celt fell onto the point of my blade and *Wolf-Fang* had just saved my life.

He was still barely alive when I threw off his scrawny body and rose to my feet and struggled to yank out the bloodied blade. I then quickly knelt back down and raised my shield over my head, as both armies hid under their shields. The waelisc archers had sent thousands of arrows onto the battlefield killing both the Saxons and Celts. I then got back up and noticed a Briton looking back at his own men that had fired the arrows and I saw a great opportunity for butchery.

I then ran behind him and thrust *Dances with Corpses* deep into the small of his back. I then looked him in the eye as his crippled body lay twitching and writhing in agony on the floor. And I walked away laughing, knowing that he would never be able to pick up a sword again and use it against my people.

Warriors and dying men filled the battlefield with screams and cries, their stomachs were split wide open, as guts and intestines flowed over the killing zone. Bodies were twitching and bleeding, as limbs, and in some cases heads, were missing from the quivering mass of blood and flesh. The Christians often talked about scenes like this in their underworld, only they added fire, brimstone and demons. But for my men this was our heaven, our *Asgard*, our *Valhalla*, our daily world.

I was drunk with blood and battle-fury as I was slashing at the horse's legs and stomachs. And as the men fell off I would introduce them to Englisc steel and might. It was cold, wet and muddy as I slipped on the guts and intestines that covered the battlefield. I didn't know if they belonged to the horses or the men, I didn't care, as only in battle I truly felt alive.

Whilst in the middle of the chaos, I heard the horn sound three times and as I looked back I could see the ten thousand men walking down the banking, being led by Hrothgar. I then looked for Aesc and saw him slashing against the skull of an unprotected black haired Celt and his head split in two and his brain flopped out in two halves onto the muddy floor.

Aesc then heard me shouting him and he rushed towards me as we retreated back to join Hrothgar and form the *Boars-Head*. The *Boars-Head* was a shieldwall that formed the shape of an arrow head, or giant wedge. I, Wynn, Hrothgar, Aesc, Aelfred, Froda and Wipped were on the front line as the rest of the thanes packed in behind us. And they kept packing themselves in until all ten thousand men formed a giant impenetrable wedge.

We were armed with saxes or spears and shields, but we were all told that our greatest weapon was the man next to us and to honour that man like a brother. We were trained to protect the man to our left with our lives, as any weak spot in the shieldwall and the whole thing would fall apart and we all die. And if that happened then our women and children would be raped and butchered by the British and our new England would die a horrible death. 'Cut their legs, ankles and balls.' Hrothgar shouted to the men behind and they passed it on to the ranks that faded into the background

The waelisc had formed their own shieldwall and our two armies began to step closer to each other with our spears and swords sticking out from the walls of steel. And as our two armies finally clashed in the centre of Crecanford field, I could feel the power and weight of the enemy, as my feet began to slip backwards on the muddy field. I couldn't see anything except for rain, feet and legs that I tried desperately to slash open.

I was being pushed and shoved from the men next to me and from the ten thousand thanes behind me. And I was already exhausted as I sucked in oxygen and told Aesc: 'I'm getting to old for this shit.'

'There's still fight in you yet old man. You're still breathing aren't you?' Aesc shouted over the grunts of the men. I then heard Hereswith blow the horn from far in the distance and the row of thanes behind us placed their shields over our heads to protect us from the bombardment of Frisian arrows. Everyone on the first fifty rows placed their shields over the row in front of them, as the British got battered by the screaming arrows.

The rain poured down hard as arrows crashed on top of the waelisc that were still holding their shields in front of them. I could hear the Celts scream and I heard the sound of the arrows that were hitting the shield above me. 'Come on, come on.' Aesc was saying to himself, as he impatiently waited for the waelisc on the front row to raise their shields to protect themselves from the arrows.

I could hear the waelisc shouting instructions to each other, but many didn't listen as they began to raise their shields to protect their heads and as they did so they had exposed their stomachs to our saxes and spears. '*Now!*' Hrothgar screamed as we all stepped forwards and began thrusting our iron and steel into the flesh of the Celts.

I rammed *Wolf-Fang* up and beneath their chain-mail and straight into the balls of the man in front of me. And as I pulled my blade back down, I took great delight as I saw blood dripping off and onto the floor. He then lay bleeding in the grass and was soon trampled on by his own men as the waelisc began to panic and push forwards. He was quickly replaced by the next man and I simply slashed at his unprotected belly and he slipped on his own intestines.

'Wooow!' Hrothgar cheered as he thrust his sax at the Celts. 'This is living.' He bellowed as he was enjoying the blood bath at Crecanford field. 'I didn't think it would be this easy.' Aesc shouted over the British screams. 'Kill the fucking bastards!' I heard Wipped shouting to the men behind as they thrust their boar-headed spears passed our heads and into the faces of the Celts. I was then slashed against the face by a Celtic spear and blood must have poured from the open gash, as I shouted at my son: 'raise your fucking shield.' I ordered, as Aesc was busy stabbing the Celts.

I began slipping on the mud and I was being careful not to trip on the corpses of Celts that lay at my feet. My left arm felt heavy and weak from holding up the shield for so long and my right arm was in agony. And I could feel my body begging for a rest, as I then ordered the thanes behind us on the second row to quickly swap places. And one at a time I, Wynn, Hrothgar, Aesc, Aelfred, Wipped and Froda began to fall back to the second ranks.

And once we had placed ourselves on the second row and we were confident that we still had the upper hand against the Celts, we began to fall back even further before finally retreating to the back of the shieldwall. I was gasping for air and my entire body was aching and bleeding as we watched the battle continue from on top of the embankment whilst sitting high on our horses. And I was later joined by my blood-drenched wife Wynn after she had been on the frontline with me.

As the battle raged on late into the evening and the sky poured down hard with rain, I could see the British begin to retreat from my kingdom, as they ran southwards and towards the seas where they were either drown or slaughtered. I saw that Woden had been present to witness my victory that day, as he came to collect his gifts in the form of a hundred ravens that feasted on the corpses of the men and horses that scattered the battlefield.

I was watching the foreign vermin running out of my country as they were being chased by Saxon, Frisian, Jutisc and Englisc swords. I was resting high on my horse as I was joined by Wynn, Hrothgar, Aelfred, Wipped, Hereswith, Froda, Aesc and Rowena. The white dragon, the white horse and the swastika flags were blowing in the wind and rain, as we all raised our right arms in the military salute to show our respect to the thanes below.

And as I looked across the battlefield, I suddenly became aware of a ghostly white figure of a young girl standing perfectly still, not taking her eyes off me. She was watching me from in the middle of the corpses that scattered the battlefield. It was the same white figure of the *Valkyrie* that I had first seen as a child.

Nobody else seemed to be able to see her as she stood staring at me, draped in a long white gown, with her long white hair blowing in the cold breeze. I smiled at the ancient spirit and held out my right arm in salute, as shivers ran down my spine.

Sludge and congealed blood was caked to my skin, as I turned to my son Aesc and said: 'Somewhere, someday, my *wyrd* will be revealed to me and I will smile on their swords. But for now the fight
  for our new England
  has only just
  begun.'

*"We must recognise that we have a great inheritance
in our possession which represents
the prolonged achievement of the centuries;
that there is not one of our simple uncounted rights
today for which better men than we are
have not died on the scaffold or on the battlefield.
We have not only a great treasure; we have a great cause.
Are we taking every measure within our power to defend that cause?"*

*Sir Winston Churchill
September 1936*

Epilogue

At the conclusion of this novel, after the battle of Crecanford, it is reported that Hengest ruled the kingdom of Kent for the next thirty years and had continually defeated the Celts until 488AD. It is believed that Hengest finally died of natural causes as he lay peacefully in his bed and was succeeded to the throne by his son Aesc (pronounced Ash). One of Hengest's thanes by the name of 'Wipped' is recorded to have been killed during a battle against the Celts at Wipped Creek, that as since been named after him.

In the year 477AD, Aelle, a Saxon war chieftain from Germany, arrived in three ships along with his three sons Cymen, Wlencing and Cissa. And after nearly two decades of fighting the Celts he finally forged the kingdom of Sussex.

Hengest and Aelle were amongst the first Germanic chieftains to independently invade Britain, but they certainly weren't the last. It is believed that over a period of two centuries, approximately thirty kingdoms rose and fell (in what is now England) as the Germanic-Nordic tribes fought against the Celts and each other.

Eventually Anglo-Saxon England stabilised with four kingdoms that had since been converted to Christianity. These kingdoms were Northumbria in the north, Mercia and East Anglia in the centre and Wessex in the south. And the tribes of southern Denmark, known as the Angles, or Engles, would later give their name to the three kingdoms in the north and they would call it 'England' which literally means 'Land of the Angles'.

In the fourth and fifth centuries southern Denmark had many names and the most common were 'Angeln' and 'Angelcynn', which literally means 'English Nation'. And so Southern Denmark was in fact the very first England and it was brought to Britain, along with the English language, by the Anglo-Saxons, or as I call them, 'the tribal ancestors of the English'. This story would be repeated the same way when the English took England and the English language to North America and later to Australia and so on.

After the Anglo-Saxons had settled and essentially created England out of the carcass of Roman Britannia, a new wave of Germanic-Nordic tribes would invade from Scandinavia and Denmark that we now call the Vikings (meaning raider). And the Vikings would simply call all the Germanic peoples in Britain 'English' and so the new identity of being English (in the modern sense) had emerged.

Later the Normans would defeat the English in 1066AD, as well as the Viking settlers of England that had since converted to Christianity. But what most people fail to realise is that the Normans were in fact Norsemen (meaning men of the north) from modern Denmark. They had defeated the French, similarly to the way Hengest defeated the Celts, and ruled over the small kingdom of Normandy before adding England to their rule. And so the English were in fact related to the Normans and William the Conqueror did have a small claim to the English throne.

The English language has been slightly influenced by Norman-French, but it still remains a Nordic-Germanic language (not British or Celtic or French).

And so in conclusion, the mix of Germanic-Nordic invaders of Britain, first led by Hengest, slowly, over the course of centuries, lost their original identities (i.e. Frisians, Franks, Jutes, Angles, Saxons, Danes, Norwegians, Vikings and Normans) and simply became known as the English.

Historical Note: Fact or Fiction?

The rise of the Saxons is based on real people, real events and real wars that helped lay the foundation of what was destined to become England. It is designed to give the reader a better understanding of who the English really are and where we really came from. All historians and historical novelist write their accounts of history with an agenda. My agenda is to educate the reader on my Anglo-Saxon/English ancestors and to tell the truth based on the evidence available, even if that truth is horrific and exposes England's best kept secret.

The story is based in the early medieval and therefore suffers from a lack of writings from historians and most of our knowledge comes from later sources. I have exhaustively researched all of the information available that is to be found in fragments scattered around hundreds of various sources, including the social, economic and religious conflicts of the age. And I have painstakingly tried to piece them all together to put our English origin story into context and show how and why the ancestors of the English came to be in Britain. And the Rise of the Saxons was the end result.

The disappearance of Latin and Celtic languages, in what is now England, suggests that the Germanic invaders did not absorb the Celts, but rather conducted a war of extermination. And scientists believe that up to 100% of Celtic blood was replaced, in what has since become England, with a mix of Germanic-Nordic blood. Modern DNA tests amongst the English have confirmed this.

I would describe this story as an interpretation of historical events based on the information available and I of course have embellished much of the story to help fill in the blanks. I have tried to piece a giant puzzle together when most of the pieces are missing or have been neglected to promote other agendas. We are taught in England that we are British and therefore we have viewed our history from a British perspective and so naturally we have viewed the Anglo-Saxons as foreign invaders. But if we say 'NO!' to the people that wish to oppress English identity and do the most un-politically correct thing and think of our history from an English perspective then the Anglo-Saxons weren't foreign at all, they were us. And we should honour their achievements and tell their stories, because if we don't, then who will?

Lightning Source UK Ltd.
Milton Keynes UK
21 December 2009

147805UK00002B/90/P